Where the
Last Rose
Blooms

Books by Ashley Clark

The Dress Shop on King Street
Paint and Nectar
Where the Last Rose Blooms

HEIRLOOM
SECRETS

Where the Last Rose Blooms

A NOVEL

ASHLEY CLARK

BETHANYHOUSE
a division of Baker Publishing Group
Minneapolis, Minnesota

Published by Bethany House Publishers
11400 Hampshire Avenue South
Minneapolis, Minnesota 55438
www.bethanyhouse.com

Bethany House Publishers is a division of
Baker Publishing Group, Grand Rapids, Michigan

Printed in the United States of America

Library of Congress Cataloging-in-Publication Data
Names: Clark, Ashley- author.
Title: Where the last rose blooms / Ashley Clark.
Description: Minneapolis, Minnesota : Bethany House, a division of Baker
    Publishing Group, [2022] | Series: Heirloom secrets
Identifiers: LCCN 2021037693 | ISBN 9780764237621 (paperback) | ISBN
    9780764239908 (casebound) | ISBN 9781493436118 (ebook)
Classification: LCC PS3603.L35546 W48 2022 | DDC 813/.6—dc23
LC record available at https://lccn.loc.gov/2021037693

Unless otherwise noted, Scripture quotations are from the King James Version of
the Bible.

Scripture quotations labeled NIV are from THE HOLY BIBLE, NEW INTERNATIONAL
VERSION®, NIV® Copyright © 1973, 1978, 1984, 2011 by Biblica, Inc.® Used by permission. All rights reserved worldwide.

This is a work of historical reconstruction; the appearance of certain historical figures are therefore inevitable. All other characters, however, are products of the author's imagination, and any resemblance to actual persons, living or dead, is coinci-
dental.

Cover design by Kathleen Lynch / Black Kat Design

Cover image by Lee Avison / Arcangel

Author is represented by Spencerhill Associates

Baker Publishing Group publications use paper produced from sustainable forestry
practices and post-consumer waste whenever possible.

22 23 24 25 26 27 28   7 6 5 4 3 2 1

To Amy Norton—
a precious friend in every season.

We went through fire and water,
but you brought us to a place of abundance.

—Psalm 66:12b NIV

PROLOGUE

Charleston, 1860

Ashley

Mama thought I was asleep the night 'fore I was sold. I wasn't. I was looking at the patterns of the shadows on the wall, but she couldn't see my eyes from where she sat.

That was a year ago now. Well, roundabouts. Maybe half a year. Guess I don't know the day, just that it was fall and still warm outside, and summer seem like it was gonna take forever to get here.

Not a minute goes by, I'm not thinkin' about her. I'll never forget what she said when she put my best dress inside the satchel, along with some pecans and a braid of her hair.

"It be filled with my love always," she said, and when Mama said *always* she meant it. Problem was, *always* wasn't ours to give.

She put her favorite buttons inside the satchel too. Those butterfly buttons I had always loved. But the buttons fell out when the men took me. And I saw that look in Mama's eyes—tryin' to tell me she gonna find me and bring the buttons with her. I just know she will. And I remind myself of that look every night when I close my eyes.

Only she'd better hurry. Because the dress Mama gave me ain't gonna fit much longer.

ONE

New Orleans, Modern Day

Alice

Alice always had loved flowers.

There was something about the blend of colors, the hidden roots, the twisting petals as they unfurled in the sun one by one. A symbol of femininity—how that which is delicate can also be strong.

Whiskey in a teacup, as her aunt always said. Well, her aunt and Reese Witherspoon, but honestly, Aunt Charlotte had been saying that way back when Reese was still filming *Sweet Home Alabama*.

Alice swept petals from the floor, beautiful yet fragmented evidence of the fullness the day had brought. She'd been running The Prickly Rose, a customizable bouquet shop on Magazine Street, alongside her aunt for several years now, and Valentine's Day always left plenty of cast-off remnants.

She was sweeping the last of the petals into the dustpan when she heard a knock at the door. A quick glance at the clock confirmed they were a quarter past closing time, and if she didn't leave now, she would be late for her date.

Not that she was particularly excited about a blind double

date on Valentine's Day, but her friend Harper had insisted, so she'd acquiesced.

Still, it was the principle of the thing. No self-respecting person thought so little of his date that he'd buy flowers at closing time. Let alone fifteen minutes after.

Alice was just about to check the bolt on the door when her aunt buzzed past, placing a hand on each side of her own face to get a better look through the wrought iron. She glanced at Alice over her shoulder. "He's handsome."

Alice stepped down to open the trash can, then dumped the petals. "They always are."

Aunt Charlotte turned to face her. "But this one looks like a young Clooney."

"I don't care if he looks like Milo Ventimiglia." Okay, that was an exaggeration. But her aunt probably didn't even know who Milo was, so she wasn't too concerned about the woman calling her bluff. Alice tapped one stubborn petal until it fell into the trash. "We're closed."

Aunt Charlotte hurried closer, glancing behind her as though he could hear them. "But the poor boy needs flowers. It's Valentine's Day, Alice. Couldn't you have a little heart?"

"I see what you did there with the pun." Alice planted her hands at the hips of her knee-length skirt. "But the answer is no. I cannot. He can abide by the store hours just like everyone else managed to."

"I didn't want to have to do this . . ." But before Aunt Charlotte could finish the words, she began racing toward the door.

Alice followed two steps behind but did manage to slam her hand on the door before her aunt could shimmy it open. "What are you, four years old?" she whispered. "He's probably seen us through the door."

"And whose fault is that, hmm?" Aunt Charlotte peeled Alice's hand from off the doorway.

Alice balked. "Why, I have never—"

But Aunt Charlotte was already busy opening the door. She smiled a warning sort of grin at Alice. "What if it *is* Clooney?" she whispered. Her eyes went wide.

"You think everyone is Clooney," Alice murmured as the man stepped inside. She managed a smile despite his tardiness because, after all, she was just the kind of person to be polite.

The bell at the front of the shop jingled as he entered.

Definitely not Milo, but—dare she say it—even more attractive.

He was tall and seemed even taller because of the way his presence filled the room. His smile revealed straight teeth, his jaw was strong but not sharp, and his shoulders, broad. He wore a relaxed T-shirt over properly fitting jeans, and faintly smelled of cedarwood.

He had on trendy tennis shoes that made him look ready to run . . . both literally *and* figuratively.

But despite his obvious appeal, he was a *customer*. And it was well past closing time. At this point, Alice was so exhausted that Clooney really could've walked into the shop, and she would've pointed to the *Closed* sign.

"How may I help you?"

One strand of the man's trimmed brown hair fell askew as he looked at her.

Their gazes locked, and Alice caught herself drawn in by a blend of curiosity and attraction. His eyes were the color of sea glass and the wild waves that made it strong.

Alice blinked, her mind foggy with the memory of waves.

After the slightest moment's pause, he pulled out his wallet. "I need some red roses."

Alice frowned. She looked at Aunt Charlotte, then back at the man.

"It's Valentine's Day," Alice said matter-of-factly.

He set his debit card on the counter and pushed it forward, as if the gesture would make a difference. "I am aware of that. Which is why I need them."

Her aunt smiled sweetly, ready to accommodate him, but Alice wouldn't be so easily swayed. She didn't like his bullying tone, and handed the card back to him.

"We're all out," Alice said.

The man rolled his eyes. "Fine. I'll take pink, then."

"Out of those too."

"White?"

Alice leaned forward, her elbows on the counter. "I'm sorry. Nope."

The man sighed as he looked straight into her eyes once more, clearly not used to hearing the word *no*. He pocketed his hands. "Let me put it this way. What *do* you have?"

Alice kneeled beneath the register and chose another arrangement to set up on the counter.

The man touched the whimsical array of baby's breath, berries, dried cotton, and pine cones as though it were a prickly cactus. He tapped the glass with his finger. "This is a mason jar."

Alice cleared her throat. "It's an antique. That's something we pride ourselves in here at The Prickly Rose—no two of our items are identical." She wouldn't mention the flowers were two days old and half-off because the petals had begun to droop. That's what he got for waiting until the last minute.

"This is stuff you could find in your backyard."

Had he heard *anything* she'd just said?

"It's organic." She swallowed to fight the tide in his eyes, hating the amount of willpower it took to do that.

"I cannot bring her a jar of berries and squirrel seeds. I'm trying to leave a good impression here."

I hope for your sake your impression on her is better than the one you've left on me.

"Sorry we can't be of greater help." Alice shrugged, thankful to soon be rid of him. Sometimes these after-store-hours customers could be equally insensitive to overstaying their welcome. "You've caught us after closing time, so it's pretty picked over."

He turned to the door with a wave over his shoulder. "Thanks anyway," he mumbled, on the very edge of rudeness.

But as the bell above the door chimed, Alice realized her aunt was smiling a dangerous sort of smile.

"Well, he was darling."

Alice rolled her eyes. Her aunt was convinced Alice's prospects for a suitable marriage expired after age twenty-nine. Which left her six months.

She shook her head and fiddled with the mason jar arrangement before placing it back under the counter. "Late for a date on Valentine's Day? Definitely not my type."

Sullivan

Obviously, Sullivan had made a mistake. Buying flowers for his blind date had resulted in unequivocal failure.

What was worse, a quick glance at his phone showed he was ten minutes late to meet his friends. And counting. He was lost. In the French Quarter. He had passed this nostalgia shop at least three times now and was walking in circles.

Maybe his date wouldn't be the flowers type.

Who was he kidding? All women were the flowers type. His mother had taught him that. And his Grandma Beth would disown him if she knew he was about to show up to a date on Valentine's Day empty-handed.

Sure, it wasn't a serious date or anything, but the woman was a friend of a friend and the day was really Valentine's

Day, so he was pretty sure those two things combined qualified her for a bouquet.

A lot of help the woman at the flower shop had been. He had every intention of giving her a one-star review, when his phone lit up with the notification his buddy Peter was calling.

"Dude, where are you?"

Sullivan spun around to get a look at the street name. "I'm here . . . ish. I just can't seem to find the place."

"Okay, I'm going out into the street now to see if I can find you."

Suddenly, he saw Peter waving from one block up. Sullivan waved back and hustled over.

The two men clasped hands. "Sorry, man. I got turned around."

"It happens." Peter smiled. "Hey, it's good to see you. Been a while."

Sullivan raked his hair back into place with his hand. "Sure has. Engagement suits you, Peter. You look happy."

Peter's grin widened. "I am." Near the restaurant, two women lingered on the sidewalk. Sullivan assumed the woman next to Harper was his blind date for the evening. They were still too far away for him to get a good look at her.

Sullivan wasn't typically the type to go for the whole blind-date thing. But he, Peter, and Harper were in town for only a little while because of Peter and Harper's wedding in a few days. Harper apparently wanted to see this woman as much as Peter and Sullivan wanted to hang out together, so doubling up seemed like a good idea. They'd insisted he and his date would get along great.

And really, Sullivan didn't make a habit of turning women down. Well, not on a first date, at least.

It wasn't until he and Peter approached the restaurant that the nagging feeling in his chest began. Something about the woman standing beside Harper was familiar. . . . He had seen her before.

Then she turned, and he saw her face. Her beautiful, berry-squirrel-seed-loving smile. He rubbed his hands over his eyes. *You have got to be kidding me.*

Peter turned, the gesture not lost on him. "What is it? What's wrong?" he asked.

"It's just . . . well . . . Is *that* my date?" Sullivan nodded his head toward where the women stood.

"Yes, and I don't see why you're not falling on your knees in gratitude right now. She's totally your type."

Sullivan held up one finger and shook his hand. "Funny you should say that, actually . . ."

Peter crossed his arms. "What's going on?"

"I sort of met her earlier." Sullivan huffed. "You could say I didn't leave the best impression."

Peter hit him hard on the shoulder. "So here's your chance to make a better one."

TWO

Charleston, Summer 1861

Clara

Coming to visit her cousin Mary made Clara feel like she was grown and capable, but the truth was, she might not be either one of those things. Definitely not grown. The capable part was up for debate.

See, she had ideas. All sorts of ideas. About justice and hope and happy endings—about a woman's capability, and the kind of world that could be possible.

But she wasn't a fool either. She was Clara Adelaide Abels, future heiress of a cotton empire. From childhood, her parents made it abundantly clear that to leave the family business would mean to leave their family completely. And even at the age of sixteen, Clara was keenly aware of all she had to lose.

So with one foot on the doorstep beneath the rose trellis and the other on the ground, Clara peeked through the open doorway and spied her cousin just on the other side.

"Clara!" Mary clutched her hand to her chest. "What a fright you gave me. I had no idea you were lurking around out here." She started laughing, absentmindedly running her hand over her intricate hairstyle.

Clara laughed too, shutting the door behind her. "How was I supposed to know you were standing there, ready to intercept me?"

Mary hugged Clara, the merriment continuing. "I'm glad you've made an appearance, however sudden, because I have something to tell you. We've received word an associate of Oliver's will be joining us for dinner."

Clara pulled back from the embrace. Mary's husband Oliver had been working furtively for abolition and had recently signed up for the Union army. The plantation where he and Mary lived had once belonged to Oliver's parents. When he and Mary wed and inherited the estate, they both knew they must do something about emancipating those who were enslaved there. But the family's livelihood rested upon a good harvest. So Oliver began training as a minister to have extra income to pay the workers as employees, should they choose to remain on the plantation. Mary said it was a far cry from equality, but it was something.

Clara didn't speak of this with her father—else he might forbid her from ever seeing Mary and Oliver again. See, Clara's father had recently been promoted to a general within the Confederacy, and it was a role he took very seriously. Their family, their friends, their community had all begun to fracture like splintered wood under the weight of ethical failures—and the last thing Clara wanted was for her father to keep her from Mary.

She couldn't imagine her life without her dear cousin Mary. Mary was her only confidante, really.

Clara looked squarely into Mary's eyes. "When you say *associate*, what do you mean exactly?"

Mary hesitated, her right eye twitching as it always did when she was hiding something.

"Mary?"

"I'm sworn to secrecy."

Clara's heart skipped a beat. "Sounds interesting."

"It is. Believe me." Mary held onto her gaze. "You must solemnly swear to me you'll tell no one about this dinner, Clara."

"Unlike you, Mother taught me never to swear, and certainly not solemnly," Clara said with a wink.

Mary sobered. "I'm serious, Clara."

Clara drew in a breath, her corset constricting. "I am too, sweet Mary—I promise you I will not say a word."

Mary nodded once. "Excellent. All you need to know is he's British, and his name is Teddy."

Clara's mind flew to the heroes in her Jane Austen novels—the ones her father didn't know she was reading. "In that case, the secret is *definitely* safe with me."

Clara wasn't typically what you would call a fiery woman. She did her best to obey all the social expectations of her society. She followed all the rules about her hair and her corset and the colors her mother suggested she take in and out of her trunk for each season of the year.

But war, even at its very beginning, had changed her.

She had never been comfortable with the thought of slavery, though her father had drilled the phrase *lives, income, tradition* into her head so many times over the years that, up until now, she had shrugged off her gall toward the institution as feminine sensitivity. Everyone said that women could not be trusted to make decisions of business and logic for this very reason.

As war began to take men into its ranks, Clara began to realize something with more clarity every single time she looked at the enslaved woman Father had assigned to her care—Rose.

She wasn't the one who was wrong.

So when her cousin Mary, who *was* by all accounts a fiery woman, wrote to Clara last week about spending the weekend at her house, Clara knew she had better keep her evolving thoughts on the political landscape to herself until she arrived here. Because she could make no promises for what might happen when she actually saw Mary and got her hands on the newest edition of the abolitionist paper *The Liberator*.

Such were among her reasons for particular interest in Mary's dinner guest this evening. She hugged her shawl a little tighter around her shoulders—for the room was drafty despite the candles on the table—and looked to Mary as they took their seats at the table.

"Will your guest be here soon?" she asked her cousin.

"Indeed." Mary smiled, eyes twinkling. Clara couldn't be sure, but she could have sworn she saw mischief there. Mary was up to no good.

Rose helped Mary's housemaid pour water into goblets and set platters of corned beef, sweet potatoes, and corn on the table, along with a large basket full of buttermilk biscuits. It smelled delicious.

Clara looked at the empty place setting beside her. A wave of nervousness went through her at the thought of making conversation with a stranger. Though she was well-versed in keeping conversation going—it was a feminine art, after all— she wouldn't say she enjoyed it. Constantly racking one's brain for another topic to discuss grew exhausting after a while, especially when a lady was expected to accomplish such a feat with poise and grace.

There were only so many graceful ways to discuss sweet potatoes.

But alas, her parents had trained her well. And she appreciated having the skill set and gaining information from people, even if doing so *did* prove wearying.

A figure appeared in the doorway—a masculine figure, as though summoned by her nerves. As he drew nearer, Clara studied him. His height was appropriate for dancing, his frame, modest yet capable, and his thick hair had been parted with a flattering swoosh of sorts at the top of his forehead.

"Pardon me for arriving late," he said, and his accent was deliciously British. "My mother would find my lack of manners ghastly." His eyes swept the room until landing on Clara, and he seemed to pause at the sight of her. Or maybe that was a girlish fancy speaking . . . for this man had the same type of arresting presence as the dawn. She couldn't bring herself to look away from him.

He filled the seat beside her and extended his hand. She took it—gladly—and with a nod, he introduced himself. "Theodore Atwood. It's my pleasure to make your acquaintance."

Why did everything British people say have to sound so charming?

She offered her name and removed her hand from his with her finest sense of etiquette, despite the desperate attraction that begged her to let her fingers linger in his own.

She had never felt this way before and truthfully, had always assumed such butterflies were the stuff of fiction. She swallowed hard when Theodore reached for his napkin and nearly brushed her knuckles with his own.

"Tell us, Theodore, are you from England?" Clara took a sip of water from her goblet, careful to set it down without the tiniest splash. She chose the proper fork from the place setting and tried to retain the utmost of social graces as she took a bite of her sweet potatoes, even as her heart raced at the nearness of the handsome stranger.

She would make pleasant conversation with him just as decorum required, and then she would do everything in her power to forget how cozy her hand had felt when he'd taken it for those few moments.

"Originally, yes." He smiled. "But I am an American now. My family and I reside in New York and have for many years."

"Oh, I hear the clubs in New York are splendid," Mary's husband, Oliver, said. "High society and whatnot."

"If you can keep their good favor." Theodore chuckled, shaking his head. "I'm afraid my poor mother expends a good bit of energy trying to secure my place." He wiped his mouth with the corner of his napkin, looking to Clara. "Then again, she is also quite concerned with securing me a wife, so perhaps it's me and not her who deserves your deeper sympathy."

Clara laughed loudly at this, then bit down on her bottom lip. She should not have laughed so freely— 'twas unbecoming. Yet she couldn't help herself. She understood what he meant far too well.

He met her eyes, his gaze dancing with amusement.

"Surely your mother means well." Clara snuck another biscuit from the basket. Being around Mary was already making her more impulsive.

"No doubt she does. Yet her good intentions seem to have no effect on how dull these seemingly endless conversations with potential wives become."

"You mean to say not a single one of these women holds your attention, Theodore?" Clara asked.

"And you're certain the problem is not yourself?" Oliver added, teasing.

"Touché," he replied, leaning forward. "But you've got it all backwards. You see, the problem is absolutely myself. I've always been surrounded by these posh social parties and expectations—in a nutshell, my parents' life—and have never really had the opportunity to create my own. Until now." He ran his tongue along his teeth as though the words were hard to say aloud. But Clara knew exactly how he felt.

He leaned a little closer. "By the way," he said, for her ears alone. "Please call me Teddy."

And her heart was light as a sheet on a clothesline, floating up, up, up.

And she knew she was in for it now.

Later that evening, Clara awoke from slumber at the sound of wooden boards creaking. Though groggily wakened from her dreams, Clara was all but positive the sound came from the second floor. She sat up, pulling the covers around her dressing gown, and wishing Rose were in this room instead of the one next to it.

Clara stood, sliding her arms into her wrap, then tightening it and carefully placing a globe over her candle.

Investigating strange sounds in the night was hardly behavior of which her mother would approve, but Clara wouldn't get an ounce of sleep until she followed this through.

She eased open the door with her free hand, the candle in the other, and peered into the hallway.

Nothing.

No sounds, no sights, no figures.

Perhaps she had imagined the whole thing. Oh, but there'd be no going back to sleep now.

So she went down the stairs as quietly as her slippers would allow and let her fingers linger on the curved banister as she turned to the first floor.

Outside, a mature climbing rose vine wove in and out of the trellis just past the back door. The effect was so charming, she wanted just a few moments of the fragrance to herself, a peace before the day's hustle and bustle.

She went outside, sat on the bench beneath the trellis, closed her eyes, and breathed deeply, careful not to knock over the candle beside her.

The fragrance was beautiful, and so were the crimson and

pale pink petals by the light of the moon—petals that littered the grass below with daubs of color.

She sat there for a full minute, feeling young and enchanted and free.

That's when she heard the leaves behind her rustling.

Her heart began to race. Who was there? Had she been foolish for venturing outside on her own in her dressing gown, with only a cape wrapped around it?

But as the man came into view, her heart eased with relief even as her breath caught in her chest for an entirely different reason.

Teddy.

His hand brushed against the side of the trellis as he turned to face her. "Clara?" he asked, in that appealing accent. "Are you okay?"

"Perfectly fine, thank you." She grinned up at him, unsure of whether he could see her expression.

Teddy swept one hand through his hair to justify the part that, at this time of evening, looked to be a lost cause. Why was he so unkempt? And what was he doing awake like this? Though she supposed he could ask the same things of her.

He sat down beside her and studied her a long moment. "Well, then. I suppose we are both just two people who enjoy the company of the moon."

Clara's stomach fluttered at his words. She folded her hands in her lap. "I suppose you're right."

"I was trying to remember where I've heard your name before. Is your father high-ranking in the Confederacy?"

Suddenly, reality fell upon her in all its crushing weight.

"He is," she shifted toward him.

Teddy inhaled slowly. "And you?" He leaned forward and caught her gaze. "Forgive me if I'm being presumptuous . . . but Mary told me you're an abolitionist."

"I think I am." It was the first time she'd actually spoken

the words. With them, her heart became unfettered—like a wild horse running free for the first time—as she confessed what the depths of her had long known to be true.

Slavery was an abomination. An offense in the eyes of the Lord, and a blight on society. She wondered, even, if perhaps there was more she could do to stop it. But was that ridiculous? Her . . . the sixteen-year-old daughter of a Confederate general?

"You *think* you're an abolitionist or you *know* you are?" Teddy fiddled with his collar. "Surely you see that you must make a firm decision one way or the other, don't you? Because if you truly believe in the cause, you must act to further it." Teddy stood from the bench but never looked away from her.

He spoke as though she were capable of changing the world. "What is it you're doing here on Edisto . . . exactly?" she asked him.

"Let me know where you come down on abolition, and then I'll tell you." Teddy's eyes twinkled, making her all the more curious.

A bundle of nerves, Clara didn't so much as blink. His presence tickled every part of her, from the buckles of her shoes to the pins of her curls. And she felt as though her heart had been awakened, and she didn't know how she would ever again sleep.

He was right in everything he said. Clara could not, in good conscience, continue to support the abolitionist cause here on Edisto, then go home to reap the vast comforts of a cotton plantation. She couldn't have it both ways.

It was time to put both feet on the same step.

And she hoped as a benefit, that step might also lead her closer to a certain British stranger.

I didn't mean to do no snoopin'.

But I heard Missus Clara tryin' to make her way all sly down the hallway, and I was worried, you see? So I followed her. She about as subtle as a horsefly, but she thinks she's being real secretive. Really she's still just a girl tryin' to figure out how to become a woman, and we all do that sometimes, don't we?

Anyway, what I mean to say is I overheard Missus talking to that Theodore fella about slaves and abolition, and now I think I've heard all I need to.

Just like I suspected, Missus don't want no part of partaking in slavery, but she don't know what to do about it. She ain't yet figured out she's got a say in the world around her.

But she will. Maybe Theodore will tell her, just like he did tonight under those flowers. Missus ain't looked at nobody the way she looks at that man. He may yet be a stranger, but he may also be our savior from this God-forsaken reality.

Clara likes him.

So do I.

He gonna help me get my daughter back—my daughter Ashley, who I haven't seen in a year. I feel it down in my bones. And bones don't lie.

THREE

Alice

"You have got to be kidding me," Alice said. The breeze caught the green-and-white striped awning she and Harper stood beneath as they waited in front of Café Beignet.

Harper reached out to take Alice's elbow. "What's wrong?"

Alice shifted her weight between her 1940s-inspired heels. "Oh, did I say that out loud?"

But Sullivan and Peter were quickly approaching, and Alice didn't have time to explain.

"W-o-w," Harper mouthed, darting her eyes to Sullivan. This was apparently her first time meeting Peter's friend.

"He isn't *that* cute," Alice murmured under her breath.

Okay, so it was a lie. But Alice wasn't shallow like that. She found intentionality and punctuality far more attractive than height and a nice face. Even a very nice face.

Sullivan's eyes widened with mirth. In the glow of the streetlamp, they were downright jolly. "You'll forgive me for showing up late and empty-handed on Valentine's Day." He grinned. "I tried to get you a small bouquet, but the florist told me they had sold completely out."

27

"Yes, Valentine's is a very busy sales day for florists. I imagine she was probably ready to put her feet up the moment the clock struck closing time." Alice smiled and raised her eyebrows.

"Well, let's go inside, shall we?" Peter shook his head and laughed, scratching his forehead above his eyebrow. How much had Sullivan told him?

Harper leaned over and whispered in Alice's ear, "What is going on?"

"Nothing," Alice whispered back. Sullivan held the door open for the group to walk through. From the look on Harper's face, she wasn't buying Alice's dismissal, so Alice added a quick clarification. "*I* was the florist," she muttered.

The slow grin that spread across Harper's face in that moment was so predictable that Alice knew exactly what her dear friend was thinking.

Oh no, Alice wanted to respond. *This is not our meet cute. He is no Tom Hanks, okay? Or Matthew McConaughey. He's the type of guy who waits until the eleventh hour to buy his date flowers, and I am a respectable florist who could never be with that type of guy.*

But Alice said none of that. Instead, she just smiled as the hostess led their group to a table. They each settled in around the table, and Alice browsed through the menu as she took in the charm of the restaurant. The brick walls and curved ceiling formed an arch that made the small space all kinds of cozy. The holiday had drawn quite a buzzing crowd, all of whom apparently knew where to find the best beignets in the city, away from the maddening tourist crowds a few streets over.

She didn't know why she was looking at the menu. Of course she was getting beignets.

"So, Sullivan." Alice looked at him over her menu and crossed her ankles under the table. "What do you do for a living?"

"I'm a business consultant, actually." He rubbed the back of his neck with his hand.

Why did he seem so uncomfortable? She was letting him off the proverbial hook and changing the subject. He should be thanking his lucky stars Harper and Peter were here right now, or she would've very politely been saying *thanks, but no thanks* because she had dated enough guys like this before to know exactly how it was going to end. Experience had shown her if you couldn't arrive on time when you were making a first impression, you were probably only bound to get less reliable as time went on. And if there was one thing Alice appreciated in another human being, it was reliability.

"That's nice," Alice replied.

"Usually." He scanned his menu before setting it down on the table. "At this particular moment, it's a little frustrating, however—because I blocked off a solid two weeks for a project in New Orleans while I'm here for the wedding, only for them to cancel on me." He crossed his arms and leaned back against his seat. "Now I guess I've got a long vacation ahead of me."

Harper spoke up. "Actually, Alice—weren't you just telling me a few weeks ago that your flower shop could use some help with rebranding?"

Sullivan raised his eyebrows, his interest clearly piqued.

Alice, however, was not humored. What was Harper doing? She shot her friend a look that she hoped conveyed her displeasure. "Did I say that?" Alice started. "Because I don't know if I said, exactly . . ."

But it was too late. Sullivan was already drumming his fingers against the table.

"You know if you're interested, I would be happy to help with that."

Harper quickly looked away from Alice, nodding on her

behalf. "Oh, that would be great—wouldn't it, Alice? What perfect timing."

"Mmm," Alice forced a pleasant expression so as not to be rude. After all, she had to work with this guy on the wedding errands, even apart from his offer to help with The Prickly Rose. She didn't want to make the situation even more awkward than it already was.

She glanced over at him and realized he was watching her. "So Alice . . . have you always loved flowers?" Her name on his lips was kind and caught her off guard.

"I have." She looked back down at her menu.

She didn't tell him her dream as a little girl was to be a singer, just like her mother. She definitely didn't tell him what happened that caused her to give that dream up.

The waitress arrived just in time.

Alice once again was able to successfully pretend, and no one seemed the wiser. As the night continued, she discovered that Sullivan wasn't quite as obnoxious as she'd initially suspected and was really even—dare she admit it?—rather charming.

"Let's take a photo before the waitress brings our checks," Harper said.

Alice wiped the corners of her mouth to check for powdered sugar and pulled her phone from her heart-shaped purse. "Here, we can use mine, and I'll text it to you."

Alice held out her phone but couldn't fit everyone in the photo. Sullivan scooted his chair closer.

"Let me help," he said. When he reached for her phone, their fingers brushed, sending an unexpected and unwelcome sense of anticipation fluttering through Alice. Mostly unwelcome, that is. Okay, so it wasn't unwelcome at all.

Alice smiled at the camera as though this incredibly attractive man were her honest-to-goodness date. She smiled at the camera as though she didn't *have* a complicated past, as though her mind hadn't been a blur ever since Sullivan asked about how long she'd loved flowers.

It was a beautiful smile. It was only a little bit a lie. But she was used to that by now.

Alice tugged her strawberry-embroidered cardigan a little closer and waved good-bye to the dinner group.

A wild auburn curl flew over her shoulder as she turned to face the path ahead. After all this time, her heart ached for her mother, for her home. She ached for home and ached because of it—though maybe, on second thought, the two were one and the same.

She'd scheduled an Uber while still at the restaurant and was only a few skips down the block from where her driver would appear in several minutes' time, when she heard someone call to her from across the street.

From the light of the streetlamps, she realized she recognized the group gathered on the sidewalk. It was one of the bands her mother used to sing with. Like a ghost from over a decade gone.

She checked for cars before she crossed the street in a haze.

"How are you, Alice?" The woman with the saxophone asked. "I'd recognize those colored tights of yours from a mile away. You've grown up, but I see your fashion hasn't changed."

Alice grinned, wondering if they could feel the tensing of her shoulders.

How was she? Did they really want to know?

"I'm well, and yourselves?" Alice's skirt stuck against her thick leggings as she took a couple steps closer.

They all nodded and smiled and exchanged general pleasantries. Alice didn't recall them playing on the street so late at night, but then again, it was Valentine's Day.

"So nice to see you," the man with the banjo said. Alice didn't recall his name, and it seemed he hadn't remembered hers either. "Tell your mother we said hello."

"I will."

Why she said these two words in response, Alice didn't know. She definitely hadn't intended to. They had just sort of tumbled out, like a rolling wave.

Personal pronoun. Future tense.

A complete impossibility.

They must not know. Alice's mother had stopped singing with them months before Hurricane Katrina, and somehow, they must not know what happened and the giant question mark that hung in the air.

Please let her be okay. Please let her be okay. Please let her be okay.

Alice had prayed those words more times than she could count, hoping it would make an impact if she said it the right number of times or the right way. Somehow, she felt like saying it correctly would better ensure God heard her. The problem was, she never quite knew how to pray *correctly*.

The Uber driver arrived, and Alice said good-bye with another round of pretend smiling before she slid into the Camry. She made it all the way to Magazine Street before her chest started hurting with waves of grief. And as waves are prone to doing, the wave brought the tide, and the tide came strong, and the current pulled her under.

Harper told her a trick once about not fighting riptides but moving parallel to them so you don't lose your strength. Then you just sort of float along until you're in a different space in the ocean where you can handle swimming.

Alice tried to apply the same idea to her own tide—the one that pulled her in different directions, sometimes tugging her harder than others until she fought back, eventually growing weary.

As Alice watched the storefronts of Magazine Street, she thought about her mother, and she missed her terribly. So terribly that her body physically ached, and she could actually smell that Elizabeth Arden White Tea perfume her mother used to get from the department store. Back when malls were the place to get your perfume—actually, back when people even wore perfume.

Nobody wore it anymore, did they? Migraine triggers and hidden plastics or whatever the danger in the synthetic fragrance was supposed to be.

Her mother's perfume *had* given Alice headaches. But secretly, sometimes she went to the makeup store and dabbed a little of the fragrance on her wrists just because she missed her mother, willing to take the migraine.

Other days, most days, she was okay.

They arrived at the small cottage Alice shared with her aunt in the Garden District, and Alice opened the wrought-iron garden gate, then carefully shut it behind her.

Alice liked living here. Aunt Charlotte bought the house ages ago and when Alice needed somewhere to stay, she brought her right in. Sometimes they drove each other plumb crazy—as her aunt would say—but they were family, and family wasn't something Alice took lightly.

She hoped that tonight she could curl up for a few moments with a thick blanket in the courtyard at the back, overlooking the garden, and she could do some deep breathing exercises, and she could find peace again before she went to sleep.

So after the Uber left, Alice lingered on the brick path leading to the cottage, her arms crossed as she looked up into the starry sky.

The winter stars had always been her favorite. So easy to see certain constellations when it was good and cold out. She stayed there and watched her breath form little clouds that floated up toward the heavens. Maybe it was five minutes, maybe it was fifteen, but soon she became aware of someone standing near the closed gate.

A very tall, very handsome someone.

"Sullivan?" Alice walked over to him, and the iron creaked from its ancient hinges. "What are you doing here?"

He stepped inside the gate, just past where she opened it, and set her wallet in her hands. "You left this at the restaurant." His touch on her fingers was warm, warmer than the cold outside and in. "How was your Uber driver?"

Alice wrinkled her lips in a wry smile. She slid her wallet into the pocket of her skirt. "Well, he didn't tell me Happy Valentine's Day, for starters."

"The nerve." Sullivan pretended to be appalled. "And how was the conversation otherwise?"

"Lacking compared to the droll humor of my blind date." This was too close to flirting and she knew it, and she also knew she should still be on guard near him because he was still the kind of guy who showed up to her flower shop at the eleventh hour—and why was she already having trouble remembering this?

But the moment got the best of her anyway.

Sullivan raised his eyebrows, sending a tug of attraction through her and all manner of alarm bells. "Have you forgiven me, then?" He put his hands into his pockets casually. "I mean, I did get your address from Peter and brought your wallet all the way over."

Alice studied him—how he stood with his feet so firmly planted in a way that evoked strength, not just because of his height but because there was also something . . . well, something else. Something engaging. Mysterious and confident. Yes, that's what she was attracted to.

Alice, stop it before you start crushing on this guy who probably has a new date every day of the week!

Several quiet moments stretched between them, but the

silence felt full as Sullivan studied her in return. And she wondered—between her red curls and eclectic style and the mystery she kept beneath her cloudy eyes—what did he see?

"Why did you seem so uncomfortable when I asked if you'd always loved flowers?"

The question was only fair.

Alice accidentally bit the inside of her lip. The sting mirrored the sudden burning inside of her. She exhaled, slowly. "Because before I loved flowers, I loved singing—like my mother." Alice hesitated. "She's missing."

Sullivan turned his head, concerned. "Missing?" he asked, clearly trying to make sense of the word choice.

"Yes. Since Hurricane Katrina."

"Oh." Sullivan took a step closer, placing one hand gently on her arm. "Oh, Alice. I'm so sorry."

Alice nodded. She started to reassure him it'd been a while and she was fine now—the usual script people liked to hear and she liked to say—but something stopped her from pretending.

Maybe it was the look in his eyes. Maybe it was the honesty. Either way, he just stood beside her, the two of them looking at the starry heavens.

Please let her be okay. Please let her be okay. Please let her be okay.

FOUR

Charleston, Summer 1861

They got a new girl over at Missus Mary's house—she says Mary and Oliver actually payin' them to work, like they white folk or something, and then she tells me her name is Hannah. She tryin' to make introductions, see, but the problem is I been "mama" so long, I forgot my other name.

Ever since the men took my baby—she a girl now, really, but she'll always be my baby—every day has been another fight to breathe. So I reckon I have to remember my name, eventually. At least if I want to get my Ashley back, because somebody bound to ask me.

Women who're slaves ain't supposed to get chillen who're slaves back. That probably goes without sayin'. So up 'til now, I have behaved as the best house slave anybody could wish for. I been making my plan, see, hopin' that someday Clara will help me.

Here's a secret—Clara's young, yes, but she's matured a whole lot since I came here a year ago and I see it in her eyes how she really feels about slavery. She looks at me, really looks at me, even though she ain't supposed to. Some days I even trust her. And I ain't foolish—believe me.

But if there's even a chance she would help me find my Ashley . . . well . . . that's a chance worth taking.

So I'm waitin' until I'm absolutely sure I can tell her about my daughter, and she won't run off and tell her father and make a mess of things—her father is a monster, see. And I keep waitin'. For another sunset, another sunrise, another hum of the songbirds.

The servants are all staring at me now like maybe I can't speak, and all of a sudden, I finally remember.

My name is Rose.

And when I remember that—I can't explain why—I feel stronger. Maybe 'cause I remember what my own mama was always sayin'—that I'm strong and smart and can do great things. So this is my great thing.

Because while I do find myself motherin' Clara, at the end of the day, I already got a daughter. And come hell or high water, I'm gonna do whatever it takes to find her. Whether Clara helps me or not.

But either way, I've got to hurry.

Clara

The following evening, Clara lay awake in her bed with thoughts of Teddy keeping her company. He had bold ideas, just like Mary and Oliver, and the three of them had challenged her into the realization she could no longer stand halfway in the familiar traditions of her family and halfway in abolition.

She had to be all in.

And it was among the presence of these ideas, multiplying

within her soul, that she heard the sound of wooden boards creaking, just as she'd heard the night before.

Clara stilled and listened with as much attention as she could manage at the midnight hour. After the initial creaking, she heard nothing.

The back of her neck was moist with sweat—either from her sudden panic or the heat of the second-floor room, she did not know. Perhaps both.

The noise stilled, but the disturbance did not settle well within her.

Clara moved to the window as the moonlight cast a glow through her room, onto her carpetbag beside the window.

She told herself the rest of the house was asleep and that she was only imagining things.

The trouble was, she knew she wasn't.

Suddenly, a baby's cry pierced the silence from down the hall, followed by a shriek. Clara jolted. She circled the brown wrapper around her nightgown, placed a globe upon her candle, and hurried from her room.

Whatever was happening?

The baby's wail faded in and out of the hallway, and Clara rushed toward an open doorway where Mary stood.

Inside the little room, Teddy and Oliver huddled around a black woman in bed, holding the baby.

Clara's eyes widened.

Who was she?

"Clara," Mary urged. "Send for Rose immediately. I'll explain soon."

The infant cried again—so tiny, so frail—and Clara's skin crawled with the realization that something was wrong with the baby. Her heart sunk in fear.

She ran for Rose. She didn't even remember what she said or how long it took her feet to travel down the hallway, all she knew was that Rose sprung into action, moistening towels and offering the mother water to drink. Clara felt helpless—absolutely helpless—because as she realized with a start, she had no practical knowledge of how to care for anybody.

It was upon this humbling realization that she met Teddy's gaze from the glow of the candles. He was wearing long trousers and a buttoned white shirt. Strange, that he would be wearing such garments in the middle of the night. Though now that she considered it, Mary had also been dressed as if ready for the day.

But Clara shook her head. She chided herself for thinking about garments when the baby was in such a fragile state.

Death had seemed to move by the very air of the clouds since the Ordinance of Secession had been signed at Institute Hall in downtown Charleston, and Clara had never felt closer to that storm as she did here, in this room.

Theodore gently took her by the hand and led her back into the hallway.

"Teddy?" she whispered. "Will the baby be okay?"

He nodded, and for the briefest moment, the glow of the candlelight caught the warm brown of his eyes.

"I imagine you have a lot of other questions."

"I do."

"Before I explain anything, Clara, I need you to tell me with every bit of sincerity if you have given any thought to last night's conversation, and, if so, what conclusions you have made."

Clara inhaled slowly, summoning her strength. "You were right, Teddy."

"About what?" he asked.

"Everything." She wrung her hands. "Now tell me—what are that woman and her baby doing in Mary and Oliver's house?"

Teddy watched her intently, as though studying her and determining how much to say. "We are helping her. Oliver, me, and Mary."

"*Helping* her?" Clara tightened the wrap around her gown. "But how did you find her?" Then another thought came. "Have you done this before?"

Teddy reached out and took her hands in the palms of his own. His touch was warm and steadied her. "For now, you're just going to have to trust me."

Clara hesitated.

"Do you trust me, Clara? Are you committed to this cause despite what it may cost you?"

She thought of all the strange noises she'd been hearing in the house at night, once everyone else was asleep . . . or at least supposed to be. How she'd seen Teddy last night as she sat under the rose trellis.

Something was definitely going on here.

Clara took a deep breath, hoping he would hold on to her hands a little longer. "Yes. On both accounts."

Teddy nodded. "Good. Then let's go back into the room, and I'll fill you in further as soon as the moment allows. But for now, we must make haste."

When the two of them stepped back through the doorway, they found the baby sleeping in the bassinet by the window.

Mary's shoulders heaved with relief when she saw them.

"Clara, come closer. Touch this woman's forehead and tell me if she's warm. I am so flustered, I'm convinced I could feel fever on a block of ice."

Clara approached the bed and reached out her hand. The woman's eyes were open, but even in the candlelight, she looked sickly. She murmured something unintelligible, then moaned.

The tips of Clara's fingers felt the heat of the fever before they had even touched the woman's skin. Never before had she felt such heat on a person.

Slowly, she looked to Mary and nodded.

Rose dampened cloths in cool water and put them over the woman's forehead.

"What happened to them?" Clara asked.

Mary took Clara's elbow and led her away from the bedside. Once they were beyond the woman's earshot, she whispered. "They are running from a plantation, Clara, trying to get to freedom. But I am worried. Very worried, for her sake and her baby's. Rose examined them while you were out of the room with Teddy, and she agrees they both have thrush and are exhausted from the journey it took to get here."

"What does that mean?" Clara asked. "Will they recover?"

Mary shook her head. "I think so. It's an infection. Before you came upon us, I applied gentian violet both to the mother and the baby and will continue that treatment. The next few days will be critical—for the mother, especially. She must regain strength. She is so very weak."

Mary tucked a stray lock of hair behind her ear and seemed to notice Clara's garb for the first time. "You should change into a proper dress. I'll tell Rose to do the same. We will likely be here all night."

Clara nodded and walked back to her room. With each step, she listened to the echo of her feet against the wooden floor. The resulting sound was most definitely not the same one to which she'd awakened.

What could that noise have been? She knew she hadn't imagined it.

Inside her room, Clara fastened the buttons of her crisp white shirt, having chosen a style she could put on without Rose's help, and pulled up her long black skirt.

She reached for her brooch—a gutta-percha design. As

she pinned the brooch against her lace neckline, she pricked her finger on the sharp end. She sometimes wore it as a mourning brooch, which, in a way, was fitting—perhaps she *was* mourning, or she was about to be. She knew that choosing this course with Mary and Oliver and Teddy was only the beginning, and after helping this woman, she could never go back to the way things used to be. She might fall fully out of relationship with her family. She might lose everything.

Well, everything except her good conscience. Her heart and her soul. The knowledge that whatever she left behind would be a worthwhile sacrifice to help other human beings . . . whatever that may mean.

The tiniest drop of blood marked her lace, and even in the candlelight, she could see the stain. The blood jarred her into the realization that perhaps nothing was exactly how it seemed.

She thought of her father. Of all those phrases he used repeatedly to justify owning other human beings, and how for so long, she had silenced her own conscience, believing she was simply too sensitive.

Clara sighed.

She had no idea what she was going to do if he put her out on the streets.

For now, she would simply do the next right thing. And in this case, that meant readying herself so she could help the woman and her baby.

Rose waited in the doorway for Clara so the two of them could walk in together.

"I know you must be confused about this," Clara said to Rose as they neared the room. "To be honest, I am too. But I trust Mary and Oliver as I trust no one else"—although she could see herself trusting Teddy just the same, but Clara wouldn't mention that part aloud. "Seeing the woman lying there so helpless . . . hearing the cries of her baby . . ." Clara turned to look at Rose directly. "My heart aches for them both, Rose. For surely any mother, any woman, any human with any empathy, cannot fault her for wanting a better life for her baby."

Tears began forming from the corners of Rose's eyes, and the air around them seemed heavy with grief. Clara had never seen Rose cry before and wondered what, through her words, she had triggered.

In that moment, the thought occurred to her for the first time—had Rose ever considered running from Clara's father? And what would happen to her if she attempted it, only to be caught and dragged back mercilessly? Clara was admittedly naïve about a lot of things, but she had overheard bits of conversation between her father and those with whom he kept company, and she knew what happened to slaves who attempted escape unsuccessfully.

Did Rose herself ever have a baby?

Clara's thoughts began to race as she realized that her own father, her own family, was the captor in this situation and that Rose, whom she loved so dearly, could have just as easily been the young, fragile mother in the other room. For the past formative year as Clara transitioned from a girl to a young woman, Rose had always simply been there—just as a housemaid might be. But Rose *wasn't* a housemaid, was she? She was a slave, and legally she was considered property. Clara's stomach turned so violently.

She needed to do something.

She didn't know what, exactly.

She just knew she needed to do something.

"Missus?" Rose asked, her hands shaking.

"Yes, Rose?"

"Before we go back in that room . . . I need to talk to you 'bout somethin'."

"Sure." Clara nodded, reaching out to touch Rose's hands, hoping to still their trembling. But Rose looked at her, wide-eyed from the gesture. "You can tell me anything."

She only hoped Rose would trust how much she meant those words.

FIVE

Alice

Alice rubbed her glossy lips, the taste of lip balm still a new luxury for her almost-teen self.

Wax, from those candies shaped like little bottles. That's what it tasted like! She'd been trying to figure out the familiar taste for fifteen minutes now. It smelled like berries, and she was sure she looked mature enough to be a pop music star.

When she first dabbed the gloss against her lips, mimicking what she'd seen her mother do many times, she'd been so dumbfounded by how grown up she looked and how beautiful she felt that she stared at herself in the mirror for the longest time. But a girl could only do that so long, and now she was back to playing outside as her father carried the last of the cardboard moving boxes from his truck to the house. He was due back on the oil rig tomorrow.

She was going to like living here in New Orleans. She could already tell.

Alice had set out to look for butterflies when she noticed the neighbor next door. The woman looked about the age

47

of her principal and was holding a pair of garden clippers, standing beside the biggest rosebush.

The flowers were so beautiful, Alice took a deep breath of the perfumed air and walked right up to the woman. "Hi," she said, waving. "I'm Alice."

The woman seemed a little startled at first, but then she set down her garden tools and smiled. She held out her hand. "Pleasure to meet you, Alice. My name is Juliet."

The fact she did not add a *miss or missus* to the front of the name caught Alice a little off guard and filled her with glee. She always liked when grown-ups spoke to her like one of them versus someone who belonged at the kids' table.

Juliet pointed at the roses. "Do you like flowers?" she asked.

Alice nodded emphatically. "Yes, ma'am. They're my favorite thing."

"You don't say." Juliet tilted her head. "You know, the lady who lived in your new house before you moved in . . . her name was Eliza, and she loved gardens. Have you seen the bushes in the back yet?"

Alice shook her head.

"Well, they're azaleas, and come springtime, they'll be lit up with color. Just wait and you'll see what I mean."

Alice beamed, but then her patience waned. "Spring seems like a long time from now."

Juliet breathed in slowly. "It does, doesn't it?" She picked up her garden clippers and trimmed one of the roses from the bush. Holding it out toward Alice, she said, "How about a rose, then?"

Alice took it gladly, careful not to touch any of the thorns. "Are you sure? Thank you!"

"My pleasure," Juliet said. She gazed back at the bush but kept talking. "There's actually a rosebush that Eliza planted in your own yard—came from the same plant as this one originally."

"That's so cool." Alice was fascinated by the story.

Juliet nodded. "You probably didn't notice it in your yard because they trimmed everything back for the real estate listings, but it'll start to flower again soon." Juliet gestured with her garden tools as she spoke. "This bush is hardy, and it's got a history that goes back generations and generations in my family. Did you know in the olden days, people used flowers as a sort of secret code?"

"Really?" Alice held the rose Juliet had given her up to her nose and took a whiff. "Like what?"

"All sorts of things . . . they'd put together combinations of flowers that had different meanings to say they had a crush on somebody, or maybe the opposite—that they were furious or filled with envy. Sometimes flowers were even used by spies."

Alice's eyes widened. "Does *this* rosebush have a story like that?"

Juliet tapped one of the stems, then searched for the best spot to make her next cut. "It's got secrets to tell, all right. Some secrets even *I* don't know about. And I'm glad to know a flower lover will be living in Eliza's old house and can tend to it properly."

"The bush or the secret?"

Juliet smiled. "You tell me."

New Orleans—Modern Day

Alice

Alice parked her Tiffany blue bicycle outside the ironwork of her flower store and locked it up securely. When she opened the door, the bell above her head chimed, and the smell of freshly cut flowers assailed her senses.

She would never get tired of that scent.

It was the perfume of color, of blooms, of beauty. It was the smell of hope on days gone awry—both for her and her customers. And when she looked at the chalkboard-painted wall and the long bar of flowers in every shape and hue, all grouped together neatly, she was as filled to the brim with joy as the water that filled the vases.

When she'd first teamed up with her aunt several years ago, The Prickly Rose was a tired, predictable shop. Now, through all their hard work together, it had earned its prestigious place alongside the rest of the charming and eclectic stores along Magazine Street, even winning a few local awards.

They had incorporated the flower bar, a make-your-own-bouquet concept, and used the shop as an event space for small gatherings, complete with floral teas. Customers could also buy premade arrangements from a table in the middle of the store, or even subscribe to a monthly service to have flowers delivered directly to their door.

In all the little in-between spaces, Alice had worked hard to provide curated gifts, from specialty soaps and handmade jewelry, to old books and antiques. Everybody in New Orleans knew most shops on Magazine Street sold antiques.

Still . . . it was hard to keep up with the fickle nature of trends, and the flower business was full of them, being so closely linked with the wedding and event industry. The truth was, Alice felt grateful for any help Sullivan could give—anything so that The Prickly Rose could continue garnering acclaim. Because she would like to be running the shop long-term.

Alice slid her hipster bag in the compartment under the ornate register where Aunt Charlotte was working, then made her way over to the two women at the flower bar.

"Hello." Alice crossed her arms and grinned as she approached. "Welcome to The Prickly Rose. Are you interested in creating a bouquet today?"

"You have a lovely store." The older woman placed her hand on the young woman's shoulder. "My daughter is planning a small but intimate ceremony for her wedding, and we're hoping to find something a little more unique than a typical rose arrangement."

The bride-to-be leaned down to take in the collective scent of the flowers. She seemed hesitant, unsure whether choosing a stem and raising it to her nose was acceptable behavior, and Alice appreciated the care she showed. Too many people came into the store and proceeded to handle the delicate flowers as though they were artificial.

They were not artificial.

They were exquisite, rare, and delicate. Imbued with meaning, and when coupled together, they made an even more remarkable and striking statement.

Just as her old neighbor Juliet taught her when she was a girl.

"You've come to the right place." Alice slid her hands into the pockets of her kelly-green skirt. "Unique is my specialty."

The young woman turned her focus away from the stems and met Alice's gaze with glittering attention. "Finally." Her shoulders gently eased with her sigh. "You have no idea how many florists we've visited in the past two weeks." She lowered her voice to a humble whisper. "I thought wanting something more eclectic would make me easy to please, but when I explained my vision, most of the places we've visited have looked at me like I've got four eyes."

"Roses and babies' breath." Alice nodded. "Maybe the occasional daisy or ranunculus. Although I do love ranunculus. They've got such a whimsy about them."

"Yes!" The woman swirled her long, wavy hair into a bun at the nape of her neck. "How did you know?"

Alice grinned. "I'm in the flower business."

"Clearly," the mother of the bride said. "I can't tell you what a sight for sore eyes you and your shop are. I want my daughter to have exactly the sort of wedding she wants—after all, it only happens one time, right?"

"Well, hopefully." The young woman wiggled her eyebrows. Alice laughed. The mother did not. "Mom, you know I'm just kidding. I take marriage very seriously."

"You can say that again," the mother murmured, looking at Alice. "Took her long enough to finally settle down with someone. All those poor boyfriends—"

"Never stood a chance, and you knew it too."

"Oh, I suppose I did." The mother rolled her eyes and offered a half grin. "The point is, Alice, we are clearly enchanted. Could you tell us a little more about what we're looking at?"

"Absolutely." Alice shifted so she could more easily gesture to the flower bar with a sweep of her hand. "As you can see, we have a multitude of steel containers here each housing a different type of stem. They range in colors, sizes, shapes, and scents. And they may seem beautiful now . . ." She leaned closer. "But just wait until you see the bouquets. The true magic comes when you mix them." She pulled a garden-variety rose stem from its housing and held it up for the two women to take a sniff.

The bride's eyes widened, and she swooned as she took in the fragrance. "That is incredible."

"Isn't it?" Alice nodded with a small grin, biting down on her bottom lip. "This flower is one of my favorites, especially for weddings."

"Not another boring old rose, that's for sure," the mother said, handing the flower back to Alice.

Alice placed the rose securely into its watery display. "Have you ever heard about the Victorian language of flowers?"

They shook their heads.

"Well, back then, people would put secret messages into flower arrangements. Sometimes these messages were just as romantic as we would expect, but other times . . . other times they could be quite ominous. Messages of war or hostility, insult or injury. Sort of like a secret spy code."

"In flowers?" the bride asked incredulously.

"In flowers." The bell above the door chimed, and Alice glanced over to see another customer walk through. Aunt Charlotte greeted the customer, and Alice looked back at the women. "You have to remember, the Victorians were a very particular people. Polished and preoccupied with social status and all they considered to be proper behavior. But those characteristics never did make anybody immune to gossip and drama."

The women laughed at that. "No, they certainly do not. Nothing new under the sun, I suppose," the mother said.

"Indeed." Alice gathered several other stems to put together a sample bouquet for the purpose of illustration. "Say I incorporate pansies, yellow roses, and peonies. Any guesses what I might mean?"

"Platonic love?" the bride ventured.

"A great guess." Alice raised her eyebrows. "But not in this case. See, yellow roses can also mean jealousy. So combined with pansies, which represent thoughts, and peonies, which represent riches, we can 'read' the bouquet to mean *jealous thoughts of riches*, which is not an entirely welcome sentiment, is it?" Alice plucked each stem gently from the grouping she'd created and placed them back into their respective vases. "And so you can see, in work like this, why a trained florist is important to have—because it takes a trained eye to read flowers."

"Bravo," the mother said. "Where do I sign?"

Alice laughed, pointing to the register counter. "If you

head over there to my aunt, she can get you set up with the paper work you need as well as some booklets with photos of the many flowers we offer. If we don't have what you want on hand, we can always try to order it, but depending on the date of your wedding, the New Orleans heat can sometimes be prohibitive to getting the more fragile varieties."

The bride beamed at her, taking Alice's hands into her own. "Thank you," she said. "You're a dream. Seriously, thank you so much."

"I'm always happy to meet someone who loves flowers as much as I do." Alice patted the young woman's hands. "Looking forward to working with you."

As the two women walked away, Alice's phone buzzed from her pocket. She swiped to unlock the screen.

The text was from her father.

Alice took a deep breath. She didn't mean to be cynical, but he had a way of coming in and out of her life as unexpectedly as a hurricane. She'd made excuses for him when she was younger, but looking back . . . well, he could have found an alternative to the oil rigs if he really wanted to raise her. In truth, he liked her fine enough to want a steady relationship but not as much as he liked his second family. The one he moved on to so quickly after her mother's disappearance that Alice suspected he may've loved that woman back when her own mother, Lauren, was still alive.

Not that she wasn't alive now. She might be alive. Alice hoped she was alive. Prayed she was alive. Desperately wanted her to be alive.

But sometimes it was easier to cope if she thought of her mother as gone. Otherwise, she had to admit her mother, too, had left her behind.

She really should return his call this time.

Reluctantly, she dialed the number.

He answered on the second ring. "Thanks for calling me

back. Listen, there's something we need to talk about. I know it's not exactly the best timing, but unfortunately it's the only timing we've got."

Here we go. . . . Alice braced herself for the sugarcoated disappointment.

"I'm selling the old house."

"You're . . . what?" Nothing could have prepared her for that.

"Selling the old house. I don't feel like keeping up with the hassle of renting it out any longer, and Trisha and I could use the money for a beach house we're looking into over in Alabama."

"You're telling me you're planning on selling our family home so you can get a beach house with Trisha?" The words felt so uncomfortable to say out loud, she felt as though they tainted her heart and the house as well—an ugly blight like an ink stain on a once beautiful portrait.

Okay, so it wasn't always beautiful. But sometimes it was, and that was enough to make Alice miss the place. Knowing the house was still in their family had soothed the thought of losing someplace she once shared with her mother. And now all of that was about to be gone.

A long pause followed. "I'm sorry, Alice." He cleared his throat. "Anyway, I'm not in town but wanted to give you a chance to go back to the place in case there's anything you want in the attic. I'm not sure if anything's left up there or not. There's a key under the ceramic frog by the door. You can let yourself in whenever you want—the renters are gone now."

Alice tried not to audibly groan. She felt faint and looked for a place to sit down—finally settling on a chair behind the register. "Okay," she managed to mumble. "Thanks for the heads-up, I guess."

"Look—I'm sorry to throw this on you. I really am. I hope

55

you can have a nice, nostalgic moment when you go back inside there and find some closure."

A nice, nostalgic moment? Did he really think it was as simple as that?

And yet she wished for it as well.

"Thank you, Dad. Take care of yourself."

"You too." And like that, the conversation was done.

Alice slid her phone back into her pocket and blew out a deep breath. She'd planned to stop by Juliet's house this afternoon anyway because the woman was helping with alterations for the wedding party's attire. Juliet was the aunt of the groom and a renowned seamstress in New Orleans.

While there, she would walk next door and go through the old house for the first time in such a long time. She didn't want to, but she would never forgive herself if she left something behind.

SIX

Charleston, Summer 1861

Now, I don't know if it was the Holy Ghost or just my own courage come suddenly upon me, but as I'm standing in the hallway with Miss Clara, I know I have to tell her everything.

She rattlin' on about mamas and babies and why we should feel sorry for that woman who done near almost died trying to escape slavery, and it's time I tell her about Ashley. I can't keep it in any longer, not for another minute. It's wasting away in me like poison, makin' my stomach cramp in pain every time I eat and waking me with terrors in the night, and it's been that way ever since my little girl was sold. I lost so much weight, I don't know if my baby would even recognize me no more.

I don't know if I recognize me either.

I don't even know how much of a *me* there is left.

And I wonder . . . I wonder if Missus Clara even knows this house's a safe place for people like that new mother, that

Clara's cousin Mary and Oliver and Theodore are organized in how they goin' about this.

I wonder if she even sees what I see so plainly. That they—these people—can help me.

Clara's watching me now, waitin' because I told her I was gonna say something even though I ain't got no words for the feelings inside me. I musta practiced this conversation a thousand times, but now I can hardly remember where to begin.

"They took her." I shake my head, and my shoulders begin to shake right along with it. And it's then I realize I'm crying—sobbing, really—and Missus Clara does something. She reaches out and she embraces me.

I can't remember the last time somebody touched me for kindness' sake.

"They took who?" Clara puts two hands on my arms, her grip far stronger than I thought her delicate hands could manage, and she looks straight into my eyes, and for some reason in that moment, I know I can trust her.

"My baby." I swallow past the lump in my throat, my shoulders still trembling though there ain't no more tears to cry.

"Your . . . your *baby*?" Clara frowns. I never seen her make that kind of unfeminine expression before. "What do you mean, Rose? You have a child?" Clara shakes her head as her eyes begin to widen.

And I get chill bumps and I bet she does too because you know how those kind of things are catchin'. I nod my head. "Yes, though she ain't a baby no more. She was nine years old when they sold her. They sold me too, just a little bit after, and that's how I came to live at your home a year ago."

Clara covers her mouth with her hand. "How could I have not known this?" she says. "How could I have been such a fool?"

"You know it now."

"But I should've known before—I should've *done* something."

"Maybe that's true." I reach my hands into my pockets, where I been keeping the buttons. "But you doin' something now." I open my hand and show her the two butterfly buttons I been holding. "I gave her a satchel full of provision for the journey, but they took her so fast these buttons fell out. I must not've sealed it up good." If only these buttons could take flight, show me where my daughter is. "When I find her someday, I'm gonna give 'em to her, you see?"

Clara looks at the buttons, then interweaves her fingers together, placing her hands above her mouth. "What can I do?" she asks. "For your daughter, I mean."

My words tumble out on their own accord. "Help me."

Clara's eyes widen further. "Find her? But is there a way?"

"I think so," I say, and maybe it's wishful thinking but I really do believe it. "Those people in there can help with all of it."

Missus tilts her head in surprise. "Mary and Oliver? And Teddy?"

I try and decide how much I should tell her. How much she's ready to hear. But this is about my daughter, so I figure I ought to put it all out there.

I look straight at her, which is something I ain't supposed to do but rules be darned right now because I'm finally feeling brave. "I don't get the impression what they doin' in there is a one-time sort of thing."

"You mean . . ." Clara glanced rapidly at the bedroom door. "You think they're in the habit of helping slaves escape?"

"That's exactly what I think." I cross my arms over my chest as the pattern in the hallway wallpaper seems to grow. "How you think they found that woman, Missus? You think she just walkin' in broad daylight down the road with her baby?"

"I hadn't really thought through the logistics . . ."

"Missus, I'm takin' a real risk by asking you this and I've waited a mighty long time to tell you, but I just can't wait no longer. I need you. I need them. Because what I really need is my baby."

Clara swallows visibly. "We'll make a plan."

I gesture with my head toward the bedroom. "I suspect they already got one, that they use in these situations."

"So we will start by telling them, then," she says. I expect to see panic flash over her eyes, as this is all a lot for her to take in, but instead I see only resolve there, and her resolve fills me with relief because I know when Missus sets her mind to something, ain't nobody gonna stop her.

Clara

Through the soft candlelight, Clara scanned the room for Teddy. She found him at the woman's bedside, and she caught his eye and whispered, "Could Rose and I have a word with you?"

He smelled like linens fresh from the clothesline, breeze mixed with the slightest sooty scent from the globed candle he held.

He nodded despite his obvious distraction, then stood and walked to the upholstered settee and chair in the corner of the room, gesturing toward the cozy corner.

Clara and Rose followed, taking a seat across from him.

Teddy settled into the chair. "I assume it's acceptable your cousin is within earshot," he said.

"Quite." Clara nodded. "Actually, your inquiry opens up

the subject. It seems . . ." She looked at Rose, who watched the woman in the bed just beyond them. Clara turned her head to face Teddy again. "Well, it's been brought to my attention that perhaps yourself and my cousin . . ."

Teddy raised his eyebrows, his interest piqued. "Yes?"

Clara sighed. "I suppose I'll just come out with it. Are the three of you helping runaway slaves escape to freedom? Is that what you've been so hesitant to tell me?"

Teddy's expression remained stoic. Clara wondered if he had been trained to react so guardedly and if perhaps he were working covertly for the Union.

None of her parents' proposed suitors, not one of them, had the strength and gumption Teddy had already shown.

Clara's delicate tone provided a sharp contrast for the clarity of her intention. She leaned forward slightly. "I need you to be honest with me. You mustn't fear repercussions. If I were so appalled by the business in this room, would I still be sitting here?"

Teddy hesitated, as though considering this.

"Prove it, then." He softened his words with a gentle smile.

Clara boldly looked up at him.

"For how long have you been an abolitionist?" Teddy slipped his hands into the pockets of his trousers. "That is not to insinuate I'm displeased with the development, but surely you can understand . . . this is quite literally a matter of life and death. Were you to change your mind about your views upon returning to your father's house . . ."

"I will not change my views." The resolution in her tone was convincing, at least. Or so she hoped, for she felt resolve deep inside her. "Rose has a daughter." The words tumbled from Clara. "Her name is Ashley." In a movement that was wholly questionable and entirely provoking, Clara reached out and took his hand—her heart accelerating like a carriage clamoring behind a spooked horse. "Can you help find her?"

Rose pulled something from her pockets then held out her hands, palms up, to show two buttons.

Teddy's eyes narrowed, and he scratched his forehead. "I mean . . . I can certainly try, but these endeavors are quite dangerous and quite complicated." He looked down at the buttons. "What are these?"

"They belong to my child," Rose whispered. Silent tears screamed from her eyes. Rose shook her head, fisting her hand around the buttons for safekeeping, as if to say their story wasn't over yet. "Please. There wasn't time when they took her, and there ain't much time now. Every day that passes is another day she might be sold again—maybe to another city, maybe to another state. Help me get my daughter back. You can trust Missus. You can trust me."

Teddy's gaze went to Rose's closed fists, then met Clara's eyes. "All right." He nodded his head. "I'll do it, but Clara . . . you need to know the truth before you commit to anything, and I can tell you right now, you're not going to like it."

"The truth about what?" Clara asked. Her hands fluttered to the tight lace around her neckline.

"There's a man named Joseph." Teddy ran the tip of his tongue along his teeth as though the name tasted filthy in his mouth. "Do you know him?"

Clara frowned, trying to think back to who he might mean. Then it dawned on her. The pompous associate of her father's who had come to dinner three weeks ago.

"The reason I'm here is to gather information about Joseph. Oliver and I are involved with gaining intelligence for the Union army, and Joseph is our assignment." He hesitated, giving her a moment's pause that she used to consider this shocking revelation. "Your cousin Mary wanted to involve you straightaway, but I insisted we first confirm your commitment. It's a lot to ask."

Clara was confused by his last statement. "What's a lot to ask?"

Teddy met her gaze and didn't look away. A long pause followed, and her heart began to thunder. "How do you feel about espionage?"

SEVEN

New Orleans, Modern Day

Alice

Juliet was putting the last pin in Alice's dress sash when Peter and Sullivan came through the door. Both Juliet and Alice turned toward them. Alice's heart skipped rather unexpectedly at the sight of Sullivan.

"Sorry we're a little early." Peter walked up to his aunt and gave her a hug.

"Oh, that's all right," Juliet said, taking the pin from her teeth and sliding it into the sash securely. "We're done here. Alice's dress fits like a dream. I just need to put a couple stitches in the belt, and she can take it with her."

Alice offered Sullivan a small smile almost involuntarily. She wasn't flirting, she told herself. Only being pleasant.

She tried to force the heat from her cheeks when he gave her a half grin.

"You have everything you need already, right? The groomsmen are renting tuxedos?" Juliet asked Sullivan.

"Yes, ma'am," Sullivan nodded. "I just gave Peter a ride here."

"Got it." Juliet patted Alice's back, turning her attention to her. "You go ahead and change, and I'll put these last couple stitches in your sash so you can take the dress with you."

"Thanks." Alice lifted the hem of her skirt, careful not to let it graze the floor—it had, after all, been hemmed for the two-inch heels she'd be wearing. She didn't dare look at Sullivan a second time. She slipped into the bathroom and changed back into her skirt and screen-print T-shirt, carrying the formal gown over the crook of her arm as she walked toward the front door.

"Oh, Alice, before you go"—Sullivan held up one finger—"I had a question I wanted to ask you about the flower shop. Mind if I walk to your car with you?"

A slew of butterflies fluttered within her, anticipation floating on the air between them. She really *had* to get over this little crush she was developing. The wedding would come and go, and Sullivan would be gone in a blink. The last thing she needed was to develop real feelings for this guy who lived all the way in Charleston.

And yet, she couldn't help the pull she felt every time she looked at him. "Sure," she said. Before she could form her next thought, he was opening the door for her.

Alice pulled her keys from her purse and unlocked her car, turning toward him. "What did you want to ask me?"

"I know the store does a lot with cut flowers from flower farms, which is really cool and everything . . . but have you ever considered selling rooted plants too?"

Alice opened her car door, set the dress in the backseat, and puckered her lips together, considering this idea. "Actually, I haven't. And I kind of like where you're headed. Tell me more."

He swept one hand through his hair. "Well, I was doing some research on stores that offer similar products to The Prickly Rose—unique bouquets and subscription boxes and that sort of thing . . . and I noticed many of them also sell potted plants that can be grown inside. What I like is that these blooms keep going, and since you're all about the meanings behind the flowers, we could market this as a sentiment that keeps giving."

His words struck a chord within Alice, and she marveled at how instantly and thoroughly he seemed to understand the vibe of her store. He really got the heart behind the flower shop, didn't he? That they weren't just pretty blooms, but messages sent and received. "I love it," she said.

His eyes lit up. "Really?"

"Really." She looked at Juliet's sprawling rosebushes—the ones she'd admired as a young girl new to the neighborhood. She gestured toward the fragrant roses, which would be blooming soon. "This plant is actually a perfect example. I've admired these roses ever since I was a kid. Did you know they survived being submerged underwater during Hurricane Katrina?"

"Wow. What a story of survival. That's inspiring."

"Yeah, I think so too. I bet Juliet would let us take some cuttings from the bush to root. We could market them as a message of hope after literal and figurative storms."

"Just imagine them planted all over the city." Sullivan snapped and pointed toward her. "I really like where this is going."

"Me too." When Alice locked eyes with him, a very unexpected double meaning seemed to pass between them with the words. Okay, so maybe the *meaning* wasn't unexpected, but she hadn't intended to communicate it.

She shut her car door and beeped the lock.

"Aren't you getting in?" Sullivan asked.

"Oh." Alice shook her head. "No, I actually need to stop by my old house next door before I leave. My father had been renting it out and recently decided to sell the property, so I'm going to take a pass through the attic and make sure there's nothing of ours still there." She hesitated, deciding how transparent she should be. "I'm kind of dreading it, to be honest."

He bit down on his bottom lip. "Well, I don't mean to impose, but would it help to have some company?"

She felt as though a huge weight had been lifted from her at the mere thought of not having to do this alone. "That would actually be wonderful." Had she sounded desperate? Maybe she should clarify. "I mean . . . I have some significant memories here and would rather not be alone with them."

"Understood." He nodded. "Maybe we can even brainstorm more ideas for the store, confidentially of course, until you and your aunt decide what you want to do."

She appreciated the distraction. "Actually, it's funny you say that because ages ago, back when I was just a kid, Juliet told me that rosebush holds some kind of huge secret."

Sullivan raised his eyebrows. "Did she ever tell you what it was?"

Alice shook her head, stepping into the grass that needed a fresh mow. "No, she said even she doesn't know."

"Well, now I'm intrigued." Sullivan followed her through the yard. "What's your connection to Juliet, anyway?"

"Just neighbors, back when I was young." Alice reached for the ceramic frog and found the key to the door right where it had always been. "What about you?"

"You know how it is in the South—everybody is connected to everybody. You know Juliet is Peter's aunt, and Peter is one of my good buddies back in Charleston. I've done some work with him here and there on architectural salvage. But I also have another connection to her through my great-grandmother, Eliza."

Alice hesitated. "Where have I heard that name before?"

"She was a renowned watercolorist and helped to facilitate the preservation of Charleston during the Charleston

Renaissance. So if you're familiar with Charleston, you may have heard of her that way. She was also friends with Juliet and Juliet's mother, Millie." Sullivan took another step until he was close beside her. His clothes smelled like espresso, and she wanted another whiff, but she told herself no. "But most likely, you've heard her name because she owned this house for a while."

Alice slid the key into the lock. "That's it! Juliet told me about her gardens way back when." She started to open the door but turned to face him instead. "So basically, your and Peter's ancestors are connected."

"Right." Sullivan nodded. "For many generations. Going all the way back to the Civil War, actually."

Alice opened the door. She had to take a quick breath and steady herself so she didn't fall through the looking glass of time. She could hear Sullivan's feet shuffling behind her, an oddly comforting reminder she was not alone.

The house was empty. It seemed both larger and smaller than she remembered, all at the same time. The air carried a slight staleness that was hard to describe, except to say it'd clearly been awhile since the windows had been opened.

There was no use lingering in these empty spaces now.

"You ready to head up to the attic?" Alice asked Sullivan. "I doubt we'll find much up there, but you never know."

"Sure." He closed the door behind them. "You lead the way."

In no time, Alice showed him the garage and was pulling the ladder down when he came up beside her to steady it should she fall.

Alice crawled on her hands and knees into the space, then got a feel for the layout and stood. How strange to be in a place that'd been home to her for years and yet to be exploring a part of it she'd never really known before.

Sullivan was close behind her. He had to use more care

not to bump his head than she did, considering his height and the angled roofline. "It's a nice attic space—much bigger than I expected. There's a lot of storage up here."

"Yeah, it is." Alice waved her hand in front of her face to clear a cobweb. "Truth be told, I think this is my first time up here. I'm just as surprised as you." Her gaze scanned the length of the attic, but she came up empty.

Just as she suspected. The realization was entirely predictable and yet surprisingly disappointing.

"Funny how you never really go up in the attic as a kid."

"You don't, do you?" She turned to smile at him over her shoulder. But Sullivan lost his footing, tripping over a raised area in the plywood floor.

He steadied himself, but Alice's smile turned into a concentrated frown. "Wait a minute . . . what is this?" She stepped closer to the board, and Sullivan did too.

"Looks like a really good place to put something for safe-keeping."

"You think?"

He shrugged. "All I know is, I do a lot of this salvage type work with Peter, and these little hidden spaces will often hold important things. People put them there then forget the spot, or unfortunately they may pass away without ever having told anyone about the hiding place."

The thrill of the possibility sent her heart lurching forward, and she lifted the plywood to reveal a compartment underneath. Inside it were a couple of framed paintings, a sweetgrass basket, and a box that would change everything.

EIGHT

Charleston, Summer 1861

Clara

Clara stood perfectly still, perfectly stunned, looking straight into the eyes of Teddy. *Espionage*. The word rolled 'round and 'round like a child's ball moving ever faster until finally rocketing down a hill forever. She feared she might be about to commit herself to something there was no coming back from. If caught, her life would change forever. She could be imprisoned. Could she be killed?

And yet her life already *had* changed. She refused to go another day turning a blind eye to slavery's horrors. She would be different now. She would have to be.

"Clara?" Teddy asked. He seemed to see right through her. "Do you hesitate?"

She chose her words carefully, for she grieved the image she once had of her father. The man who left her little coins and chocolates and promised that someday he would take her to Italy. She grieved the comfort she'd found in her illusions.

She had lived a sheltered life, considered herself safe from whatever wars raged around her. And now it was becoming increasingly apparent that she would have to break from all those falsities. She wished she could say that was easy, but the truth was, a part of her would probably always grieve for the family she must now let go of—even if they were not the beacons of character she once thought them to be. She grieved not so much for the coming conflict but for the people they'd become—for the people they perhaps were all along. No amount of relational reconciliation would ever make up for their lack of integrity.

She raised her chin markedly. "No, Teddy. Do not mistake my contemplation for hesitation."

He shifted, seeming surprised by her declaration. "As you say."

"What will I need to do?" she asked, wishing she could loosen her corset to allow for more air, as the room was beginning to spin around her. Still, she retained her composure.

"Our best bet would be for you to play the part of naïveté, using active listening during any of your father's social engagements, especially if Joseph is there. Doing so will allow you access to conversations and people with whom Oliver and I could not interact without raising suspicion. You won't need to incite anything, but rather to be patient and careful. Do you know what a mnemonic device is?"

"Pairing the first letter of a word in a new combination? The memory trick?" Clara gripped the edge of the sofa where she and Rose sat together, hoping it might ground her.

"Precisely. You will want to begin utilizing methods such as these to remember as many names and as much information as possible. Then as soon as you're able—without drawing unnecessary attention, for we certainly don't want you getting hurt in this—go back to your chambers and write it all down."

Clara nodded, strangely exhilarated by the thought of performing such important work. She was struck by the way

Teddy clearly believed her capable, and spoke to her as an equal. She had been raised among people who never considered a woman's intellect worth addressing. And perhaps . . . perhaps that blind spot would be how she would get away with this.

She met Teddy's gaze. His warm brown eyes sent a tickle down her spine. "Then what will I do with the papers?"

He rubbed his face with his hands. His exhaustion was palpable. "We will need to work out some sort of code. Our first step should be to establish a rendezvous point as well as a means by which you can ferry the information discreetly—an object, ideally. What is something you or Rose uses daily?"

Clara's mind went blank. All she could think of was this blasted corset strangling her, and she wished she wasn't using *that* daily. The lacy neckline of her garments scratched her skin, so with gloved fingertips she pulled the fabric away.

She looked at Rose and immediately knew what to say. "Your embroidery." Clara blinked—it was as though everything was suddenly coming into focus.

"Embroidery?" Teddy questioned.

Rose nodded.

Clara continued. "Rose is a highly skilled seamstress. She mends all my clothes, but beyond that, she also does hand embroidery that's decorative. Needlepoint samplers and so forth. They're so good, she's even sold a few to my mother's friends."

"Really?" Teddy sounded as though his curiosity had been sparked. He rubbed his hands together. "That's very interesting. . . . Yes, that actually could be exactly what we need." He met Rose's gaze directly. "Do you think you could place a hidden code within the embroidery?"

"A code?" Rose asked, her voice hoarse with hope. Clara could only imagine how Rose must feel about a plan that might help her reunite with her daughter. What trauma must

Rose have gone through—and to have kept this a secret alone for so long. And what ignorance had Clara allowed that she'd been blind to it?

Teddy ran his hand over his mouth and chin, contemplating. "Yes, I'm thinking something like . . . like maybe flowers? Could you stitch flowers into these samplers? And you're sure it wouldn't raise suspicion if you sell them?"

"Yessir," Rose cleared her throat. "Missus's daddy lets me sell my samplers early in the morning, save up a few coins for my fabric. That way I can make my dresses. I'm real good at sewin' flowers already."

"She is. Her floral work is spectacular. And I usually drink my morning tea while she stitches."

"Okay," Teddy nodded. "We may be on to something here. Do you use a particular teacup? Drink it in a certain place?"

"If the weather's nice, I sit out on the front piazza and watch the passersby," Clara said. "And yes—I do typically favor one teacup over the others. It's porcelain, and I painted it several years ago with a rose pattern."

"A rose teacup." Teddy's lips pulled into a grin. "How unexpectedly fitting."

It may have been Clara's imagination, but she could have sworn she sensed Rose's countenance lift at his words.

"You mentioned these flowers could be some sort of code?" Clara tried to follow his meaning.

"Yes . . ." Teddy took a deep breath, resting his hands on the arms of his mahogany chair. "You're familiar, of course, with floriography. The language of flowers."

Clara nodded. "Of course. My mother gave me a flower dictionary just last year so I could interpret the meaning of any bouquets I receive now that I am of age in society." She paused. "You're suggesting we use the flower dictionary to assign secret meanings within Rose's needlework pieces?"

Teddy's feet shuffled against the floor. "That is precisely

what I am suggesting. I don't think anyone would expect it—do you?"

Clara shook her head. "No, I don't." She turned to Rose. "Are you comfortable doing this?" she asked. "If not, I'm sure we could figure out some alternative."

Rose did not flinch nor hesitate. "Comfort be darned. Ain't nothing I wouldn't do to get my baby."

Teddy nodded slowly. "All right, then. It's settled." He tugged at the wrists of his shirtsleeves. "You'll need to make sure that you order the flowers and their messages left to right, as you would if you were writing words. We will also be sure to assign an arbitrary flower to key figures, such as Joseph, who will appear in the messages. You'll have to memorize those, and we will create a journal to be kept under lock and key with the meanings. You can study it whenever you visit Mary."

Clara thought of something. "What will we do with the needlepoints?"

"Well theoretically, you will use the teacup as a signal when you have new information. From now on, you'll drink out of a different teacup when there's nothing to say. We can plant someone to look like an ordinary passerby on the street, then as you sit on the piazza and enjoy your tea, you will say *good-day* and exchange the usual brief pleasantries, such as a wave. On these mornings when you do have information, the passerby will take note of your teacup and feign interest in Rose's needlepoints. Then he or she will 'purchase' the coded information."

"Clever." Clara was impressed by Teddy's quick intellect. In fact, it may be even more charming than his accent—if that was possible.

"If we ever need to ferry information to you rather than from you, we will do so in the payment exchange—either verbally or on a written note that looks like money. You must both remember this, however—if ever someone does communicate to you via a physical note, read the words and then destroy the evidence immediately."

"That sounds very somber," Clara said, a heavy feeling settling over her.

"It is." Teddy stared into her eyes, hesitating. "Clara, there's one more thing you should know . . ."

Chills ran down the length of her arms at his earnest tone. "What is it, Teddy?"

"Your father's associate, Joseph . . . well, from what I've heard he thinks very highly of you. I would prepare yourself for the idea that he may be romantically invested."

The thought of that humorless man, at least fifteen years her senior, expressing his interest turned her stomach. She was grateful Teddy had warned her, but at the same time, she so hoped he was wrong.

"What am I to do if he tries to approach me?"

Teddy took his next breath slowly. "I haven't a good answer. The truth is, I'm fond of you, Clara, and I despise the idea of a man like that courting you. But on the other side of the token, we both have a job to do. If he fancies you, he may be more apt to communicate information we could use." He looked into her eyes, and the warmth in his gaze comforted her. "My best answer would simply be that you please privilege your safety. If at any point this gets too dangerous, or something unexpected happens, you and Rose will plan to come here to Mary and Oliver's house. They will hide you, and we will make an escape plan." His attention went to Rose, then back to Clara. "Neither of you are to take any unnecessary chances, understood? You may be collaborating, but you are not formal spies for the Union like me and Oliver, and I do not want either of you caught or tried as though you were."

Clara nodded. But she couldn't help but notice Rose never did.

The next morning, Clara pulled the black lace collar from her neck, but the pin about the top button kept it from budging. Her mother had arranged to have more clothes sent over to the estate, as she'd decided to stay a few more days with Mary under the guise of the pleasant, warm temperatures.

Yet the morning humidity had reached an unseasonable level, and the shift in weather had affected Clara's headaches. The pins in her hair had begun to exacerbate the pain, and she thought she might get a breath of fresh air outside to lessen it. And if that were not successful, at least she might distract herself with the garden's beauty—it wouldn't be long before autumn took the colorful blooms.

Clara stepped outside the grand estate toward the expansive fields of cotton and swung her skirt as she stepped onto the pebbled pathway, imagining she were dancing.

With Teddy.

Truthfully, she had daydreamed this way more times than she cared to admit in the brief time she had known him—if not dancing, then going for a walk through the cotton fields or practicing poetry. A Keats collection, perhaps, or her beloved Longfellow. Teddy would never object to a woman reading. Why, Theodore was so radical in his views, he was likely to say a woman ought to vote.

And slowly, he had begun to court her heart without even trying. Actually, without even knowing. For he had made no advances or articulation of his intentions. Clara realized that in all likelihood, their romance may stay solely in her imagination. Perhaps it would be for the best, anyway, given the circumstances.

But the look in his warm chocolate eyes was one she would never forget so long as she was living.

She hummed softly and breathed deeply.

She did not expect the sting at the back of her throat and wiggled her nose to keep from sneezing. As she turned toward the garden, ash caught along the breeze.

What was burning?

Clara hitched up her skirt and hurried around the corner of the house, interested in whether she could see anything.

When she got there, she clutched her hand to her chest. The entire horizon was on fire!

Thick bands of bright flames grabbed whole stretches of sky, smattering the expanse with shades of grey. And the bands of grey stretched far over the horizon, as far as Clara could see. She knew that under each grey cloud hung destruction unlike anything else she'd ever seen.

Her stomach turned at the thought.

Clara hurried back to the door of the estate as the horses in the stables neighed their displeasure. She must warn her cousin, and quickly.

But the woman, as it turns out, was sitting down at the table beside Teddy, leisurely having a cup of tea.

"My!" She set her cup down on the dainty saucer. Clara knew the tea was watered-down, for they'd begun using each tea bag twice in a sitting, but Mary still liked to use the nice table settings. She said it added elegance to the crude times war brings. "Clara, why are you running about so? You look pale. Have a seat."

Clara did as instructed, then reached for her cousin's hand. "It's just awful, Mary."

"What's wrong?" Teddy's beard was freshly trimmed, and even the worry lines at his eyes were handsome.

"Fires." She shook her head. "Fires as far as you can see."

"Ah." Teddy nodded and looked down into his cup.

Clara's eyes widened. "Ah?" She pointed at the estates across the way that were burning and sending up pillars of smoke in their wake. "When I tell you a portion of Edisto is burning, all you can say is, 'Ah'? You act as if you knew this was happening."

Teddy took a deep breath and said nothing. When he finally met her eyes, she knew.

"You were *aware* this was happening?" Clara's gaze shot to her cousin, who also seemed unshaken by the news. "Mary, you too?"

Clara felt as if she might be sick. "But all those people's homes will be destroyed."

Teddy held onto his cup with his hands but made no move to take a drink. "No one said it isn't a tragedy." He looked up, catching Mary's attention and then moving his gaze to Clara. "But such is the nature of war."

Clara's mind rushed with thoughts of who might live in the estates that were the direction from which the fire came. She didn't know any of them personally, but her parents did.

"Wait a second." Clara's pulse raced as understanding dawned. She hesitated, summoning the courage for the question. "Did the Union set those homes on fire?"

"Clara," Teddy's tone was more direct that she had heard before. "I know it's startling, but think of this in the proper terms. Fire is one of the most powerful weapons of war."

Fire is one of the most powerful weapons of war.

He said these words as if they were the most natural thing.

And suddenly, she became aware of the impact her espionage would create. She was not simply playing a part against Joseph and the institution of slavery. She was making decisions that would destroy livelihoods and family homes. And she was likely to destroy both for herself in the process. Was she really ready for this?

She couldn't believe the Union would do such a thing to civilians' homes. And she remembered her father's words at the start of all this, as he spoke of everything they were in danger of losing.

Lives. Homes. Income.

Before her very eyes, homes were burning. Homes just like the one that belonged to her own family. Fields of crops were torched, and the cotton that provided income, utterly destroyed. All that cotton, burning. Its ashes scattering, and with them, families' very way of living. Clara wrung her hands.

Her nostrils were still stinging from the flames every time she tried to breathe.

But then she thought of Rose, and Rose's daughter Ashley.

She heard the desperation in Rose's voice last night as the woman asked Clara to help her. And Clara knew. Clara knew that even still, she was doing the right thing.

"Clara." Teddy folded his hands, almost as though in prayer. "You have to understand—there is less suffering if the enemy is cut off by the root."

"Less suffering?" she asked. "Less suffering for whom?"

"Everyone." His response was quick. "Fire has a fierce impact on the economy while minimizing casualties."

She considered this a long moment. But before she could respond, Teddy said something unexpected as he lifted his teacup to his lips. "While the Union army *does* use fire when needed, in this case, the sea island cotton farmers themselves are to blame."

What was he implying?

Clara allowed herself an unladylike frown. "I don't follow your meaning."

"Edisto is a helpful island for the war, strategically. Many farmers here have abandoned their homes, leaving enslaved people behind to fend for themselves. But others . . . others are setting fire to their crops rather than risking their harvest falling into the hands of Lincoln's army."

Clara covered her mouth with her gloved hand. "You mean to tell me the farmers are burning their *own* land? Out of spite?"

But that didn't make sense. Her father had said the reason plantation owners must continue with the ugly business of slavery was because its undoing would destroy homes and livelihoods. Yet that was precisely what these Confederate landowners were doing to themselves.

"I suppose they consider themselves war heroes," he added.

"And you?" Clara asked. "What do you consider them?"

He met her gaze with his warm brown eyes. "Foolhardy."

NINE

Alice

Alice held tight to the box of embroidered samplers as she scuffled down the attic stairs, curiosity getting the best of her. Did the embroidery hold any significance beyond being decorative? Why had they been stored up here? Had they simply been forgotten?

"Alice, hold up." Sullivan followed after her. "Tell me what's going on here."

"I'm taking these to Juliet," she said. "I bet she'll know what they mean." Alice hurried through the grass toward Juliet's house. As she did, a car pulled up to the residence, and Juliet's mother, Millie, stepped out, waving to the driver.

Alice hesitated. "Millie?" she called. Though Alice didn't know Peter's grandmother well, they'd met at a wedding in Charleston last year and had chatted occasionally whenever Alice called her friends in Charleston and Millie was in the same room. Millie was . . . well, she was not one to pass up the chance for a conversation. Millie had a way about her, a way that drew people.

"Alice?" Millie ambled to the sidewalk leading up to Juliet's door. "Fancy seeing you here," she said.

Alice grinned. "Was that an Uber?" Given Millie's age, Alice hadn't expected her to be so comfortable with ride-sharing.

"Yes, and let me tell you"—Millie was standing just two steps from her now—"they are a remarkable invention. I'm staying here with Juliet for the wedding, and I had a taste for beignets, but no one could get away to keep me company. So I scheduled an Uber and"—she snapped her fingers—"Presto. I'm in the French Quarter before you can say *powdered sugar*."

Alice chuckled. "Sounds like a fun adventure."

Millie grinned, straightening the red cloche she wore carefully pinned to her hair. The hat was clearly authentic vintage. "I'm of the mind we could all use a little more adventure in our lives." Her gaze seemed to catch on the box Alice held. "What do you have there?" She smiled at Sullivan as he came to stand beside Alice.

"Oh, these are some things we found in the attic of my old house next door," Alice explained. "I wanted to show them to Juliet because . . . well, I just have a hunch about them. Maybe it's wishful thinking."

Millie frowned. "What am I missing?"

Alice tilted her head. "What do you mean?"

"Why would Juliet be able to help you?"

"Oh." Alice nodded, shifting the weight of the box in her arms as she started once more toward the door. She looked to her side at Millie, who walked toward the door too. "Because these predate my time in the house. They belonged to the woman who lived there before my family, and she was very close to Juliet." Alice stopped in her tracks. "Actually, come to think of it, you knew her too."

"I knew a great many people." Millie put one hand on her

cloche to protect it from the breeze. "I'm a bit of a people-person, if you hadn't noticed." She looked back at the house, as though suddenly recognizing it. "Wait a minute . . . you don't mean Eliza?"

Alice smiled, glad Millie was here to shed even more light on her discovery. "I sure do."

Alice set the box down on Juliet's coffee table. "I found something in the attic of my old house," she said. "Several somethings, actually. You need to see this for yourself. I'm hoping you can tell me more about it."

Juliet stepped toward the box, and Millie leaned closer from where she sat on the sofa. Sullivan and Peter huddled around too. Juliet pulled several framed needlepoints from the box. Each one showed a beautiful series of flowers, sin-gular stems ordered as though standing in a line.

Juliet brushed the dust off the glass. "I've seen these before," she said. "Your mother brought them over once, long ago, wondering if I knew how she could return them to their rightful owner. At the time, I didn't know who their rightful owner would be, given that Eliza had passed by then. I told her I would research it, but I just never got around to it."

"So they definitely belonged to Eliza?" Sullivan asked, his rich voice drawing Alice's attention.

"They did." Juliet nodded. "Well, at least, at one point they did. But the original owner would have gone way back before Eliza. Judging by the stitching and style, as well as the fabric, these were likely made near the antebellum period before the Civil War. Maybe just after, during Reconstruc-tion. They're in remarkable shape—probably from being kept away from sunlight in the attic. I'll bet that's why she had them up there. She must've forgotten they were there when she sold the place. Eliza had so many things she was always saving, you see."

"So you think they go back to Eliza's ancestors?" Alice asked.

"Yes," Juliet said. "Probably all the way back to her grandmother, Clara, judging by the timeline. Eliza told me about her grandmother on a few occasions. Clara lived a fascinating life, and may have even been involved with the Great Fire of 1861 in Charleston . . . possibly as a spy. But that's hearsay, of course. No one knows for sure."

Millie's expression sobered. "Millie?" Alice asked, before Juliet had a chance to answer her other question. "What's wrong?"

"It's just, the way that rose is stitched . . ." Millie's voice trailed off. "I've seen a likeness of it before."

"Go on," Peter encouraged her.

"There was a dress we always kept in the family—a little girl's dress that once belonged to my great-grandmother. Ashley." Millie hesitated, as though to emphasize the name. "Ashley was just a child when she was sold, and her mother sewed the dress and embroidered a rose like that one on it."

"Kind of reminds me of the color of that huge rosebush at Eliza's old estate in Charleston," Sullivan said, and Peter agreed. "I mean, I know it's comparing a real bush to an embroidered one . . . but isn't it strange Eliza would have a bush with that color rose in her yards both here and in Charleston, and a collection of needlework displays with it in her attic?"

Alice shrugged. "Maybe, maybe not. Roses are very popular flowers and were especially popular during that time period. It certainly could mean something, but I'm more interested in the sequence of the flowers this person chose to embroider and the connection Millie mentioned to that dress." Alice leaned closer. "Millie, are you sure the stitching is the same?" As a renowned seamstress, Millie's eye could be trusted.

Millie nodded emphatically. "I have no doubt about it," she said. "The gentle curve of the petals shows remarkable craftmanship. I remember admiring it when I was a little girl myself. It's one of the first memories I have of falling in love with textiles."

Alice's mind was racing, trying to sort through the puzzle. She chose her words carefully. "So that would mean these . . ." she gently touched the framed works Juliet was still holding. "Were created not by *Eliza's* ancestor, but by *yours*."

Juliet appeared speechless, and like her mother, that was a rarity. But after a moment's pause, her words came quickly as she put together several more pieces of the mystery. "Before she died, Eliza told me she believed there was a connection between our families, but I never found any more information about it and didn't know where to look. Records of enslaved persons' personal lives are hard to come by, as they weren't often kept." She looked at Millie. "All Mama and I ever knew about our ancestors is that they were separated when Ashley was sold. I always accepted that was all we *could* know—that time had erased the rest of the story."

Millie's voice caught with hope almost imperceptibly. "You really think there's more to uncover?" she asked Alice.

"Oh, absolutely. Do you see these flowers? Their alignment?" She pointed to the row of flowers stitched on the needlework. "This is why I rushed the box over to you. You're the one who first told me about the Victorian language of flowers when I was a young girl, remember? Well, I think this is an example of it. . . . This is a code."

Everyone was looking at Alice, and the only sound was the twittering of bluebirds just past the windows.

"A code?" Peter was the first one to voice the question, almost incredulously.

Alice nodded. "First we see the two carnations grouped together—pink and white. The pink carnation symbolizes a mother's love, while the white carnation symbolizes innocence."

"For Ashley and her mother?" Juliet wondered aloud, her eyes widening. She covered her mouth with her hand as it clearly all began to sink in.

"I think so . . ." Alice said.

"What is that next flower?" Millie asked. "It's beautiful but very unique."

Alice drew the cone-shape of the flower in the air with her finger. "Yes, that's called a protea. It can symbolize diversity, but I think in this case it symbolizes courage because it's paired with an anemone, which means protection against evil." Alice hesitated. "The only thing I can't quite work out is this last flower, this rose. Roses have many meanings, most along the lines of admiration, beauty, or love. But I can't sort through why it would be included here. What does it add to the message?"

"Alice?" Millie said, looking straight into her eyes. "Rose is the name of Ashley's mother."

Chills ran down Alice's arms. Yes, that made so much more sense. "So the rose is like a signature, then, to clarify who the message is from."

"I'd bet my buttons." Millie nodded.

"This is incredible," Peter said. "I can't wait to tell Harper."

Sullivan looked equally interested. Since he was a distant relative of Eliza, Alice realized, this could all relate to his history too.

But as Alice's attention turned to Juliet, she saw hesitation in the woman's gaze. "There's just one thing . . ." Juliet shook her head, speaking to Alice. "I didn't say anything at first because I didn't want to upset you, but it's now obviously important."

The somber lines tightening around her eyes caused Alice's adrenaline to catch, then still. "What is it?" she asked.

Juliet tapped her fingers on the framed needlepoint. "Well, it's just . . . when your mother first brought these over to me, there were more than three of them."

"What do you mean?"

Juliet took a slow breath in, choosing her words carefully. "I think it's possible your mother still has them. I mean, they could've gotten lost, I guess, but . . ." Juliet hesitated. "But it's also possible your mother is still alive and has the rest of this story."

Alice's heart stopped. "But I don't know where my mother is. . . ." She felt faint just by saying the words.

"What if I help you?" Sullivan blurted out. But why would he be willing to help her? She wondered if she must have sounded pathetic.

"I mean," he continued, "I'm already going to be working with you on new ideas for your store. We could talk through all this too. I know you're the flower expert, but I can be another pair of eyes, at least. We can sort out the messages in the needlework we have already, and then maybe if you're up for it . . ." She filled in the words he couldn't seem to say: *If you're up for it, I can help you find your mother.*

"I don't know . . ." Slowly, Alice met the gaze of each person in the room, and she began to flush from all the attention being on her. She looked back to Sullivan, but taking in his gorgeous grin did little to still her heart, which had suddenly begun racing.

"I hate to disappoint all of you, but . . . well . . ." Alice blew out a deep breath. She would have to say this directly. "If you don't already know the story, my mother went missing after Hurricane Katrina. We don't know if she's even alive, much less where she is."

Sullivan's gentle expression showed his empathy. But she

didn't want his empathy, kind as it was. She didn't want to be in this situation at all—to be the girl with the missing mother. It wasn't fair.

Alice rubbed her eyes with her hands, probably smudging her mascara, but at this point, she didn't even care. "We searched for her day and night for over a year." She hesitated. "It's hard to explain how that feels . . . when everything in your life is going according to plan and then suddenly the ground opens up beneath you. You doubt everything about yourself, everything you've always believed in—why God would let this happen, and why He would have abandoned you." She shook her head. "Many victims of Hurricane Katrina were never identified, and many missing persons were never found. My mother is far from the only case."

Alice looked at the ceiling. "Eventually, gradually, we stopped looking. I moved in with my aunt, and we both began to speak about my mother as though we'd accepted she was dead. I think, in a way . . ." Alice lowered her gaze to look at everyone, their expressions somber. "In a way, that was easier to accept than the alternative—that maybe she left us because she didn't want to be my mother any longer."

"I'm so sorry for mentioning it," Sullivan said. "I really meant to be a help, but I apologize if I was insensitive."

"No, no. It's okay. I know you were trying to be helpful." Alice waved her hand, looking once more at the embroidered flowers. As she took them in, she felt a sudden awareness of purpose—that she was uniquely equipped as a florist to translate this artistry. She didn't want to let Millie and Juliet down. She always had loved Juliet, ever since they moved into the house when Alice was a child.

But she didn't know if her heart could handle the answers she may find if she went searching for her mother. As it stood, she was uncomfortably suspended between what-ifs—but to weigh the scales might bring devastating closure.

For the time being, she would offer something that made her a lot more comfortable. "Tell you what." Alice glanced at Millie, then Juliet. "What if I take photos of the artifacts we already have, and do some research with my Victorian flower dictionary? We may not even need those other needlepoints."

"That's kind of you to offer," Juliet said.

"Yes, we would appreciate any information you can find," Millie added. "You know, before I die."

"Millie Perkins, you behave!" Juliet hissed, laughing as Millie offered a sly smile. "It's not up to this girl to uncover all our family secrets."

And yet, in her heart of hearts, Alice knew it was precisely up to her to find them.

TEN

Clara

Tucked neatly into the newest copy of *The Charleston Mercury*, Clara read from *The Liberator*—the abolitionist paper her cousin had mailed with her last correspondence.

Careful should anyone suspect the paper-within-the-paper, Clara looked up and smiled, nodding, and pretending to engage in what her father was saying about the developing war.

The parlor door opened then, seemingly on its own accord, to reveal a very stately Joseph Thomas, with his hair parted sharply and his beard neatly trimmed, wearing a suit of dusty grey. He smelled like gunpowder, and Clara wasn't sure why, exactly, but the truth was that he always smelled like gunpowder, if she really thought about it.

Her heart thundered in his presence—and not in the way it did when she was around Teddy. 'Twasn't a good sort of thundering at all but rather the clamoring of nerves at the thought of what she must do. This afternoon marked the first time she'd seen Joseph since learning Teddy and Oliver had orders to spy on him—and that currently, she did too.

She knew she should put away her reading material. Careful to arrange both papers so no one was the wiser, Clara set them down on the table beside her upholstered armchair and instead reached for a pair of trousers she was mending for the soldiers—a cause her mother had insisted upon.

Mr. Thomas raised his cap and dipped his chin to her. "Evening, Clara," he said.

"Evening, Mr. Thomas." In and out, in and out, Clara pierced the fabric to steady her racing thoughts.

"Your father and I have discussed it thoroughly, and Clara, I would humbly like to ask for your hand."

Clara scanned the room aimlessly until she met Rose's gaze. The concern she saw in Rose's eyes comforted her. Yes, Rose was probably far more invested in securing her own daughter's safety than she was with Clara's situation—as she should be—and yet it was enough for Clara to know she was not alone.

Clara's thoughts darted around like a panicked squirrel. What should she do?

She would absolutely be expected by her father and mother to accept this proposal. *Not* accepting this proposal would never be an option in their eyes. To them, she was a prize to be bargained for. Were she to voice her own opinion on the matter, she would elicit all manner of suspicion, and yet the alternative . . .

Her stomach soured at the mere thought of it.

She glanced up to find Joseph and her father talking to one another as though the matter had been settled. As though she had given her permission. As though her permission mattered to them.

So that was it, then. She was as good as married to him.

Clara only noticed the tiny drops of blood at her thumb after they'd stained the garment. She'd pricked her fingers so many times, she could scarcely feel it anymore.

Clara sighed. Another garment for the wash. She was absolutely ruinous at this patchwork business.

She pressed her hand to the tightest part of her corset—she hoped to catch a deeper breath before the prospect of marrying Mr. Thomas wound its way like mythical tree roots around the room.

Clara had always had a gift for sensing things. Bad things. Good things. At least, that's what her mother called it. A gift of discernment. Clara wasn't so sure it was a gift, though. Sometimes it seemed more like a curse, for she felt so deeply. But she hadn't sensed how this would feel.

The room began to spin as she considered her next steps. Of course she wouldn't actually go so far as to marry the man, but for however long Teddy and Oliver needed information from him, she would have to pretend she intended to.

"Shall we set a date, then?" Clara brought her pinpricked thumb to her lips and forced herself to smile at him.

Joseph turned his attention toward her with a smile that would have been pleasant if he had a different moral compass. How strange to think she scarcely knew this man, but her family wanted her to spend the rest of her life by his side. And what type of man was he, really? Besides one who wholly agreed with her father?

What would he do if he knew her interest in current affairs and papers like *The Liberator*? She imagined he wouldn't take to that part very kindly. But not many men would. At least not the type of men who, as she already mentioned, wholly agreed with her father.

"I fear in my haste, I have gotten ahead of myself." Joseph pressed his hand to his chest as though pledging a flag, not talking to his betrothed. Could she really fool everyone into believing she planned to go through with this marriage? At only sixteen years old, Clara imagined the man to be at least fifteen years her senior. She felt absolutely no attraction to him. Not that he was ugly . . . well, at least not physically speaking. But his ethical standing was a different story entirely.

Joseph rubbed his beard between his finger and thumb. "I may be needed on the battlefield at any time, so the way I see it, there is no sense in us wedding only for me to depart shortly after. It's not as though you're in need of my name or my fortune, as a good many women might be in the event they were widowed." He glanced over at her father. "That said, my thought was to have the wedding a year from now. Does that suit you?" he asked her.

Clara trailed her finger along her forehead, searching for the invisible strand of hair that had fallen near her eyes. "That suits me just fine," she said. She only hoped she would not have to keep up the charade that long.

"It's settled then," he said.

"Yes." And what she meant, of course, was the very opposite of that.

Mother insisted the evening's dance would be a three-petticoat sort of occasion.

Clara tried to adjust the hairpin at the nape of her neck, the especially tight one that was causing her head to ache already as the carriage plodded down the road. Rose had created an intricate braid with her hair that overlapped as though woven—the beauty of it, apparently expected and entirely worth the pain. Or at least so Clara kept telling herself.

But nothing about this evening seemed entirely grand, entirely fetching, or entirely lovely. In fact, it all seemed a very elaborate yet bleak stage for Clara to step onto, and yet step onto it she must.

After all, that's how these things were done. She may pine for a romance like the ones in her Jane Austen novels, but the world simply did not work that way, and she'd no choice but to follow her parents' plan.

She struggled to breathe, all the while, from the extra half inch her corset pulled from her waistline. Why she bothered with this extra half inch when she knew she would be out of breath from waltzing, Clara couldn't tell you, but tradition preferred a smaller waistline. And so Clara, like all the others, contorted herself into the assemblage.

Sometimes she had a mind to go without a corset entirely and just see if anyone noticed.

Sometimes she had very rebellious thoughts.

She knew she must make a good impression because the ball at St. Andrews Hall was her first formal occasion on the arm of her would-be husband. They would arrive alongside her mother and father to make a statement as much about politics as it was about her future.

Which meant this was her first opportunity to gather information.

"Such a beautiful place for a ball." Mother peered through the small carriage window. "Don't you think, Clara?"

"Indeed." Clara lifted her chin. Her gown dipped a little lower along her neck than she was accustomed to, and she found herself reaching for her dress trimmings only to find an elaborate bertha that left the bare and tender skin exposed instead.

The little buttons trailed down, down, down until they reached the delicate ribbon at her waistline. And an intricate ribbon it was, acquired by her father from an embroidery shop somewhere in Europe. The pattern of the butterfly wings mingled with the flowers, and as Clara ran her fingers over the ribbon, she wished she could interpret the story it had to tell.

She was always thinking that way, of the meaning behind the meaning, and despite her mother's many attempts to curb the impulse, she simply could not seem to stop it. Seeing beyond, that is. And maybe feeling beyond too, but that was something else entirely.

The carriage lurched to a stop as Clara's thumb gently grazed the buttons tightening her gloves. Tiny buttons that'd caused all manner of trouble when she'd discovered she'd once again misplaced her buttonhook. Rose had come upon the scene just before Clara was about to give up and go with loose gloves.

Joseph reached for Clara's hand to help her from the carriage, and she took care with her silk skirt as she climbed down. A lady must consider so many confounded pieces of clothing at any given moment, it was no wonder men considered the female mind less capable. Women were too distracted with the effort it took to properly dress and breathe.

Joseph smiled at her pleasantly, the corners of his mustache upturned into a sharp point. Clara managed to smile back at him. See how well she could handle feigning interest? Why, she was quite fit for espionage.

Together, she and Joseph, along with her parents, stepped through the arched doorway and into the grand hall, the interior of which was quite something to behold. Lush garlands with beautiful ribbons had been draped beneath the windows. And the ceiling climbed so far upward, Clara liked to imagine it might reach the heavens.

Though the evening outside held a distinct chill, hundreds of candles brought not only light and merriment but also warmth to the sprawling room, such that Clara fanned herself lest her skin glisten before the first dance had even begun.

In no time, Clara was square in the arms of Joseph and waltzing along to the music with posture that would make her former girls' tutor proud. At the song's end, Joseph held on to her hand a moment longer than necessary.

"Any further news on the war?" Clara asked, and Joseph looked at her quizzically.

"None I might imagine to be fit for a lady." He smirked.

"Why, I suppose that depends entirely on how you imagine her." Clara fiddled with the fastener at the wrist of her glove.

Joseph regarded her a long moment. "A rather clever response, Clara." His grin widened. Good, he was pleased. That meant he believed Clara was trying to make pleasant conversation and *not* the reality—that she was trying to gather information Teddy and Oliver might use to help both the Union soldiers and the escaped slaves on their way to freedom.

Father had begun to catch wind of her interests in abolition—how, she had no idea, for she had been the very picture of subterfuge—and quit discussing the topic in her presence lest she, as he odiously reiterated, develop a distinctly unladylike investment in the matter.

It seemed Joseph would fall for her charms far more easily, which frankly, was a relief because Father could be quite cunning when he put his mind to it.

Joseph continued to hold her gloved hand within his own. "I can appreciate a woman with a knack for adventure." He kept his voice low. "But I wouldn't worry your pretty self, Clara—my boys and I will do whatever it takes to keep your family's fortune safe."

"I am so grateful to hear that." She feigned a sigh of relief. She wanted to say, *I'll bet you desire to keep the fortune safe, considering you plan to profit from it,* but she, of course, said no such thing. Instead, she appealed to his ego, which seemed to be growing by the moment from her flattery.

"In a few days, I'm afraid we must part ways once again, as I will be traveling to Virginia to consort with Beauregard and Jackson—the latter of which has earned himself a new nickname after recent victory . . . Stonewall." Joseph sighed, clearly pleased with himself. "Ah, 'tis an honor to be in the company of these men. Nevertheless, you needn't worry yourself, Clara—we will win the fight in time."

"A few days?" Clara spoke the question with greater surprise than she intended. The last thing she meant was to make such an impression upon Joseph that he relayed her interest to her father. She must make a concerted effort to speak more coolly. She decided to move the subject forward. "I had so hoped war might be over by Christmastime, but I overheard Father saying the bloodshed at Manassas is a harbinger of things yet to come." This part held no deceit at all.

"Indeed, I believe your father is right." Joseph nodded.

"Will you stay in Virginia a while?" Clara asked innocently enough. Perhaps his answer would lead to some information Teddy and Oliver might find useful.

"For a time, yes—but I believe there are plans for an attack west of the Mississippi. Missouri, most likely." Joseph fussed with the looped knot of his tie. "Yes, and I plan to be an asset among them."

Clara wanted to groan with exasperation, but thankfully, had acquired a great deal of experience keeping her emotions hidden—frowning and carrying on was anything but ladylike, of course, and if there was one thing her mother had taught her, it was proper etiquette. Little did her mother know how those lessons were already serving her well in deception—and Clara could only imagine what her mother's response might be if she ever found out. Clara giggled inwardly at the mere thought of it.

Nevertheless, Joseph was not providing the sort of detail Clara had been hoping to acquire through their conversation, so she decided to more intentionally prompt him.

"My father speaks highly of your military ability," she said, tilting her chin ever so slightly and offering a fetching, dainty smile. "What radical implications abolition would bring. . . .

I, for one, cannot imagine my life without Rose." She locked onto his gaze and held it, hoping he would never expect the attention to be intentional flattery. "In fact, I do wonder if you could find out more about Rose's history. . . . Once we're wed, I would like to find another woman like her."

Joseph held tightly to her hand. "If that's what pleases you, I'm sure I could have a conversation with your father to discuss how and where she was bought."

His phrasing soured Clara's stomach, yet she carried on. "Thank you," she managed to say, in her most feminine fashion. "I've no doubt there are a good many women capable, but Rose is uniquely skilled." She considered saying, *It seems to be in her blood—perhaps we could see if she has any family relations*—but Clara didn't want to arouse suspicion and knew that might be taking it too far.

For now, she would simply plant the seed in his mind, and later find out what sprouted from it.

ELEVEN

New Orleans, Modern Day

Alice

Ten hours and a short Netflix binge later, Alice leaned back on her bed and rubbed the stinging mascara from her eyes. Her Victorian flower dictionary lay open beside her. Alice's mind spun from what Juliet had said earlier this afternoon . . . that her mother may have the rest of this story.

Alice's eyes fluttered closed.

In a haze and with her eyes still closed, Alice drifted off to sleep, emotionally spent from the day. She dreamed she was wearing the beautiful crimson gown her mother had bought for Alice's birthday two months before Hurricane Katrina— the dress that'd hung in her closet ever since, though she'd long outgrown it. The last gift her mother gave her.

With a flick of her wrist, Alice twirled her dress so it flooded the space all around her. And in that moment, she felt alive. Really and truly alive. As though all that'd been broken and all that'd gone missing in her life had returned, restored.

She stood in that space between—between dreaming and happening, passion and doing. And she felt so sure of herself—so strong—as she slowly filled her lungs with breath to say something. But when she parted her lips, no sound emerged. No matter how hard she tried. Only silence filled the void.

She crumbled to the ground in a heap, but no one could see. No one was listening.

"Alice," her mother's voice said in the dream. In desperation, Alice looked everywhere, trying to locate her mother but seeing nothing. "Alice," the voice said again, calling her so clearly. But Alice could not find her anywhere.

She began to panic. The feeling of wholeness shattered, and in its place came an unrelenting sense of doom. The dress ripped as she began to run, looking around every corner to find the source of the echo—the source of her mother's voice, calling her name—but she found nothing.

All that was within her grieved. The deepest sort of grief. She felt the despair she wouldn't allow herself to feel during her waking moments. She felt the loss that would cripple her ability to breathe if she entertained it during the day.

Awakening from the nightmare, Alice sat straight up in bed, gasping. Her pulse raced, and her llama-patterned pajamas were sweaty.

It was only a dream, she told herself, trying to breathe. *Only a dream.*

But the sensation she was choking was still a reality. And the grief she'd just felt . . . that part wasn't just a dream either. No, that part was trauma, and it was very real indeed.

The wake of the dream left dizziness and uncertainty. She realized in her half-conscious state she'd forgotten to turn off the television, so she reached toward her nightstand, fumbling for the remote to mute the sound.

Where is God in all of this?

The thought surprised her, and she immediately felt guilty.

What if God held it against her that she was questioning, doubting where He might be?

And in the deepest part of her heart, the thing Alice feared most began to stir—that God might love the rest of the world but still have forgotten her.

That God, in all His supposed majesty, had simply failed to see.

And there she was, in a crumpled heap—voiceless, broken, and unloved.

Alice reached for the glass she always kept on her nightstand and took several big gulps of water. She worked to steady her breathing, and cleared her throat to assure herself she really could speak, just as her counselor taught her.

She told herself it was just a nightmare and had no bearing on reality.

The trouble was, she knew she was lying.

Because her mother really might be out there somewhere. She could be anywhere, really. But it was time Alice took another shot at finding her. Even a death notice, the worst case scenario, would at least bring closure.

She fired off a message to Sullivan and Juliet on a social media account, afraid to text them at this hour. Though she might regret her hasty message, she was determined she would meet them in the morning. She would agree to help find Rose's story. Because she couldn't go on like this much longer.

Before turning off her phone, she glanced at the photos of the samplers once more. One of the patterns caught her eye, and she flipped on the bedside lamp and held it up, squinting. Now that was certainly odd . . .

Alice gulped back the fear clawing her throat as she found herself at Juliet's doorstep the following afternoon. She fingered the bun twisted at the nape of her neck and nervously checked to make sure no hairs had fallen out of place. Then she straightened her floral skirt, as well as the long strand of beads at her neck, and smacked her red lips together.

You are going to be okay. One step at a time. You are going to be okay.

But no matter how many times she tried to stop herself, her heart kept tugging her to the house next door—the one she once lived in—like a stubborn child pulling the hem of her mother's skirt.

Everything that happened after the hurricane seemed like a blur. Yet the past had become a cloud so large, at some point it settled permanently over the landscape—changing her. She could never look at that house the same way again.

She could never look at her life the same way again either.

She was terrified of what she might learn about her mother but even more terrified at the prospect of leaving it be. The lingering question of what happened to her mother pulled Alice in, despite the emotional danger, like the glittering of the sun against the water's deep tide.

Alice stood until she couldn't stand there any longer.

Finally, she squared her shoulders and raised her fist to the door to knock.

Juliet opened the door with the same sparkling smile she'd offered yesterday. "Alice." She gestured toward a hallway lined with beautiful watercolor paintings. "Please come in."

At the sight of her smile, Alice's nerves eased.

This *was* going to be okay. She took a deep breath and followed Juliet to a navy couch at the center of the room.

A couch where Sullivan was already sitting.

"You beat me here," she said. His presence brought immediate comfort, which caught her off guard, given how little they knew each other.

He drummed his fingers against the top of the sofa and

grinned at her. "I was told I needed to work on being more punctual."

Alice smirked, her gaze trailing over the white crown molding and the eclectic mix of colorful picture frames on the fireplace mantel. She liked Juliet's decorating style. It was mismatched yet charming. Almost like a garment.

Juliet sat in the patterned chair across from Alice. An antique turquoise table filled the space between them. Juliet crossed her legs at her ankles and leaned forward. "Before you say anything, Alice . . . there's something I need to tell you. It's about your mother."

At the mention of her mother, a fight or flight response kicked in, and Alice resisted the urge to run. She had spent years upon years trying to move forward with her life, haunted by the giant question mark of her mother's absence. Now that she had the opportunity to face it head on, she felt as though she may have a panic attack.

She tried to calm herself with more deep breaths before anyone noticed how flustered she felt.

But Sullivan looked at her, frowning. "You okay?" he mouthed.

She nodded. Though in reality, she was not. Maybe coming here had been a mistake. Maybe she should just leave, avoid Juliet at the wedding, and go back to only seeing her old neighbor once in a blue moon.

Maybe it'd be better to continue living with that question mark after all.

Alice reached for the strap of her purse, fiddling with it. But before she could consider an escape, before she could overthink what she was doing, Juliet's words pierced the haze.

"The night before Hurricane Katrina, I was trying to find a gas station and a store that still had bottled water in stock, and I recognized your mother." Juliet's words were unwavering. "She was getting out of her car on the bridge, and at first, I thought she was checking traffic. So many people were evacuating, the roads were gridlocked for miles. But it quickly became apparent to me she planned on jumping."

Alice stared, wild-eyed, her purse falling from her hands.

Juliet quickly reached out, taking Alice's hands in her own. "Sweetheart, I believe she's still alive."

Alice parted her lips to speak, but found them numb. She was beginning to feel fuzzy-headed, dizzy. "I don't understand." She shook her head.

Alice tried to swallow, but her tongue was putty. She felt a wave of relief to finally be getting answers, followed by alternating tugs of panic about what this might mean. She tried to shift her position on the sofa, but her legs were too wobbly to move.

"Alice," Juliet said, pulling her back into the present. "I parked my car as soon as I recognized her, and I hurried over. She didn't jump off that bridge."

Alice hesitated, biting down on her bottom lip and staring back at Juliet. "You're sure it was her? It must have been dark by then, and storming . . ."

"I'm sure," Juliet said.

Alice closed her eyes, daring for the first time in years to truly *hope* her mother might still be living.

Please let her be okay. Please let her be okay. Please let her be okay.

But the anxiety pulled so deeply, the usual prayer did little in the way of calming her panic. Alice's pulse raced, and her mind did too.

Alice adjusted one of the throw pillows behind her back. "What happened next?"

Juliet met her gaze. "I offered to take her to the hospital, but with the storm coming . . . she convinced me she would be safer staying the night with a friend in St. Bernard Parish."

Alice swallowed hard, the implications of this new information hitting her with the weight of a freight train.

Sullivan leaned forward. "St. Bernard Parish? Isn't that the neighborhood . . ." But his words were a hushed whisper, too hard to say aloud.

"Yes." Juliet nodded sadly. "At first, the media didn't even cover how dire the situation was in the parish because they couldn't get in. The destruction was unlike anything we could have imagined. Unthinkable, really."

"Did *anyone* survive the storm in that neighborhood?" Alice dared ask her. She was so young at the time, she really wasn't sure.

"Yes." Juliet's answer was quick. "Some people cut holes through their ceilings and climbed onto rooftops, where volunteer firefighters and even a Canadian rescue team came to help them." Now, she hesitated. "I don't mean to present this in a rose-colored way. It was *bad* in the parish, Alice. At one point, everyone going in had to wear a hazmat suit because the floodwater was toxic. But"—she leaned forward—"I have reason to believe your mother is alive. About a month after the storm, I received a letter in the mail from her, thanking me for stopping her on the bridge that day. While it's possible she put it in the mail the night before the hurricane hit, I find that highly unlikely—especially considering some of those mailboxes aren't even standing, let alone getting mail service."

"What I don't understand is . . ." Alice looked down at the floor, then slowly lifted her gaze to meet Juliet's. "If all this is true, why did she never come back for me?"

"Maybe she tried." Juliet shrugged. "I don't know, sweetheart. Depression is an ugly thing. It convinces folks the world is better off without them. Maybe she believed her illness was too much for you to take." The woman sighed. "My own mother made some radical decisions when I was a baby that changed our family dynamic forever. When I first found out, I was angry. So angry. But as I've grown older, I've come to realize why she did it—why she felt she had to. And now I realize I always looked at the situation as a daughter, but maybe if I had been the mother . . . Look, I'm not saying that's the case with your own mother. I don't know where she is or why she stayed away. But what I am saying is, give her the opportunity to explain."

"I don't know. . . ." Alice rubbed her hands over her face. "None of this makes sense. None of this seems like something she would do."

"I'm just sorry I didn't get the message to you. After the storm, I left town for three weeks to stay with a friend in Shreveport until power was restored, and by the time I returned, you were gone. But then all these years later, you showed up again. And looking at you yesterday—your expression so full of interest when you found those old heirlooms—well, I went out on a limb, and I don't regret doing it." With one firm nod of her chin, she added, "People deserve to know the whole truth about their families, no matter how painful it may be. I really believe that."

Juliet stood and walked over to the wall to remove a framed needlework that was exquisite. Alice took the frame from her outstretched hands but frowned. Why was Juliet giving her this to hold?

"I'm boiling some hot water for tea. Would you like a cup, Alice? What about you, Sullivan? You've been awfully quiet."

"I'd love some," Alice told Juliet. "English Breakfast, if you have it."

"None for me," Sullivan said. "But thank you anyway."

When Juliet returned, she held a teapot and two delicate cups, each with a tea bag inside. She set them on the table in front of the sofa, then poured boiling water into the cups.

While it steeped, she took the frame back from Alice, gently touching the embroidery. "You see these stitches?"

Alice nodded. They were so intricate in their design and color, she'd assumed it was yet another family heirloom.

"I stitched them by hand. Each flower petal and bird and tree." Juliet set the cross-stitch back down and opened her palms. "These hands of mine aren't what they used to be. They're riddled with arthritis now, and well, it's a struggle most days even to bend my fingers. But my mother, Millie, taught me the art, and with it, something even more important."

Juliet looked into Alice's eyes. Her gaze unraveled Alice like a sudden pull to a spool. Alice reached out and took her teacup in her hands, testing the temperature of the liquid.

Juliet tapped the glass of the frame. "Brokenness abounds—it is the state of this world." She patted the stitches once more with her wrinkled hand. "But if we look hard enough, we can find spaces, pierced by a needle. When threaded together, they create something beautiful—a story, our story, and through the threads and the holes, we grow."

Alice sat still, moving her gaze down to her own teacup. That was all very well, but what did it have to do with her mother?

"I don't think it works for everyone that way," Alice whispered. A small cut from yesterday's rose thorns was barely visible beneath her sleeve.

Why did she expect God's answers here, through an old neighbor's story, late on a Sunday afternoon?

"The stitching really is beautiful," Alice said. Perhaps it was time for a change of subject. She rubbed the rim of her cup with her finger. "Speaking of stitching, I wanted to talk with you about something I noticed late last night in the heirloom sampler." Alice pulled her from her purse, pointing to the photo and stitched flame. "This is an obvious break from the consistent floral presentations we see in the other needlework. What do you think it means?"

"Hmm," Juliet murmured. "Let me go grab something, and you two can tell me if you think there may be a connection."

When she returned, Juliet set a worn antique journal down on the table in front of Alice. Meanwhile, Alice's mind was still turning with all Juliet had said about spaces and holes and stitching. Her fingers trembled ever so slightly around her teacup, and her breaths came quick. She wondered for the five-hundredth time what on earth she'd gotten herself into. Juliet's words had resonated within her.

Alice's own struggle had changed her. And not for the better. Far from Juliet's beautiful embroidery, most days Alice still felt like a broken arm reaching to grasp things and ever reminded of the pain of the fracture.

Secretly, sometimes she wondered . . . would she ever be the same?

Juliet made herself comfortable once more in the chair across from Alice and Sullivan. She turned the journal slowly and pulled out a page near the front—time had detached it from the rest of the diary, its edges rough. The ink was faded. Juliet used care even looking at the piece—its worth, to her at least, must be incredible.

Alice waited, wondering. What might that script have to say?

Juliet gently held the page out to Alice, her bottom hand supporting it, protecting it even from gravity's pull.

"Go on," she said.

And so, needing no further prompting, Alice did.

August, 1917
My, I never thought I'd see the day I'd be sittin' at a window, lookin' out at my own yard and writin' in a diary.

Alice stopped. "Wait a second. Who wrote this?"

A small smile lit Juliet's face. "Ashley. My great-grandmother." Juliet took another sip of her tea. "Keep reading."

Alice read the words aloud.

Sometimes when I close my eyes, I still see that fire spreading like the waves of the sea in holy terror. But maybe in a way that fire freed me.

I met a woman named Clara yesterday, and she explained it to me. How the fire happened all those many years ago, and how without it . . . things would've turned out differently.

Sometimes I look back on all that happened and my heart gets caught in the ditches. I always wondered if maybe I'd find Mama again—but I knew I wouldn't.

For a long time, I was real, real mad. And deservedly.

But the ditches—they only part of the story.

The mountains and the valleys, the night and the morning. They made a person stronger, and braver too. And one day I wondered, if things had been different as I used to dream—if maybe I wouldn't be all these things.

Maybe we all got a bigger story.

—Ashley

When Alice set the page down, her hands were shaking.

She knew exactly what Ashley meant by a *bigger story*. And yet at the same time, she couldn't begin to conceptualize all Ashley had been through.

Juliet laced her wrinkled fingers together and rested them on her knee. "Have you heard of the Great Fire of 1861?"

Alice shook her head.

"The fire destroyed much of the city of Charleston and played a hefty part in helping the Union win the war. In more ways than one."

"What do you mean?" Sullivan asked.

Juliet looked at him. "I think I mentioned yesterday that

113

years ago, your own great-grandmother—Eliza—gave me several precious heirlooms and told me she believed our families share a history. I've done some research since then, and Sullivan, I think the Clara who Ashley references . . . your ancestor . . . was a spy."

"A spy?" Sullivan asked, incredulously. "But if that's the case, why wouldn't my family have passed down the story?"

"Probably because back in that day and age, they would've kept these things a secret. For everyone's safety. Trust me . . . I know a thing or two about secrets and safety."

Juliet carefully placed the journal entry back inside the diary. She looked from Sullivan to Alice and back again. "I think Clara started that fire intentionally, and I'll bet that little fire Alice found stitched into the sampler collaborates what's already here in this journal."

Intentionally? Alice's eyes widened. What kind of woman was Clara, anyway?

TWELVE

Charleston, Fall 1861

Clara

Several months of acquiring information from Joseph and pestering him with little hints and suggestions about finding another slave like Rose was finally paying off. Two days ago, he told her the name of the plantation where Rose had been prior to being sold to Clara's father—the plantation owner was a friend of Joseph's family.

The timing was in Clara's favor, as she'd already planned a visit to Mary's house—where both Teddy and Oliver were currently on a break between assignments.

The four of them—Clara, Teddy, Mary, and Oliver—all took afternoon tea in the garden, as the weather had recently given way to a pleasant autumnal temperature, and the gentle breeze tickled the ends of Clara's pinned hair.

Everyone was looking at her, for she had just announced she had important information to share.

"The Middletons' plantation," Clara said. "That's where Rose and Ashley came from, prior to being sold." Her hands trembled as she held onto her cup and saucer. "Joseph told me."

Teddy took a half step closer, as though he wanted to run to the plantation right then and there. "You're certain?" His eyes pled with her for confidence in her answer.

"I'm certain." Clara nodded. "He seems quite proud to have addressed my suggestion we find someone like Rose for our own household."

"And he thinks he is to wed you . . ." Teddy cleared his throat. As Clara met his gaze, she saw a flicker there that was strong enough to send its warmth over her skin and into her heart, and her pulse began to beat faster. Had he felt a similar spark of attraction?

Clara swallowed. "In six months' time." Her stomach turned just thinking of how close he'd come to kissing her last week. Feigning actual interest in him, rather than disgust, was growing harder and harder to do as she learned more about his character . . . or lack thereof.

Teddy's swallow was visible just above his ascot. "And you are . . . still comfortable with our plan?" His gaze softened from something akin to passion to something akin to protection.

"Comfortable?" Clara pressed the stiff silhouette of her waistline, at the spot the yellow fabric gathered tightly before billowing out down to her ankles. "No." She smiled gently at him. "But confident? Yes."

"What I said before . . ." Teddy began. "About your safety? I meant that, you know. Oliver and I both would never want you and Rose in harm's way."

For a full thirty seconds, Clara had forgotten Mary and Oliver were even standing there. She shook herself from her reverie and forced her gaze toward her cousin.

One corner of Mary's small grin lifted upward mischievously. Had she witnessed Clara's momentary stupor over her attraction to Teddy? And likewise, had Mary also seen what Clara fancied to be Teddy's own attraction?

Clara moistened her lips, carefully choosing her words—for the truth was, she would gladly put herself in a little bit of danger if the tradeoff was helping Rose reunite with her daughter. She was tired of living a careful, dangerless existence—a life that had, up until now, impacted precious few other people. "Rose and I are both very intentional with our words and actions," she assured Teddy.

Slowly, he sipped his tea, still studying her. He seemed to read between the lines of all she was not saying. His attention singularly upon her sent a giddy, fluttering sensation through her limbs, as though her nerves were trying to lift her from the ground upon which she so firmly stood.

"The Middletons' plantation," Mary mumbled, turning to Oliver. "Don't you know one of the Middletons?"

"I do." Oliver bit down on his bottom lip, deep in thought. "As Clara was talking, I was considering how I could orchestrate a social call without arousing suspicion. Teddy and I are always very cautious not to be seen together in public, so no one would suspect ulterior motives with regard to our work or even Clara's connection to Joseph. I just need a reason to call on them."

Mary took a slow sip from her tea. "Perhaps you could ask about their water buffalo?"

Oliver looked back at her incredulously. "Mary, you would have me believe you think it's a good idea for me to casually inquire about their *water buffalo*? And that would not raise any eyebrows?"

Mary giggled.

"Do they truly keep water buffalo?" Clara asked. She could not believe her ears.

Mary nodded. "Sure do. They are beautiful beasts too."

"Why am I of the impression you would not mind me *actually* acquiring a water buffalo?" Oliver asked, teasing.

Mary raised her chin playfully. "Surely no one would blame

me. They are of great interest to a good many people, I will have you know."

"Whatever you say, sweetheart." Oliver clanked his teacup against the saucer. "Perhaps, though, I might instead say I'm interested in a plant or flower from their garden?"

"Indeed," Mary agreed. "You could tell them you'd like to purchase one to get back in my good graces after having been cross with me."

Clara met Teddy's gaze, and they both smiled over the married couple's banter. Truthfully, Clara envied Mary and Oliver. How she would love to someday wed a man who cared enough to make her smile . . . what a luxury Mary enjoyed. And Oliver too, of course.

Clara wondered to herself . . . was that the sort of husband Teddy would make?

But she needn't wonder, really, because she already knew it.

The danger lay in considering Teddy as hers for fancying. Why, for all she knew, he might have plans to travel the world over after the war, or to marry a woman back in New York.

Still, her heart was soft toward him—and she knew if he ever advanced his interest beyond a few stolen smiles and passionate gazes, she would not, for one moment, resist him.

Oliver's voice broke through Clara's thoughts. "The question remains how I will get any information from them about Rose's daughter, though . . . but I'll figure something out."

"No." Clara shook her head, looking over at Oliver to find him staring at her in surprise. "I'll do it myself. I have the most obvious reason for approaching the Middletons, given the backstory I've already built up with Joseph. I'll host them one morning and see what I can unravel."

Oliver hesitated. "I don't know, Clara . . . asking you to listen for information Joseph brings up about military plans and associates is one thing. Make no mistake—you and Rose have done a great job with it. But initiating these conversations is something else entirely, and you don't have formal training as a man would."

"Maybe I don't need formal training," she replied, but even as she said the words, she knew he was right in his objection. Inviting the Middletons over and manipulating the conversation would require an advanced skill set that Clara had not needed before, aside from prompting him to research Rose's daughter. Up until now, she and Rose had simply worked on coding the names of people and places—details, really—and then handed them off to a courier. The work, while helpful to Teddy and Oliver's assignments, required little in the way of actual espionage. This would be something different entirely.

"This could be quite dangerous," Teddy interjected.

"You kid yourself if you think it isn't already," Clara said, and that much she knew was true.

Teddy and Oliver looked at each other.

"It *would* make a lot more sense than Oliver's water buffalo scheme," Mary suggested, casually sipping her tea as a cardinal behind them began to chirp.

"All right." Oliver sighed. "It makes me nervous, but I agree—this is our best bet. Thanks for your courage to offer, Clara."

Teddy reached for her, gently moving a wisp of hair from her forehead with the swipe of his thumb. His touch magnetized her instantly, though she tried not to show it. "Be careful," he said quietly. "Please." He rested his hand on her shoulder.

Slowly, Clara nodded, mesmerized by his touch. "I will." Without thinking, she reached up to cover his hand with her own. She looked at him and didn't look away. "I *will*." She hoped this emphasis would assure him.

And yet, nerves battered her resolve as she considered

that even best-laid plans sometimes failed. Still, she had to do this for Rose's sake, and for Rose's daughter.

So she summoned more courage than she felt.

One week following the visit to her cousin Mary's house, Clara and Rose were out on the long piazza of Clara's family home—Clara, drinking tea from her floral teacup, and Rose, putting the finishing touches on a needlepoint.

Clara had gained new information from Joseph two nights ago that she hoped Teddy and Oliver could use to tip off the Union army about a planned attack in Virginia. Rose had been hard at work ever since, coding the name of the Confederate general with the flower they had assigned to him when they first made the ledger months ago.

Clara watched as Rose pulled the needle through the fabric then tightened the thread, tying it off to trim the loose ends. Within the next quarter hour, the courier would pass by, purchase the needlepoint, and then take it back to Teddy and Oliver for their interpretation. The plan was simple, but consistent—and it consistently worked.

Everything was going as it should this morning, too, until the sound of a carriage stopping pulled Clara's attention away from Rose's work and to a visitor.

A visitor who was anything but the courier. The woman stepped forward toward the long, inviting porch.

"Well, isn't this piece stunning," the guest said of Rose's embroidery. "She always did have a special skill with a needle and thread."

Ida Middleton.

Though the woman spoke of Rose, she spoke *to* Clara, and Clara's blood ran cold. Ida was not due to arrive for another hour. Clara had expected plenty of time between the courier's pickup and the woman's visit. She had not expected this.

Flustered by this new development, Clara looked at Rose—but Rose simply stared down at her work, her hands shaking as she held the fabric tightly. The detail was not lost on Clara. Seeing Rose so undone by the woman caused a fiery resistance to rise up in Clara—for she was beginning to realize how, in many ways, Rose had treated Clara with more maternal instincts than Clara's own mother ever had, and Clara felt very protective of her.

"Ida," Clara forced a tone that was sweet as the sugar they had been rationing. "I'm so pleased you could visit for tea."

"Indeed, I was delighted by the invitation. The war has created such a somber mood with the men away, and it seems I'm always in want of a good conversation these days. Do you find yourself feeling the same?" Ida held her chin high as her gaze trailed over Rose's needlepoint work. Before Clara could respond, she added another question. "I assume these needlepoints are for sale?"

Clara stilled, save for the widening of her eyes. She swallowed hard, trying to think of an answer, any way out of this, but couldn't come up with anything. "Yes," she said, when she feared a longer hesitation may make Ida suspicious.

Usually, Clara and Rose only pulled out the coded needlepoint whenever the courier was here . . . but since the courier was due anytime now, they'd mistakenly thought it was safe. But perhaps Ida would not be interested in that particular work. . . .

"I'll take the one Rose just finished." She fished several coins out of her coin purse with the hook of her finger. "Will this cover the price of the sampler?"

The coins totaled twice what Rose usually sold the regular, uncoded needlepoints for, and still Clara could not think of a retort. "Absolutely." She forced another smile.

Ida made no effort to interact with Rose, apart from taking the sampler from her. Clara watched Rose hand her the fabric, and along with it, the floral code. And Clara felt as though all the air in all the earth had been taken away from them.

In all likelihood, Ida would have no reason to suspect there was more to the meaning of the floral embroidery. She would take it home, where she would frame it, and then put it on display—however ironic that may be, given that the work was essentially a flag for the Union effort.

No one would be the wiser—now or ever—as the years went on and the war eventually ended, and the world changed a hundred times over.

And yet being here with Ida—as she treated Rose more like a fixture than a human being—stirred something in Clara she couldn't quite put into words. That Ida would act entitled to Rose's embroidery filled Clara with indignation. She felt uncomfortable having to carry on this charade. And she felt rageful, that Rose had ever been in this position in the first place.

But she also felt determined that none of their efforts would be in vain.

So with all the charisma she could summon, Clara turned her attention to Ida. "You're right about what you said. Rose is so talented with embroidery." She hesitated, hoping the pause would help her collect her thoughts. "You know, this is a wild idea—but since you're familiar with her and her history, perhaps you'll humor me—do you know if Rose has any relations? A sister, or . . . even a child, perhaps?" Clara took a sip from her teacup nonchalantly. "You see, I've grown rather fond of Rose, and if I must lose her when I wed Joseph, I would at least like to acquire someone similar."

"I do know what you mean—it's hard to get used to some-one new, isn't it?" Ida took in the needlepoint she'd just purchased, studying it and tracing the patterns of the petals with her thumb. "I remember Rose having a daughter, but the girl was young. I'm not sure she would have the same skills due to her lack of experience. Although she would have inevitably watched her mother work and probably did learn a thing or two." Ida slipped the embroidered sampler into her purse. "My family sold her to the Calhouns. After Father died, Mother needed the money. You may try contacting them, see if they're willing to sell her." Ida said it all so casually, as though discussing a shoe buckle rather than somebody's daughter.

Clara's heart raced with this new information. She dared not look at Rose, for she did not trust herself to keep her emotions and expressions collected. The Calhouns were a respected Charleston family, which meant Ashley had not been taken across state lines. In all likelihood, with some careful planning, they could find her—they could perhaps even help Rose and Ashley both escape to someplace north of here.

"Thank you for the information." Clara kept her tone steady and her words brief. "Her young age is a deterrent, as you mentioned, but even still I think she may be a good fit." Clara shifted toward the front door, hoping Ida may read her body language and accept the end of this conversation. "I fear I've left you out on the piazza too long—please, come into the parlor and have a proper cup of tea."

"I would be delighted," Ida said, holding her purse close.

Clara did not know how she managed to get through the next hour making mindless conversation with Ida and arousing no suspicion about the burning plans in her heart, yet somehow, she did.

When Ida finally left the parlor, Clara rushed Rose back out to the piazza, hoping the courier may yet return. Hastily, she told Rose to stitch C-A-L-H-O-U-N into a previous needlepoint, one letter hidden in each petal, with a scripted letter *A* as a curled, red root—the symbol they had all agreed upon should anyone come upon information about Ashley.

And blessedly, a half hour later, the courier did return—taking all manner of hope with him in each step he took.

THIRTEEN

New Orleans, Modern Day

Alice

From the confines of the wrought-iron fence around their second-story patio, Alice sat with Aunt Charlotte—their hands around teacups and their feet warmed by a one-eyed and slightly deaf dog affectionately named Freckles.

Aunt Charlotte's current foster attempt had already been with them a month and a half, and Alice had a feeling the dog was here to stay, given her unconventional fear of the microwave, bathwater, and plastic bags. But Freckles loved to snuggle and watch Doris Day movies, so Alice understood why Aunt Charlotte liked her so much.

"So, what are you going to do?" Aunt Charlotte's blue eyes were wide. She set her cup down and twisted her hair into a low bun at the nape of her neck.

"About Mom?" Alice drummed her grey-painted fingernails against her own teacup and shook her head. "It's certainly a lot to process, especially with the wedding in a couple days."

A car honked at pedestrians running across Magazine

Street, which they could see from the upstairs patio where they sat.

Alice looked down, thinking. She took a slow sip of her tea. "Part of me thinks this whole thing is too farfetched and that I should just let it go and move on before I get hurt in the process."

Aunt Charlotte leaned forward, resting her chin on her hand. "But the other part of you needs to know if it could be true and will think of nothing else until you get an answer."

The solid branches of a huge oak tree spanned from the edge of the patio down to the street, and Alice watched as a squirrel chased a falling acorn all the way down. With what ease that squirrel decided where he was going next. Alice wished she could scurry about so freely.

"Exactly."

Aunt Charlotte leaned back against the wooden bench where she sat and took a sip of her tea. Her tea was always as sweet as her southern accent. "You don't think she would have tried to find us?"

Alice sighed, propping up her feet. "That's what I keep asking myself. But Juliet seemed to think Mom was in a bad place, and maybe she wanted to start over."

Sadness marked the wrinkles at the corners of Aunt Charlotte's eyes.

A pickup truck at the corner squealed its tires at the stop sign. Freckles popped up and let out a startled bark.

Alice reached out to the dog. "You're okay, girl." Freckles sat, ears perked at attention and looking to Aunt Charlotte for confirmation all was well.

Aunt Charlotte patted the dog's head, and Freckles' ears eased back down.

"Honestly, I have to try," Alice said. "Even if the chance is slim. Even if what I find devastates me. I need to know the truth."

Aunt Charlotte reached over for Alice's hand and gave it a squeeze. "I'm proud of you for doing the hard thing, Alice." The scent of jasmine caught on the breeze, and Alice was reminded of the time she'd spent in Charleston for a friend's wedding. With a change in her tone, Aunt Charlotte added, "And I'm looking forward to hearing more about a certain tall and handsome man who will be accompanying you."

Alice took another sip from her tea, looking down into her cup. "You are unrelenting, you know that?"

Aunt Charlotte laughed, scratching Freckles' ears. "Am I going to have to spy on you to get any information?"

Alice rolled her eyes, grinning. "That should go over well. You're about as subtle as an elephant."

"I will take that as a compliment, thank you very much."

The sun swept shades of pink across the New Orleans skyline as it slowly sunk from the sky. And twilight fell, suspended in that glow—that place between the day just finished and the day yet to come.

After a few minutes in comfortable silence, Aunt Charlotte turned to Alice, draining the final sips of tea from her cup. The twilight had sobered the air between them. "I really am proud of you, Alice."

Alice blinked several times, hoping Aunt Charlotte wouldn't notice the tears forming in her eyes.

Aunt Charlotte had a way about her. Always *always* pushing a person to really think about her own heart. Always helping others find their way home . . . whether a stray dog or her niece.

Maybe the preoccupation with home came when she couldn't help her sister find her own way back. Maybe that's why she started helping everyone else. Alice wondered—what would this search mean for Aunt Charlotte? Would she be able to handle whatever secrets Alice unraveled?

Alice breathed out the twilight air. "Let's just say, I don't like a story without an ending." Somewhere, far down the road, a band played jazz. The music reminded Alice of her mother, and she covered her mouth with her hands as she slowly shook her head.

Because while Juliet may have saved her mother in that moment, she did not have the power to *keep* her safe. The storm had still come—both from within and without. Both tides strong, both waters rising.

So while yes, Alice did not like a story without an ending, she and her aunt both knew the truth.

She may not like the ending either.

Alice tucked one of her long auburn curls back into a clip behind her ear and was getting to work cleaning out the tall canisters of single-stemmed flowers when the bell above the front door chimed. Her friends Harper and Lucy stepped inside The Prickly Rose, and the widest grin spread across Alice's face at the sight of them.

She had first met these friends at Lucy's sister's wedding in Charleston a year ago. What started as small talk about her and Harper both owning businesses had turned into a deeper conversation and, in the weeks that followed, a deeper friendship. Ah, the benefits of living in a digital age. Honestly, she was probably closer to Harper and Lucy than she was with any of her in-person friends. There was just something special about them both—Harper, with her love of vintage fashion and old stories, and Lucy, with her artistic talent and determination.

During twice-a-month virtual coffee sessions, Alice enjoyed hearing about Harper's engagement and wedding plans, and all the progress Lucy was making on her house—as well as her relationship with Declan. Declan had a history of dating a lot of women but melted into an adoring puddle around Lucy, and Alice wouldn't be at all surprised if the two soon had their own engagement news to share.

This was the first time she'd seen Lucy in person since the wedding in Charleston, and she couldn't be more excited to give her friend a big hug. The three of them ran to each other.

"I can't believe you're here, Lucy!" Alice said, beaming. She squeezed Lucy's hand. "And Harper, that you're about to get *married*! Has it sunk in yet?"

"Not really," Harper said, laughing. "I oscillate between absolute glee and total panic that I will drive him nuts with my extensive shoe collection. Or that he will drive *me* nuts with his refusal to drink morning coffee."

"I think that's very normal." Alice let go of Harper's hand and led both women to the flowers she'd been working on. "Well, maybe except the whole not-drinking-coffee thing, but the rest of it is. I mean, you're committing yourself to somebody for the rest of your life. That's huge." The thought of her own father abandoning their family welled up in Alice's mind, leaving her heart aching in its wake. Sometimes she wondered if things might have been different if only he'd . . . but there was no use thinking that way. Wouldn't change anything.

"That's what I keep telling her," Lucy chimed in. "Knowing each other's quirks and accepting them is the sign of a healthy relationship. And marriage should be a little overwhelming, right? It shows you're taking it seriously." Lucy twirled her long blond hair up into a bun at the top of her head. She had a classic sort of beauty that reminded Alice of Grace Kelly.

"Thanks, you two." Harper smiled, tugging at the hem of her vintage cardigan. "Honestly, when it comes down to it, I realize these are all jitters. Because the truth is, now that I know Peter is out there in the world, I could never *not* spend the rest of my life with him. I would spend every day dreaming of him, wondering what he was doing. Even with his nerdy history facts and all."

"Aww," Alice and Lucy both chimed in unison.

"That is the sweetest thing." Lucy held her hand over her chest. "I hope Declan feels that way about me."

"He does," Alice said, and Harper nodded. "Even I know that, and I live all these miles away." Alice laughed. "Every time he's there when we're doing virtual coffee, I see him in the background gazing at you lovingly."

Lucy smiled, scrunching her nose. "I really like him."

"We know." It was Alice and Harper's turn to speak in unison this time.

"Do you want to see what I've done so far with the flowers?" Alice pulled a few stems from the containers and pieced them together, holding the makeshift bouquet out to Harper. "I was thinking these for the bridesmaids. Full of color and yet with the tiny buds woven in, the mix is also a little unexpected."

Harper drew the bouquet toward her nose and breathed in. "Oh, that smells amazing." She handed it back. "And looks amazing too. You are so good at this."

"Thank you." Alice pulled each stem apart from the bouquet, placing them back into their respective containers. "Are you still happy with the flowers we chose for your bridal bouquet?"

"Yes, and get this"—Harper turned to Lucy—"back in Victorian times, flowers used to have hidden meanings. Alice explained it to me. People would send messages via bouquet! Can you imagine?"

Lucy quirked her eyebrows. "What? That's so interesting."

"I know, right?"

"So what does your bridal bouquet mean?" Lucy slid her hands into the pockets of her knee-length sweater.

"Love goes before me," Harper replied. Alice had chills

every time she said it—especially as she thought about the implications of the sentiment, both for the past and future.

"It's perfect," Lucy said, and Alice smiled as she placed the last flower back into its casing. Yes, she was good at this job. Harper was right about that much. Even if Alice never planned any of this.

Sometimes life simply takes unexpected turns.

Alice reached for her phone to take a quick picture of Harper with the bouquet-in-progress, but instead of launching the camera, her phone brought up her photos . . . in particular, one of the needlepoint samplers. Alice started to close out the app, but then she noticed something she hadn't seen before. Using two fingers, she enlarged the photo and confirmed her suspicion.

The letters C-A-L-H-O-U-N were stitched into each of the petals, along with the letter A, as though written into a code. You had to really enlarge the image to see them.

Alice blinked, trying to take all of it in. Maybe Juliet was right about everything. . . . Maybe Clara *had* been a spy, after all. But how were Rose and Ashley connected?

Sullivan

Sullivan was looking forward to a night out with his buddies Peter and Declan. The three of them stayed so busy that even though they all lived in Charleston, they rarely hung out. Sullivan was the first to admit he was a big part of the problem, often floating from city to city with work projects.

"Dude, you excited about the big day?" Declan rolled up the cuffs of his shirtsleeves and glanced at Peter.

Peter adjusted his glasses. "I've been excited since the

moment she said 'yes' to marrying me. We all know I'm marrying way out of my league."

"You can say that again." Sullivan grinned, and Peter responded with a smirk. "I'm kidding." Sullivan nudged Peter's elbow. "Don't sell yourself short, man."

Peter smiled. "I just keep hoping she doesn't change her mind."

"You and Harper are like a couple from a movie or something," Sullivan teased. Peter led the way down the sidewalk, toward the restaurant where they'd planned to have a low-key bachelor party dinner.

"Yeah, you kind of are," Declan said, shaking his head. "Although I get what you're saying because I feel the same way about Lucy."

Both Sullivan and Peter quickly turned their heads to stare. Peter was one thing. But Declan had never spoken that way about a woman before. In fact, at this point in the relationship, he was usually bolting faster than a cat with a dog on its tail.

"Wow," Peter said. "You really like her."

Declan came to a sudden stop under a streetlamp. Sullivan and Peter nearly tumbled into him.

He crossed his arms and looked up a moment, taking a deep breath. "I wasn't going to say anything because I don't want to take away from Peter's moment . . . so I'll just drop this here and we can pick it up later. But guys"—Declan looked from Sullivan to Peter—"I want to marry her."

Sullivan felt his jaw drop. "Never thought I'd see the day."

Declan ran his hand along the back of his neck. "Neither did I, but Lucy . . . she's incredible. I'm honestly fifty-fifty about what she will say."

Sullivan rolled his eyes. "Don't be stupid. She loves you. All women love you."

Declan raised an eyebrow.

Peter nodded. "It's true, man. They do. You've got the hair and everything. Like that actor in the old *Pride and Prejudice* adaptation Harper is always making me watch. . . ." He snapped his fingers. "You know, the guy from *The King and I*."

"I was going to back you up until you said that." Sullivan covered his face with his hands and groaned. "You're talking about Colin Firth. And it's *The King's Speech. The King and I* is a musical."

Declan cleared his throat. "Can we . . . uh . . . find a new topic that I understand?"

"Absolutely."

"You got it." Peter smacked Sullivan on the back. "Let's talk about how Sullivan is the last bachelor standing."

Declan grinned. Peter did too.

Oh no.

"Nope." Sullivan shook his head. "I do not like where this is heading."

"The thing about Peter out kicking his coverage with Harper is that she's bound to have a lot of charming friends at the wedding. Am I right?" Declan asked.

Peter shrugged. "I can't argue."

Sullivan waved his hand and started walking down the sidewalk in hopes his movement would distract these goofs. "I can do just fine for myself, thank you."

Declan and Peter were a few steps behind.

By the time they rounded the corner near the restaurant, Sullivan frowned, realizing something. He hadn't even considered the women he might meet at his buddy's wedding until now. Which was very unlike him.

And with startling clarity, the reason caught up with him: there was already one particular woman he was looking forward to seeing.

A certain whimsical red-haired florist.

FOURTEEN

Charleston, November 1861

Clara

A mere week had passed since Clara last saw Teddy, and yet she missed him as though it'd been years. Now, in a fiery farewell, autumn bid summer's final flowers adieu.

Until this point, her espionage had involved little more than listening to Joseph drone on and on, then scripting what he said in hopes it meant something to one more familiar with the ins and outs of a functioning militia. She knew little about the significance of the names and places she notated.

But now—a full day after she and Rose sent the coded message about Ashley—Clara had never been so exhilarated by possibility. Most notably, the possibilities for Rose and Ashley but also the possibilities for Clara's own future. Perhaps her time feigning interest in a marriage to Joseph was nearly over, and she could get on with living her own life away from all the deceit.

A life she dreamed she might share with Teddy.

She had returned to her art supplies and was painting more roses on her special teacup—her flower dictionary on the desk beside her—when Joseph walked in.

Clara startled, not expecting to see him already. "Joseph?" She held tighter to the paintbrush in her hand.

Even his grin was somber. "Are you looking forward to this evening's dinner party?" he asked. They both knew such an extravagance was rare, perhaps even the last dinner party for a while. War was rumbling the ground around them. And not a little war, as wars go, but a terrible one. Clara had felt it in her bones for a while now—for one could no longer find fresh air. Inside and outside, the world smelled like gunpowder, and where there was powder, an explosion would inevitably follow.

"I am." Clara dotted the center of the rose she was painting with a crimson hue. "I even ordered a new gown for the occasion." She used to look forward to the feeling of exquisite fabrics and the anticipation of dinners and dances. Now, they simply felt uncomfortable in every way—both the lace and the conversation.

"And are you also excited to begin making preparations for our wedding?"

"I am, indeed." Clara swallowed hard, wishing she could gulp down the words. The lie clanged like a broken shoe buckle through her heart, clamoring with a racket over the fondness she held for Teddy. "Though we do have many months left on that front," she added, speaking the words more for her own reassurance than as a reminder to Joseph.

"I must admit, I've doubted the wisdom of that decision for some time now, as I'm frequently home between posts and we've no longer any idea how long war may last. The Yanks could continue shooting cannonballs at our city for years. Perhaps we should reconsider. . . ." His hand on her shoulder felt slimy, like the skin of a snake.

"No." Clara blurted the word out before she could think better of it. She composed herself, forcing her hand to cover his in the gentlest gesture she could manage. "What I mean to say is, you wouldn't want to put pressure on Mother and Father, would you? After all, I was under the impression you and Father wanted the wedding to be a social statement—a display of the finest caliber to boost morale and remind our city why it should continue fighting for our way of life."

These words did their magic. Slowly, the off-putting expression that tightened Joseph's brows eased into a smirk of satisfaction. "I rather like the way you worded that, Clara." He squeezed her shoulder and *finally* let go of it.

She needed to talk to Mary at the next possible opportunity about an exit strategy. She would not, under any circumstances, actually marry this man. But what would she do if he once again broached the topic of changing the wedding date?

She would have to prepare a speech about why she did not want to marry right now, just in case she needed it. But the reasons would have to be persuasive, because rejecting Joseph made no logical sense. He was wealthy, a man of power, and would help her secure an impressive social station—not to mention the favor he'd find with her father. On paper, the match seemed perfect in every way. If she wasn't persuasive enough, he may get suspicious . . . and that . . . well, that could be a problem.

"What is this?" Joseph moved closer to the table in front of her. "What are you reading?"

"My flower dictionary." Clara smiled up at him meekly. "Are you familiar with it?"

"I am not." He crossed his arms over his chest. "Men of my station do not have time for matters so delicate as flowers."

Clara nodded, looking down at the laces of her boots so as not to look at him a moment longer.

"However, I'm glad you've found something to engage your feminine charms. You worry me sometimes, what with all this academic reading." He motioned to the bookshelves behind them. "Your father and I both agree some of the world's realities are simply too harsh for a woman's mind."

Perhaps because a woman's heart was fierce enough to fight them, Clara thought.

The door creaked open further, and Rose stepped inside. "Clara, I—" Rose stopped herself short at the sight of Joseph, and the hem of her skirt spun. Realizing her mistake, she hung her head, looking down at the floor.

Joseph aggressively stepped toward Rose, grabbing her by the arm, hard. "How dare you! To think you would directly address my intended by her first name when you are no more consequential than a rat in this house. You will never do it again." He slapped her so hard on the face that Clara's teacup shook across the room, and Clara jumped from her chair.

She lunged at Joseph, grabbing his fist between her own slender fingers. Every fiber of her being wanted to punch him in return, but yanking him by the hair and throwing him out on the street was hardly an option, particularly if she wanted to avoid suspicion that she'd grown sympathetic to abolition.

"Joseph—sweetheart," she whispered. She hated herself for pretending to admire his wicked heart, but she knew she had no other option. "Must you resort to violence?"

He hesitated, his mouth parting as he slowly moistened his bottom lip. Clara began to panic, knowing clear well that stopping him in this way might elicit his response to Rose toward her as well . . . a response to which her own father would probably not object, as Clara would be seen as having provoked him.

Joseph's fist tightened from under Clara's fingers. He freed himself from her grasp, firmly taking hold of her by the shoulders as Rose's eyes flashed fire.

"Now you listen to me," he spat. His fingernails dug into her tender skin, and she was sure she would be marked by this display with a set of bruises within the hour. She only hoped she could cover them with the cut of her new gown. "If we are to marry, you will never disrespect me again. Do you understand?"

Clara boldly looked straight into his eyes and was astonished to see not anger, not fury, but the cold resolve of a soldier on his way to battle. The clouds over his eyes filled her with terror, as a thought occurred to her for the very first time.

When and if this man found out she'd betrayed him, he was not above killing her.

She needed a plan. Just in case they had to run at a moment's time.

She would pack a bag for herself and one for Rose. She would leave them underneath her bed, hidden behind her hope chest. No one would be the wiser.

At least, she hoped not. She needed to consider how she might get the information to Teddy.

But for the time being, Clara simply lowered her head and nodded. "My apologies," she murmured, unsure how much longer she could keep up the ruse.

Rose

Clara done nearly sabotaged the whole thing. Bless it.

Tellin' Joseph 'bout the flower dictionary like that, she may as well have put the spy code in the papers. Oh, she didn't mean nothin' by it, but she needs to be more careful. I had no choice but to barge in, make a scene 'fore Joseph put the pieces together. Try to get his mind off what she was saying.

The girl's got a good head on her shoulders, and a good heart too. I know she'll help me find my daughter and she'll be faithful to Teddy. Well, at least, I *think* I know. Guess the only real way to know somebody is to see how they respond when it really comes down to it.

What worries me sometimes is how little she really knows of the world. She doesn't have the honest to goodness knowledge that comes from livin'. 'Cause you live long enough and you see things, you become things, and then you get stronger. And sometimes, the hard things come and in a moment's time, they grow you straight up.

Happened to me all over again when those men took my daughter.

I wouldn't say I was a child or anything before that 'cause I already had my fair share of hardship, but that day, my heart broke so bad it was like my soul grew older.

Missus, she mean well, but she's never really lost anything. She thinks she's ready to, and maybe she is, but she also naïve.

It's gonna be real hard on her to never see her family no more, even if her daddy is wicked and her fake fiancé, even wickeder. She's kind, you see. And I guess what I mean is she's never broken before.

But she's gonna be. She's gonna be real soon.

I just wonder if she'll know how to put herself back together.

Clara

The morning after the dinner party, Clara took extra care readying herself for the day—from the buckles of her shoes to the pins in her hair. She had yet to hear a response from Teddy and Oliver, but she suspected Mary might reach out to her soon. Either that or a courier could come by with a message.

She'd learned several names of Confederate spies, so she and Rose had stayed up late after the party coding those into a new needlepoint.

And she was glad they'd gone to all those lengths as she sipped tea from her painted china and watched Rose, who stood at a distance embroidering from the piazza beside her. Because something was different about this morning. And she was ready to strike the match on it.

The passerby approached, wearing the distinctive rose lapel pin that Mary and Oliver had suggested to help Clara and Rose identify him—for it would not, of course, be the same courier every time.

This particular man wore a suit of grey with a vest of cream and a fashionable hat with a band of black around it. She recognized him immediately, though she hadn't seen him in days—well, that wasn't entirely true. She had dreamed of him just about every night this week.

His presence pulled her with attraction, yes, but it filled her with something even greater than that. Hope for a better life. Not only for herself, but also for Rose and Ashley, for so many others for whom trauma had become what they were used to.

"Good morning, ma'am." When Teddy tipped his hat to her and smiled, Clara's heart raced with the thrill of their meeting. She went to bed last night feeling lost after an evening tolerating Joseph's opinions, but now, she found her way home through Teddy's warm eyes.

She noticed a tiny new scar above his eye. The mark added character, a sign of courage. It suited him. But how had he gotten it?

"Good morning, sir." She offered him her most satisfied smile. Could he feel the pull she had toward him? How desperately she wanted to throw herself in his arms and run away together?

His gaze never wavered from her own. He seemed to be reading her, memorizing the details, and she wondered what he saw there. She hoped he wouldn't notice the bruises on her arms, though she'd taken great care to cover them with her lacy shawl.

"Exceptionally lovely," he whispered.

"The morning?" she asked.

"Sure," he said, with a widening grin. He filled her heart with a thousand fiery sunsets and the promise of shooting stars.

"Are these embroidered samplers for sale?" Teddy stepped toward Rose, and Clara admired the confidence in his stride. He turned to Clara, addressing her with the question.

"They are. Rose makes them all herself."

Teddy picked up a small basket. Pretending to show him its features, Rose slipped Clara's note from her pocket into one of the basket's compartments.

"Thank you," Teddy said to Clara, smiling. He caught her gaze and didn't let go. "This one will be perfect to give my girl."

"Are you married, sir?" She gave a mischievous smile.

He held her gaze with his own. "Not yet."

Clara's heart felt like it skipped a beat, so light she thought she might float away on the breeze. When he offered payment, he tipped his hat once more, and he was gone far too soon.

It took a long moment before she realized Rose was standing in front of her, placing in Clara's palm what Teddy had offered in payment.

Rarely had couriers left messages in return, and it hadn't occurred to Clara that Teddy could be one of these few. What might he have said? She hurried to unroll the paper, hoping it wouldn't convey he was in danger.

Dearest Clara, the message read. *We received your message and are working on the details. I have thought of you every day since our departure. I think I'm in love with you. —Teddy*

Clara reread the note again and again, for the words were more beautiful than she could have imagined. And the thought of his affections bolstered her own courage. Knowing a life with Teddy might be at the end of all this gave her the persistence to keep going.

She held the note to her chest. She knew she had to destroy it, just as she'd destroyed the few other courier messages she'd received. But she would hold onto it for just a *little* longer, for the sentiment would bolster her will and keep her going.

Clara covered the little note with her fist and shoved it into her pocket for safekeeping until later, when she planned to throw it into the fireplace.

FIFTEEN

New Orleans, Modern Day

Alice

The next day, Alice was halfway through eating a cinnamon roll and jamming to a dance song in her kitchen when the doorbell rang.

She hurried over, cinnamon roll in hand, and looked through the privacy hole. Then she frowned, hurrying to unbolt the door despite the mismatched fuzzy-robe-and-Christmas-pants ensemble she was rocking.

"Harper?"

Harper's hair was frizzy and her pink T-shirt half untucked. Alice couldn't remember a time she'd seen her friend so unkempt.

"You've got to help me," Harper said.

Alice pulled her friend inside and closed the door. "Are you okay?" She searched Harper's eyes.

Harper nodded, but the blank way she looked past Alice and into the house said otherwise.

"What is going on?" Alice took her friend by both arms. "You're scaring me."

The wedding was tomorrow. Alice could only hope nothing

huge had gone wrong. At least she knew the flowers were under control. And she *knew* it didn't have anything to do with the groom because Peter adored this woman.

"I'm so sorry, Alice, but she's sick and hoarse and can't sing, and I didn't know what else to do. . . ." Panic filled Harper's voice. "I need you. Will you do it?"

"Wait. Back up. Who is hoarse?" Alice led her friend to the couch, where the two of them sat down. Alice adjusted a velvet pillow behind her back. "I think you skipped a few steps. . . . What are you asking me, exactly?"

"I need you to be our wedding singer." Harper met her gaze so fiercely, Alice was afraid to look away from the desperation she saw.

But she couldn't. She just . . . couldn't.

Right? She had told herself she would never sing again. Not in front of a group of people, at least. It was far too painful, tied to memories of her mother. There was no telling how she might lose her composure if she tried.

"Harper . . ." Alice started, but she couldn't think of what to say . . . how to refuse helping one of her best friends.

Harper rubbed her eyes with her hands. "I'm sorry, Alice. It wasn't fair of me to ask you that. I know you don't like singing in front of crowds. Forget I mentioned it, okay? I'll figure something else out."

Harper began to stand, but Alice caught her by the arm. "I'll do it," Alice said, surprising even herself with the declaration.

"Oh my goodness," Harper's shoulders fell in relief, and she gave Alice the biggest hug. "Are you sure?"

Was she sure?

No, she wasn't sure at all.

"Of course! It's your wedding. This is a big deal. I can get over my baggage . . . for a day, at least." She softened the joke with a wink, hoping Harper wouldn't read the truth behind the jest.

"You are a total lifesaver," Harper tucked her hair behind her ears. "I owe you one, okay? I'll embroider a cardigan with a thousand flowers on it."

Alice laughed. "Make it a thousand and one, and you've got a deal."

Harper held out her hand to shake on it. "It's a deal. So, I'll tell Sullivan to call you, and the two of you can set things up."

Alice stopped. "Sullivan?"

Harper hit her hand to her forehead. "I'm a blubbering mess. I didn't even mention that part, did I?"

"Definitely didn't." Alice smiled.

"Sullivan is playing the piano to accompany the vocalist. He's an incredible pianist. Apparently it runs in his extended family. You didn't know he loves jazz?"

Alice bit down on her bottom lip even as her pulse picked up speed. Sullivan was a jazz fan too? Maybe they had more in common than she'd realized. . . . "Definitely didn't know that."

"There's probably a lot you don't know about him," Harper said with a mischievous smile.

Five Hours Later

Sullivan

Sullivan was alone, sitting behind the piano that had been moved to the sprawling outdoor garden in anticipation of tonight's dress rehearsal for the wedding.

No one else had arrived yet.

No one, that is, apart from the woman coming his way now.

Her floral skirt trailed behind her as she walked down the aisle toward him. Well, not toward *him* exactly, so much as the instruments, but that was beside the point.

Sullivan cleared his throat.

"You look . . ." He shook his head as she approached, trying to find the words.

"I went ahead and got ready for the rehearsal dinner." She gave her skirt a twirl, beaming at him as she slid her hands into the pockets. "It's a fun skirt, right?"

He was actually going to use the phrase *jaw-dropping*, but *fun* worked just fine.

"Alice," he started again. Seemed the least she deserved was for him to articulate a complete thought. "You're stunning."

She stepped closer, one corner of her dark-stained lips pulling up into a grin. "Oh, I bet you say that to all the girls." She stopped after she rounded the corner of the piano. "You clean up well yourself, Sullivan."

Her sass defied his composure, and he was having a hard time reminding himself he wasn't the long-term-boyfriend type. And even if he was . . . well, they lived many states apart. Long-distance relationships had never done him any favors in the past.

Still . . .

"Ready to start?" he asked, his fingers over the keys.

"Show me what you've got." She seemed unexpectedly confident in this environment, as though she had professional training or something.

He began to play, and she began to sing, and her voice was like gold dust that settled over everything it fell upon.

Sullivan was so immersed in the sound that he nearly missed several chords.

She was enchanting. Absolutely enchanting.

And she was enchanting him despite his determination to play it cool.

But then something happened. Her voice broke. It was subtle, at first, then turned into something more. And she shook her head, waving her hand mindlessly over her face and mumbling she was sorry, and she didn't know if she could do this.

Sullivan stopped playing, pushed out the piano bench, then stood. He stepped closer to her, and that's when he saw the emotion puddling in her eyes. What had this song triggered in Alice?

"Are you okay?" He reached out to steady her with a gentle touch on her elbow. It was such a dumb question to ask when she was so obviously anything *but* okay, yet he could think of no other way to bring it up.

"Not really." She scrunched her nose as though doing so may help her regain her composure. "I have some . . . hesitation about this, I guess."

"Yeah, I can see that. I'm nervous too, believe it or not." He chided himself for being a little too transparent.

"Really?" Her tone was surprised. "But you seem so . . . so . . ."

"Confident?" He slid his hands into his pockets, giving her a mischievous smile. "Yes, I like to keep my reputation intact."

At that, Alice smiled back at him.

Good. He was getting somewhere now. His heart tugged with concern for her, and he hoped he could help somehow.

"Can I ask you something?" He looked around at the garden encircling them, drew in a deep breath of the fragranced air. "What happened? Why this song?"

She ran her tongue along her teeth as though turning the words around and around before letting them out. "I don't know if I told you, but my mother was a jazz vocalist."

He let his hand fall from her elbow, realizing all at once that he'd probably kept it there longer than he should have.

"Ever since I lost her, I haven't been able to sing jazz without getting really emotional thinking about her." Alice looked down at the dirt of the garden.

"I think that's understandable. . . . I mean, it all had to be so heartbreaking."

"It was. And still is." She blinked, shaking her head. "Anyway, I'm sorry to interrupt the song. You probably think I'm a mess."

Sullivan crossed his arms. "Quite the contrary, Alice."

"Yeah?" She looked to him in earnest.

"I think it's very brave that even though you're struggling, you keep going." He met her eyes then, and the look she gave him unraveled his resolve to stay emotionally detached. "That's the very definition of bravery if you ask me."

"I guess I've never thought of it like that."

He held on to her gaze for several very full seconds. His stomach rose and fell in a tangled tumble. It'd been a while since he'd been this attracted to someone. She was dangerous for him, and he'd do well to remember that. Yet he couldn't seem to turn away from her eyes.

"Well, I'm happy to offer another perspective. The truth is, I went through an awful breakup a couple years ago . . . we were really serious and I caught her cheating on me . . . anyway, it's only been recently that I've let people back in. I put so many walls up. And that's nothing like the trauma of what you've been through. So yes, I think you're strong for carrying on even when it's hard. Because not all of us are bold enough to do that."

Her eyes flickered with surprise. She had clearly not expected his words, and he didn't miss the way she leaned slightly closer. "Thank you," she whispered.

He grinned at her in reply. "You're welcome."

"Ready to get back to the song?" she asked.

"Take it away."

The Following Day

Alice

The part of Alice's heart that had once been solid unceremoniously became Velcro one morning.

She didn't know which morning—whether it happened at twilight or midnight or somewhere in between—just that it happened, and that some days she woke up in two pieces, trying so very hard to reattach herself to the stable side of who she used to be. But sometimes it seemed as though her real identity was off floating, catching against her softest blankets and her most delicate cardigans, leaving little bits of damage wherever they may be.

Today was one of those mornings. And as Alice used her straightener to loop defined curls into her fiery hair, she tried to sort through how she felt and who, today, she would be.

Well, she supposed she was herself any day of the week, but it *wasn't* every day of the week she felt she could get up in front of a crowd of people, just like her mother, and sing. Or sing well, at least.

But today she had to sing anyway.

Today was Harper and Peter's wedding.

Today would be a beautiful day.

Alice would make it beautiful, no matter what. She would place flowers in every vase from here to Shreveport if that's what it took for beauty to work its magic.

She would arrange flowers until she forgot the memories that kept springing up. She would touch them and smell them and look at them until they hummed a song she could sing.

And she would put herself into that song with Sullivan until she forgot the memories of her mother and remembered how to be happy.

Alice and Aunt Charlotte were the first to arrive at the garden wedding venue. Together, they spent several hours stringing garden-variety roses from the altar, from the guests' chairs, and every nook and cranny in between. The fragrance was what she imagined the English countryside to be. And yes, her own monthly budget took a little hit from going above and beyond like this with no extra cost to Harper, but Alice wanted this wedding to be everything Harper dreamed it would be.

When Harper arrived, her smile was the grin of sunbeams. She wore more makeup than usual, bringing out the striking color of her eyes, and her hair was up in pin curls. She tightened the silk robe she wore over black leggings, looking around the garden, slowly taking it all in.

"Alice . . ." She turned to her friend, wide-eyed. "This is too much. This is . . . perfect."

"You like it?" Alice smiled.

"It's a dream," Harper whispered, closing her eyes and breathing it in. "Everything about this day is a dream."

Slowly, Peter's grandmother, Millie, stepped out from the car, looking around the flowery venue herself.

"My, my," Millie said. "Now this is really something."

Alice would take the compliment as high praise, coming from the ever-feisty Millie. Harper stepped back to the car and carefully pulled out a dress that was protected by a garment bag. "Now come on, y'all. Let's get inside and finish my hair. I'm ready to wear this wedding gown." And she and Millie shared a smile then that was sweeter than ice cream.

Good thing the four of them made it inside the little guest-house when they did, because soon afterward another car drove up—turned out, it was Sullivan driving the groom. And everybody knew it was bad luck for the groom to see the bride before the wedding.

Alice's heart went topsy-turvy as she watched Sullivan from the corner of the window. She'd expected he would clean up nicely. He didn't disappoint. She was careful to hide behind the window curtain so he wouldn't catch her staring.

"Peter's here," she said to Harper, stepping closer to help tuck curls and bobby pins into the bride's beautiful vintage-style updo.

"Does he look like he has my dancing shoes?" Harper asked. "I forgot them, and he offered to pick them up for me."

Alice walked back over to the window, confirming Peter was, indeed, carrying a shoebox, and she used the opportunity as an excuse to watch Sullivan for a few more moments. She glanced up at the clock in the charming little room where they were getting ready. In a few minutes, she and Sullivan would need to do a sound check together, which made her stomach somersault for a whole different reason.

Singing on stage . . . in front of everyone . . . well, she wasn't so sure how this would go. To her surprise, a text message from Sullivan interrupted her train of thought.

Ready for practice?

She was quick to respond. *You're four minutes early.*

I told you . . . I'm turning over a new leaf, he typed. *I've been informed tardiness is unbecoming.*

Alice grinned, moving a long curl of her auburn hair behind her ear. *I'm glad you heeded the lesson. You know what they say—better late than never.*

Two hours later, Alice stood at the front of the garden venue beside Sullivan and took a deep breath as his fingers lingered over the first few notes of the keys. Harper and Peter stood at the end of the aisle, both of them beaming, the air perfumed by all the freshly cut flowers.

It was the fragrance of new beginnings.

Alice anchored herself with that breath—filled her lungs with it before she began to sing. She told herself that maybe if she could just breathe deeply enough, the breath would sustain her through all the measures and all the feelings that were coming.

So she sang. She sang as a girl sings with her arms wide open, running through a field of flowers. Freely. Boldly.

And surprisingly, for a few moments, she fell in love with music again, and fond memories of her mother returned. Love made her forget all the pain and grief in between. She met eyes with Sullivan—who, as it turned out, was a very good pianist—and his grin warmed her innermost being. And they fell into the ups and downs of the measures, the ups and downs of the music, perfectly in sync.

She was supposed to have her guard up around him. His life was in Charleston, and when the work was done, he was going to leave.

But she also forgot these things.

For a few moments, at least.

SIXTEEN

New Orleans, August 29, 2005
Early morning during Hurricane Katrina

Alice

Alice stretched her arms from under her little cocoon of blankets, then yawned and blinked. A glance at her clock said it should barely be light outside, but the windows were dark as midnight as the wind whistled sharply, and then she heard a boom.

Must have been a tree.

She had almost forgotten about the hurricane.

Alice rubbed both eyes with the palms of her hands, remembering all of a sudden that she hadn't removed her clear mascara. Her mother said she wasn't old enough for *real* mascara, which was ridiculous because all her friends wore it, and it wasn't like she was trying to be Lindsay Lohan in *Mean Girls* or something. Not that she had even seen *Mean Girls* because it was rated PG-13, but you know, from previews, she knew some things.

"Mom?" Alice called. She slid her arms into the fuzzy purple robe they'd gotten from Justice. She'd tried to talk her mom into the one at Abercrombie, but Mom said everything in that store reeked of cheap cologne, and even though Alice—okay, she could admit it—had pouted about it at the time, now she was actually pretty thankful because she liked her purple one better.

No one responded.

The wind was probably too loud to hear over.

Her father was supposed to be back before the storm, but he had texted Alice to let her know he loved her and he couldn't get to New Orleans safely before the storm. A bad accident happened on one of the bridges he used to get home, and he got stuck in traffic on his alternate route. He worked offshore on an oil rig. Her mother had just left for more groceries when Alice got the text message, and then she fell asleep watching TV in her room.

Alice tightened the belt of her robe and walked into the kitchen.

Her mother had put two loaves of honey-wheat bread on the counter, as well as some juice boxes, water bottles, a family-size jar of peanut butter, chips, and Alice's favorite . . . Fudge Stripes cookies.

Two envelopes lay on the counter. One for Alice, and one addressed to her father.

Alice opened the one addressed to her. That was odd. It looked like her mother's handwriting.

> *Dear, sweet girl—*
> *I know you will not understand, but trust me when I say I love you beyond words. I am so proud of you.*
> *I am so sorry.*
> *I love you always.*
>
> *—Mom*

Alice stuck out her bottom lip. How strange.

"Mom?" She called out, holding the letter. She kept walking through the kitchen, toward her parents' room, then opened the door.

Only there was no one there.

"Mom!" She began to yell, running around the room so that her purple robe floated up like feathers behind her, so fast she could nearly fly through the air and maybe walls too.

But there was no trace of her.

Something was wrong.

Something was very wrong.

Where is my mom? She prayed. *Please let her be okay.* And then she prayed it two more times for good measure, as if that would help make it count.

With one finger, Alice inched the corner of the blinds open so she could see between the slats. A tree in their modest-sized front yard bent and wobbled in the wind. Would it break soon?

She needed to get help. And quickly.

She hurried to the house phone, but the landline was out and so was the electricity. So she did the brave thing. The only thing she could think.

She grabbed her raincoat, galoshes, and umbrella, and she raced out the door, heading for her Aunt Charlotte, who lived one block away.

The first thing Aunt Charlotte did when they got back to Alice's house was to open Alice's father's letter.

That worried Alice.

Because Aunt Charlotte was usually all about the shoulds and should-nots of etiquette, and opening other people's private notes was definitely a *should not*.

Aunt Charlotte must have thought she would find answers there.

And she must have found them. Because moments into

reading the letter, she slid with her back against the cabinets, all the way to the floor, and she started shaking.

The wind whipped hard now against the home, and Alice heard several trees snap all around them. "I knew we shouldn't have moved to this city," she murmured. "Your mother and your father and you, and me . . ."

Alice made eye contact with Aunt Charlotte, who simply shook her head. She held up the letter in her hand. "I don't know how to tell you this. She's gone, Alice."

Alice tightened the belt around her purple robe, yesterday's clear mascara stinging her eyes. "What do you mean . . . gone?"

Aunt Charlotte swallowed, then bit her lip. "I think the best way of saying it is that she . . . well . . . she's sick, Alice, in her heart and in her mind, and it's making her confused. She thought your dad was coming home last night, apparently. That you wouldn't be alone."

"But I don't understand. She left all this bread." Alice pointed to the counter.

Why would she buy all that bread if she didn't care about Alice anymore?

She loved Alice.

Sure, her mom had been sad ever since she was pregnant and lost the baby. That was no secret, though she tried to hide it—crying under the covers in her room every day.

But she *loved* Alice, and Alice loved her.

Why would she do this?

Please let her be okay, Alice prayed, because it was all she felt like she could manage. *Please let her be okay. Please let her be okay.*

Eventually, Hurricane Katrina did pass, and the weeks and months passed too.

Alice never saw her mother again.

And on one particular afternoon, her aunt Charlotte—who she now lived with since her father had to work weeks at a time on the rigs—bought the same type of bread Alice's mom used to. And Alice looked at it inside of Aunt Charlotte's house, and she picked it up, and threw it as hard as she could against the kitchen wall.

God had not heard her prayers.

He had left her, if He even existed. He hadn't cared.

And the truth was, she had spent the last months in denial—believing that maybe God *did* still see her and maybe He *did* hear or care.

But this was what it'd come to—despair.

One time when she was really little, Alice had a goldfish that was sick, only she prayed and prayed and prayed over it. The next day, it started eating again, and her daddy said, *"Would you look at that? Your prayers must've cured her."* And Alice believed him for all that time after.

But what she couldn't figure out—what she *really* couldn't figure out, was why God would save her goldfish and not her mother.

∽

December, 2005

Alice

Four months had passed with no sign of her mother. Only fliers with her mother's face on them, posted everywhere her aunt could think. But there were hundreds, maybe thousands, of other missing people from Katrina. Who would pay any attention to her own missing person?

Yesterday, one of Aunt Charlotte's friends stopped by to catch up, and they didn't know Alice was listening. But when Aunt Charlotte asked her friend how they fared during the hurricane, that woman said the strangest thing: "Oh, we came out just fine. I just kept praying, speaking protection over our property and trusting God to take care of us. Take care of us He did. Not a lick of damage, save a small tree limb that we couldn't have put in a more convenient location if we tried." And Aunt Charlotte nodded and smiled and sipped her tea and said, "Good. That's good," or something along those lines.

But the woman's words struck terror within Alice for a reason she hadn't considered before. What if the reason God hadn't kept her mother safe was because she hadn't prayed correctly? What if this woman was right—that God always answered prayers for blessing and safety—and He hadn't answered hers because she didn't mean or believe what she was asking enough for it to matter?

And so on one not-so-particularly-significant evening, Alice slipped on her purple fuzzy robe and brushed her teeth and settled into bed where she should be warm and cozy only she wasn't, and it was then she knew.

She knew the feeling—or the lack of feeling—that made her mother leave.

She couldn't have understood it before. But now she had felt it, and that was a new thing for her.

She knew the emptiness that came from disappearing . . . like the old version of you that everyone had known before wasn't *you* anymore, and you wondered who your real self was in the first place.

As a little girl, she and her mother went to Sunday school, and she learned about Jesus and asked Him into her heart and was baptized and all those things.

She had meant it at the time; she mostly meant it still, but she knew what the verse meant now when it said "help my unbelief"—because the very real absence of her mother had instilled a very real fear: what if this life was all there was? What if, at the end of this life, was nothing?

And the utter hopelessness of that thought, that grief, hollowed her out completely. At least it felt like completely.

But it couldn't have been completely. Because when she closed her eyes, she did eventually sleep. And she dreamed of her mother—a beautiful dream.

She woke up again the next morning and wondered if, on some spiritual level, she was alone in the world, and she still felt afraid.

But she also saw a rainbow while the flowers were still wet with dew. For a moment—for the briefest moment—the fear went away, and the nothingness was filled with peace. The presence of something—of beauty, maybe—calmed her, for a little while.

Then the rainbow faded, and she was once again a girl who needed her mother.

SEVENTEEN

Charleston, November 1861

The crows cawed outside Teddy's window as he adjusted his ascot and looked at Oliver. Though the day was new, the storm clouds just on the other side of the glass gave the library a pallor. He wished the grey would hurry up and move on so the sun could shine freely once more.

Fiddlesticks. The ascot was crooked. Teddy untied the knot so he could try again.

"The intel I received from Clara this morning proved quite useful," he said. "Probably the most useful information she's acquired yet."

"Oh?" Oliver held to his fat cigar and took a puff. "In what way?"

"Last night, Joseph and Clara's father hosted a dinner party—I suspect as a glamorous means of rallying support for their cause, as well as to garner their own information. Ever the level head, Clara managed to get the names of several of Joseph's associates with whom we had been intermingling, thinking they were ambivalent about the war."

Oliver paused. "But they are not?"

"Indeed." Teddy looked out the window once more, as the gathering clouds billowed over the cotton. He turned to Oliver. "She also retrieved some very troubling information regarding plans to attack the islands."

Oliver nodded slowly. "It makes sense, of course. They dislike the growing number of refugee camps and likely fear an insurrection by these people who were formerly enslaved. With Charleston a mere twenty-five miles from us here in Edisto, the island also serves as a helpful plotting point for attacks against forces in the city."

"Forces on both sides, it would seem," Teddy murmured.

Oliver sighed, setting his cigar down on his tray. "So, what are we going to do about it?"

Teddy looked in the mirror and tried his hand at tying his ascot once more. He wanted it right this time. "I think the best thing to do is to see if Clara can get anything more specific regarding dates or times, and create our own countermeasures so we have a plan ready if we do need to mobilize it."

"I agree. Also as an update, several of the men were able to gain information about the daily routines of those enslaved at the Calhoun plantation. I think we may be able to develop our plan to help Ashley as soon as next week." Oliver straightened a leatherbound journal on his desk.

"That's wonderful news."

"Agreed." Oliver nodded once. "On the topic of Clara, how did she seem?"

Enchanting was the word Teddy wanted to use, but that hardly seemed appropriate. In conversing with Clara he had come to realize there was something special about her, something that had captured him wholly. Any time he thought of her, and especially when he saw her, he was useless in accomplishing all the other tasks that lay ahead of him. All he could think about was Clara. She was his sunshine, his glee, in an ever-stormy war world.

"She seemed well." Teddy tried to sound casual. He didn't want to let on how frequently she occupied his thoughts.

Oliver raised one bushy eyebrow.

"Why do you watch me as though a detective?"

Slowly, Oliver grinned, resting his elbows on the desk. "You've formed a romantic attachment with Clara."

"I never said such a thing," Teddy sputtered.

"You didn't have to." A humored expression lit his eyes. "Tell me I'm wrong."

Teddy hesitated. He didn't want to admit love had made him a fool, but he also could not bring himself to tell a lie.

"Your delay speaks volumes." Oliver took another puff from his cigar. "Truly, I think a match between the two of you would prove wonderful. I think highly of you both, and Mary does as well. Tell me—have you made your affections known?"

"Only recently." Teddy looked down at his hands, rubbing his palm with his thumb. "I gave her a note just this morning."

"Ah, always the charmer, aren't you?" Oliver teased. His tone turned serious. "Though I do hope she knows she must destroy the physical paper it was on, keeping the sentiment squarely in her heart."

Teddy frowned. "We need not worry. We were very clear with Clara early on that all correspondence needs be destroyed."

"Yes, but she may not classify a romantic gesture as *correspondence*. Women are very different creatures, my fine man. You will learn this soon enough. They like to keep little mementos and go back and smile upon them."

"What do you suggest we do, then?" Teddy straightened his jacket by the lapels.

Oliver drummed his fingers on his desk as though playing a pianoforte. "Ah, nothing now. I don't see it as an immediate threat—certainly not worth risking recognition by flagging her outside her home. We'll broach the topic the next time she's visiting."

"Very well." Teddy nodded, but a little part of him feared what he might've gotten them into. Perhaps he shouldn't have left that note after all.

∽

Clara

"Well, this beats all." Clara paced back and forth in the library, as though marching this way may relieve her fury. "The nerve of them both!" She whispered it vehemently to herself. Two days had passed since she'd seen Teddy, and she'd been blissfully walking on air until moments ago, when she had that conversation over breakfast with her father.

Carrying a tea service tray, Rose stepped into the open doorway. "Missus?" she asked, likely wondering what on earth Clara was up to. "Would you like a cup of tea?"

"That would be quite pleasant, Rose. Thank you."

Steam clouded above the cup as Rose poured Clara's tea. Despite Joseph and Father's outlandish dinner party display, on normal days the household was conserving sugar. But this was a double portion sort of morning.

"I'll have a full scoop of sugar, please."

Rose's posture stiffened. "Of course." She dunked in the sugar and stirred until it melted completely, handing the cup to Clara.

Clara sipped it. The warm liquid provided a swirl of comfort almost immediately. "Perhaps this will also soothe my nerves," she muttered. Holding the delicate cup by the handle, she met Rose's eyes. She was certain her mother and father were still in the other room, and dared speak freely for a fleeting moment. "Father has promised my silver to Joseph," she spat at whispered volume, looking beyond Rose to be sure no one passed behind her in the hallway. "As though dowries were still fashionable and he needed to pay someone in exchange for marrying me." She took another sip of her tea, careful not to scald her tongue. "This beats all. This simply beats all . . ."

"Your silver, Missus?" Rose asked, frowning. "Forgive me, but I do not know what silver you mean."

"Of course you wouldn't. I'm making no sense." Clara shook her head. "Let me start from the beginning. When I was a young girl, I watched my mother use the family silver set on special occasions. The silver is very valuable, not only monetarily but also in sentiment—it's Paul Revere silver. She would let me 'help' her set out the pieces before holiday meals, though I suspect my helping doubled her own work later. Anyhow, I always admired this one particular spoon. My mother told me that the spoon would be mine someday when I ran my own household. It's silly, I know—but I have looked at that spoon each holiday and felt hopeful for the days ahead—days I might finally have my own home, my own choices."

"Missus, there ain't nothing silly about that. Just plain ole' human nature." Rose poured a little more steaming liquid into Clara's teacup.

"Thank you, Rose, though I recognize in the big scheme of the war, my own silver is meaningless. I suppose it's the notion of the thing that upsets me so. How could Father promise it to Joseph when it was already promised to me? Now, as we near the wedding in coming months, Joseph will take that spoon back to his estate, and when I break our engagement, I will never see it again."

Rose set the teakettle back down on the serving tray.

"I realize my father believes the silver spoon is going to

the same house where I will be living regardless, but the principle of it remains. Our family's heirloom silver, in the hands of that awful man. I can't believe Father is treating this marriage as though I'm incapable. To think that the two of them negotiated this exchange of treasure for my hand in marriage . . . though for all I know, Joseph might have requested a dowry! It wouldn't surprise me. Nothing at this point would surprise me." She met Rose's gaze. "How could I have been so blind to their inadequacies?"

Rose stepped closer. "This ain't about the silver, is it?"

Slowly, Clara shook her head, swallowing the knot that'd formed at the back of her throat. The steam from the hot tea met her fiery anger, melted it into a trickle of unexpected tears. She felt burdened for Rose and Rose's daughter, grieved she may never make amends with her own family, and exhausted for the charade of feigning interest in a man as horrible as Joseph. She felt shame for the length of time it'd taken before she recognized Father's true colors, and even some fear that if she ran, Joseph might come after her. That Father would come after Rose. And that blessed Teddy might endanger himself in the process.

She missed the simplicity of the world she used to know, even while she grieved from the realization she never really knew it. At a moment's notice, if anything went wrong, she would have to run. She would have no sense of home. But on second thought, had she ever really?

"No, Rose . . . I suppose it isn't."

But even these ruminations were insignificant when she considered all Rose had gone through, and how light the burden Clara's own worries and woes were by comparison. For Clara could not comprehend the horror of a human believing they owned another. She was frustrated by Joseph and her father's disrespectful behavior toward her—which was a drop in the bucket compared to someone treating a person like actual property. The longer she thought of it over these past weeks and months, the more sickened she became.

To think that anyone could look past the glaring injustice of separating a mother from her daughter. To think that anyone could turn a blind eye or have a cold heart toward such trauma. To think her own father had become so hardened . . . that maybe he'd *been* so hardened all along.

And to think it'd taken Clara this long to see.

Yes, she grieved.

She grieved for Rose's trauma, she grieved for Rose's daughter, and that silver made her grieve for her own future that would not be. For in choosing what was right and just— even in choosing love with Teddy—she also had chosen to leave behind every nook and cranny of her childhood. The rooms. The smell of her mother's perfume and her father's library. The sidewalks and gardens surrounding her home. She would likely never reconcile with her family, who would view her as a traitor.

She would have to start anew.

Clara didn't realize her hands were shaking until the teacup fell from her grasp, shattering and splattering hot liquid all over the room, ruining the rug and her mother's curtains. One shard of porcelain scraped her arm as it ricocheted off the floor.

Confounded thing.

She would have to paint another this afternoon.

She hurried over to the desk drawer where she'd stashed two extra kerchiefs as Rose rushed to clean up the spill.

When she used them to lap up the tea alongside Rose, she could have sworn something fell from her pocket as she bent down—but she could not see anything on the floor and was busy cleaning up her mess, anyway.

Too busy, it would seem.

EIGHTEEN

New Orleans, Modern Day

Alice

Alice awoke to the sound of three knocks at her bedroom door as fresh sunlight flitted through her window. "Just a minute," she called, sitting straight up and yawning.

Expecting to see Aunt Charlotte, she belted her robe over flannel pants and her llama shirt. It was a charming combination. But when she opened the bedroom door, she had quite a surprise.

Sullivan, dressed in the nicest-fitting T-shirt and jeans she'd ever seen, stood in front of her. Behind tortoiseshell glasses, he blinked as he took in the sight of her. His bookish appeal mixed with his raw attraction stirred her feelings for him in the most unwelcome way. She'd always had a weak spot for men who read books, or at least who looked the part.

Alice glanced up at him. He was tall. Taller than yesterday. And he held a cup that smelled like it was an expensive coffee.

To his credit, he didn't chuckle. Though he did seem like he was struggling to keep the shock from his face. "I thought I'd get here before The Prickly Rose opened. I wanted to talk with you about some branding ideas."

He held the coffee out to her.

"We open late on Mondays." She took the cup from his hand.

He nodded. "Well, then . . ." He awkwardly shoved his free hand into his pocket.

Might as well address what they were both thinking. "You act as if you've never seen someone wear a llama shirt before." When she offered the smallest smile, he burst into laughter.

She laughed along too. "At least I don't show up at people's houses at the crack of dawn."

"Your aunt let me in." He raked his right hand through his hair.

I'll bet she did.

"Besides, it's six-thirty, not dawn."

"On a *Monday*." She took a sip of her coffee, then looked down into the cup. "This might be the best coffee I've ever had."

Satisfied, he gave her a half grin.

"Don't get too cocky. I still haven't made up my mind about you."

He took half a step closer. "I like a challenge."

"I'll bet you do." Her heart stirred.

He stood still, hesitating at the doorway. "Are you going to wear the llama shirt outside the house?"

"Now that you've asked about it, maybe." She grinned.

"Fine by me." He shrugged.

She reached for the door handle of the bedroom. "I'm just a little worried I may get chilly . . . you know, with the breeze this early in the morning. I think I'll change into some jeans and a sweater."

"Mmhmm." He wasn't buying it for a moment—she could tell.

Alice shut the door, then leaned against the back of it.

What was happening? And why did she have to be wearing such ridiculous pajamas?

She took another sip of her coffee. "I'll be just a second," she called to Sullivan from the other side of the door.

"No problem."

She hurried over to her armoire and dabbed a little cream blush on her cheeks, then swiped mascara twice over her lashes. She didn't want to look like she was trying too hard to compensate for the llama incident, but at the same time, her aunt would say she was peaked.

Let this serve as a reminder you need more Vitamin D.

Alice tugged on a pair of skinny jeans, then scanned all the sweaters lining her closet. Ironically, none of them screamed the I-woke-up-like-this vibe she needed. So instead, she turned to the pile of just-washed sweatshirts in a heap beside her bed, and pulled on the softest one in light pink.

She glanced in the mirror.

Ugh. Too boxy.

Alice wiggled out of the sweatshirt and tossed it back on the pile. What about that oversized crochet sweater she usually wore with leggings? She shuffled through the hangers once again until she found it.

Bingo.

Pulling her arms through the sweater, Alice slid her feet into her black ankle booties—the ones that made her look a good three inches taller, because had Sullivan been that tall before?—then twisted her hair into a knot.

With one hand, she opened the bedroom door, and with the other, she grabbed her coffee. Sullivan stood across the hall, arms crossed and smiling.

"You were quicker than I expected." He removed his glasses and wiped them with the hem of his T-shirt.

She led the way to the back door. "What can I say? I'm low maintenance."

"Apparently." He held open the screen door for her, and Alice took the steps down to the lower-level courtyard.

The screen flapped shut behind them, and Sullivan took the steps two at a time as he caught up to her by the courtyard fountain. "You're still wearing the llama shirt under that sweater, aren't you?"

Alice didn't meet his gaze, but she couldn't hold back her grin.

∞

Sullivan

Sullivan ducked under long tufts of Spanish moss that hung from the oak trees like a slow-growing beard. Early morning sunlight brought a particular glow to the haze of the sidewalk, and the birds chirping and dogs barking almost sounded like they were back on Edisto Island where he'd grown up.

Sullivan blinked, his eyes adjusting to the brightness of the sun over the street. He wasn't used to the glare on his glasses, but he'd lost a contact lens this morning.

He cleared his throat and looked over at Alice. Her fiery hair sparked in the sunlight, and though she'd just awakened, she seemed to glow right along with the morning.

How was he going to start the conversation he needed to have with her? He needed to tell her what happened at the wedding reception after their song together, but . . . well, he wasn't sure how to broach the subject, exactly.

He took a deep breath and opened the door to the donut shop. Everyone liked donuts, right? Especially if those donuts regularly made it into the New Orleans media buzz. Exposed bricks lined the wall as Sullivan and Alice stepped forward to the display of oversized specialty donuts.

She ordered a regular glazed—he took note of her conservative choice—and he chose a Nutella flavor. Hey, when in Rome, right?

Alice picked a booth along the wall while he waited for his coffee by the industrial-style lights over the bar. The barista didn't take long making his drink, and when Sullivan joined Alice at the table, he found her sipping her coffee in the most delicate way. Her manners would impress a queen.

Alice reached for her donut and took a nibble. Did she always eat like a mouse? At this rate, it'd take her hours to finish that huge pastry.

"Hey, you did a really nice job singing at the wedding." Sullivan twirled the cup of iced coffee in his hands, the ice clinking.

"Thanks. So did you." Her grin could've lit the morning. Alice's bun loosened, and she let it out, fingering her long curls.

Sullivan watched her. His gaze moved from her uncontrolled curls to her shoulders and then down her arms. She was stunning. Like a redheaded Snow White. He wouldn't be surprised if she sang and squirrels came running.

And for some reason Sullivan couldn't explain, he hoped she would trust him. Alice held secrets—he could see that in her eyes. But secrets didn't scare him.

That said, he needed to focus, not stare at her curls. He wasn't sure how to approach the subject, but he *had* to approach the subject, one way or another. He'd told her he had a business idea, and that was true, but first they needed to discuss a personal matter.

Alice took another sip of her coffee, looking back at him. "What's the deal? Why are you acting strange all of a sudden?"

Sullivan ran his hand along his chin. "Okay, so the thing is . . . at the wedding reception last night, after our song, a woman came up to me. She was looking for you but couldn't find you, and she wanted me to pass along how much she enjoyed your singing."

"How nice of her." Alice took another nibble of her donut.

Sullivan blew out a sigh. "The thing is, Alice . . ." He moved his hands as he spoke, holding his palms upward. "She told me she recognized you from a band that plays at Preservation Hall."

Alice frowned. "I don't understand."

"At first, I didn't either . . . I corrected her." Sullivan crossed his arms over his chest, leaning forward. "But she insisted. She said no, you have a particular tone in your voice that she would recognize anywhere, and that she goes to Preservation Hall a few times a year in hopes of seeing you perform."

Alice gasped as understanding dawned on her. "You don't think—"

"That she was talking about your mother?" Sullivan leaned back against the booth. "Actually, that's exactly what I think. Preservation Hall is an acclaimed jazz venue, right? Did you ever look for your mother there?"

Alice set her donut back down on her plate, and he wondered if she'd lost her appetite after hearing this update. "I did . . ." she started. "But only a handful of times, and Preservation Hall has a house band and hosts other bands too. If I didn't have the right night of the week, it makes sense I could've missed her. Plus, it's been so long since she went missing . . . even if she *is* singing there, which is still a big *if*, she could've joined them at any point recently and started performing again. It would've been next to impossible for me to have tracked her down."

With an elbow on the table, Sullivan rested his chin on his fisted hand. "So what are you going to do now? I hope I didn't make you uncomfortable telling you all this. . . . I just felt like you had a right to know."

"Yeah, no, I absolutely appreciate that." Alice shook her head, looking down and fiddling with the napkin in her lap. "Honestly, I feel like I have to go . . . I mean, don't misunderstand—I'm terrified of what information I may find. But I know if I don't pursue this, I will regret it."

"Can I help?" He cleared his throat. He may've been too swift in offering his help to the beautiful florist, and he didn't want to seem desperate. . . . But he genuinely wanted to do whatever he could so she wasn't at this alone.

"That's very nice of you to offer." She shook the ice in her cup and stuck her straw further inside to get the last little bit of coffee. "And really, I would be happy to have your company. I mean"—she seemed flustered, quick to change her wording—"to *have* company period, you know, and not be sorting through all of it by myself."

A slow smile pulled the corners of Sullivan's lips into a grin. Because he was pretty good at reading women, and he was pretty sure the florist liked him.

"Oh, one more thing." Alice snapped her fingers. "The embroidered samplers . . . I looked at them a day or two before the wedding, and I recognized the name Calhoun. I wouldn't have seen it had I not been looking for hidden meanings, but there it was, clear as day. So I put the name into a search engine last night to see if I could find any records. Sometimes plantation owners would notate what kind of work enslaved people did."

Sullivan stilled, wiping the ring of condensation from his coffee cup with a napkin and setting the cup down on the table. "And?" He wondered if she could have found anything, given how few historical records existed about people of color. Even the graves of those bound by slavery were often left unmarked.

"I found Ashley's name there." Alice hesitated. "I read more about the Great Fire and looked at the flowers in the embroidery, and . . . Sullivan?" Alice leaned forward. "I think there must be a codebook somewhere. I mentioned it to Juliet, and she told me there was some sort of diary or ledger among the needlepoints my mother brought over all those years ago, but at the time, it looked unsensible to her."

Alice watched his reaction. Sullivan wondered if she could read his attraction to her through his surprise over this new development with the heirlooms.

"A codebook would corroborate the work you've already done to translate the meanings of the flowers and explain to us if any other flowers—like the rose that was Rose's signature—represent arbitrary people, rather than their traditional meanings. . . ."

"Exactly," Alice said. "With the flower shop and all, I feel like I'm uniquely equipped to put two and two together when it comes to those deeper meanings, but some of the messages still don't make sense, and I think this is what I've been missing."

"Just imagine all we could learn if we could crack those codes," he said.

Alice grinned, and he grinned back at her.

NINETEEN

A couple days gone by since Missus and I had that conversation about her family and she shattered her teacup. I been worryin' she may spook any minute and want to get out of this place, away from these people, before the plan's ready.

Can't say I'd blame her.

I got Ashley's butterfly buttons in my pocket for safekeeping. I guard them with my own tight fist throughout the day—always checkin' they still there and always remindin' myself I'm one day closer to seein' my baby.

Sometimes I still can't believe they took her so fast I couldn't get the buttons back in the satchel before she was gone. I should've sealed the satchel up tighter so they didn't fall out in the first place.

But maybe it's better this way—me havin' the buttons. Maybe it gives me something to hold onto, and that reminds me to hold on to hope as well. Hope I will hold my daughter once more, yes—but also hope she will live a better life than I've lived. Hope this war, despite all its fires, will set her free.

I hope for a better life for my family, in a better world, in better decades, then better centuries.

I hope these butterfly buttons fasten fabrics once torn and frayed. I hope they tell a story.

Maybe then something good can come from all the heartache.

Maybe then all the caterpillars will grow wings.

I'm passing the library on my way to the kitchen out back when I see Joseph inside, and I watch as something on the rug catches his eye. The whole scene begins to move real slow, like the man is stuck in the mud and exaggeratin' his movements.

I take half a step back so I can watch him without him catching me spyin'. And that's when it dawns on me what he just saw.

The little note Teddy passed to Clara.

Must've fallen from the girl's pocket.

My throat burns—it goes so dry—and I want to run to tell Clara but my feet can't seem to move from the ground where they're planted. So I keep watchin' as Joseph reads the note, and even from a distance I can see his shoulders straighten up real fast.

He pounds his fists on the table, hard. So hard I jump and fear floods my body. In a blink, I'm at the plantation all over again, hiding from that awful man. I swallow, but even swallowing is hard as I force his disgusting face from my mind.

He dead now. I won't never see him again.

But he haunts me still, in memory, and I don't know how I'll ever get over it. You can't outrun ghosts—my mama used to say that. I think she believed in real ghosts and course I don't believe in *those* but there is some truth in the sayin', isn't there?

"What is this . . ." Joseph mumbles, and I manage to move enough I can stick my back to the wall. I'll still hear him from here, though—just fine.

"Unbelievable!" Joseph's voice grows more aggressive. He begins to move frantically through the room, talking to himself as though searching for something. Finally, hidden in between the records Clara's father keeps on the shelves, he pulls out a notebook.

A notebook he furiously scripts something upon. "There." He puffs air in a proud sigh. "Now it's ready to take tonight to General Lee . . ."

I hear shuffling and know I have to move from the doorway, even though my heart is thumping so fast I can't make right from left.

I manage to take two steps backward and slip behind the doorframe of the neighboring room, just barely out of sight before I hear his footsteps rough against the floor in the hall.

With a courage only a mama could know, I go back into that library with no hesitation. I know he got some kind of information in that notebook, and it right well may have to do with my daughter . . . or Teddy and Oliver's cause in tryin' to free her.

I fumble through the shelves until I come upon the notebook where Joseph wrote something, flipping the pages real gently in my hands, knowing each one may as well be gold.

Now, I don't know how to read *real* well, but Clara has taught me a thing or two, and I know Teddy's name when I see it—I do. And I recognize other names in there too, like Oliver's.

And it's then that it dawns on me: Joseph is a spy too. Why else would he be keepin' a list of names real secret in a book hidden away, like for his and Missus' father's eyes only? Why else would he be mumblin' on to himself about meeting with General Lee? He tryin' to get information the Confederates can use against the Union army—that's what he's doin'.

And all the blood seems to drain from my body as the realization of a new level of danger hits me.

Somehow through the fog in my mind, I end up in Missus's room.

She looks up at me and honest to goodness the innocence in her eyes puts me in mind of a puppy. This is gonna be hard, but we got no choice. We goin' be brave for everybody.

We have to be. See, sometimes you don't know how brave you are until brave's the only thing you got left.

"Missus." My tone is sharp. "We got to go. Now."

Her eyes widen.

"Joseph found your note. From Teddy."

"No!" Clara covers her mouth with her gloved hand.

"That's not the worst of it." I take a sharp breath, trying real hard not to panic. "He got some kind of notebook down there, and he wrote Teddy's name in it. I looked once he left the room." I run both my hands over my hair—pulled tightly up so it stays out of my way. "I also heard him talkin' to himself about taking the ledger to General Lee. Clara . . ." My eyes meet hers. "I think he's more dangerous than we realized. I think he may be gathering information on the Union, like we gathering information on him. We got until tonight to leave . . ."

Gaining her composure, Clara lifts her dainty chin. "We aren't going anywhere. Not yet, at least."

"But we got to go now . . ."

Clara's eyes search mine, real desperate, like she's trying to plead with me but I don't know what about. "We aren't going to run because instead we're going to follow him. We'll let him leave that notebook, then pick it up before anyone else sees."

Oh mercy.

I hesitate, mulling over all she just said.

"Consider this . . ." She reaches out and touches my sleeve. "What happens if we do flee, and something goes wrong? There is no backup plan. No way to warn Teddy and Oliver, and likely no way to get Ashley." She lets go of the fabric of my dress and brushes my hand with hers gently. "I wish it were not so . . . believe me . . . but the only way to handle this is to retrieve the notebook. Joseph will likely still give General Lee the information about Teddy eventually, but at least then we'll have a day or two—maybe more—to make our getaway and get Ashley. " Clara plants her hands on both sides of her waist. "Once we get the notebook, we can see what other names are implicated, and Teddy and Oliver will make a plan to secure those individuals' safety too."

She's right, of course. I know she is.

I close my eyes and squint, as though light may spontaneously pierce the darkness behind. But no answers come. Maybe because the answer already has.

"One more thing . . ." Clara says, bringing my mind out of the haze.

"Yes, Missus?"

"There's something I want to do, and I need your help. But we have to act fast."

"I don't understand. You already packed your bag in case something like this caught us unexpectedly. . . ."

"It's not my bag," she says, and something about the way she says it—well, I know. She talkin' about that silver . . . first promised to her, then promised to Joseph. The heirloom, the inheritance.

And both me and Clara are terrified, but maybe despite being scared, together the two of us can do something to change the world for our daughters, and for our daughters' daughters after.

"Rose?"

"Clara?"

"You're a hero, you know that?" She says it with a little smirk, and I can't help but think how young she looks when she does it, and how much older she's soon gonna be.

"Nah, I'm just a mama." I sigh, as a whole heap of nerves washes over me. "But bein' a mama is plenty enough for me."

Clara

With dirt still smudged under her fingernails, Clara pulled her cloak a little closer to protect herself from the evening's chill.

When she woke up this morning, Clara wasn't expecting that the sight of her bedroom window would turn her heart so deeply nostalgic. But it wasn't the window exactly, just the way the sunlight streamed through it, lighting the room with a growing flood of warmth.

And she knew then, as she maybe hadn't known before, that there was something about this space she would long for. Maybe the longing was only for an ideal that never actually *existed* but even still—still, the longing part was real.

Maybe this is how it felt to grow up. Maybe she had to recognize all the windows and leave them be before she could open them.

Perhaps her spirit knew she would need this moment of recollection to look back on—in the weeks and the months and the years that would follow. Because though she couldn't be certain, she thought one of these mornings would be the last time waking up to that particular pattern of light and shadows.

Now, this evening, a cold front was coming through. High winds were sweeping Charleston like an angry housemaid.

All along, the plan had been for Rose and Clara to commission Mary's friend Harriet if ever in trouble. She lived around the corner from Clara's family and had a carriage ready if needed.

Tonight, it was needed.

The two women snuck their luggage into Harriet's carriage for her to watch over. After taking the notebook, the three of them would easily slip away . . . or at least, that was the plan.

So as Joseph approached the Mills House Hotel on foot, Clara and Rose left Harriet and followed stealthily behind him, careful to hide within the shadows, lest he catch sight of them. And as Clara held tightly to her lantern, a deep shiver seized her—body and heart—for what must happen next.

If she and Rose were caught retrieving the notebook Joseph had left for General Lee . . . but no, Clara could not think about it now. Ruminating over the possibilities would do no good when there was only one path to forge, and that path was forward.

Joseph crossed the road ahead, and Clara pulled her cloak a little higher to discreetly cover her features in case he recognized her. He knelt on the ground, looking all about him, and Rose shoved Clara against the wall of a historic building they passed so neither of them would be spotted.

Then Joseph tucked the notebook behind a rosebush. Satisfied no one had seen him, he hurried off around the corner. And like that, he was gone.

Clara tugged on Rose's hand, and the two hurried over to the spot where Joseph had left the notebook. Realization dawned on Clara that this location was most likely a regular rendezvous point, and that perhaps more messages could be intercepted here. So she tugged an offshoot of the rosebush out of the ground and slipped it into her pocket. She would later show the rose to Teddy and Oliver so they might use it to verify the location.

She reached for the notebook.

Rose hissed. "Missus," she said. "I see a man up on the balcony watchin'. I think that's the general."

"We'll have to move quickly," Clara said.

But Clara's skirt caught among the thorns of the rose-bush, and as she tugged herself free, a man crossed the street on horseback. The clomp of the horse hooves sent puffs of dust into the air. When she took a deep breath, her nostrils burned. Rose turned to her.

The dust cleared and the man on the horse continued onward, and a figure appeared in front of them—a figure who had seen what Clara was about to reach for.

Joseph.

"I have to say, Clara, I am impressed by your little display." From the glow of the lantern, his grin was smug. "Though surely you realize this will present a few . . . complications . . . for you. And your slave too."

Panic shook Clara and wouldn't let go. A cold sweat dripped down her back, dampening her so she felt even colder. She reached out for Rose's hand, trying to think of something to say.

Despite her panic, she looked back at him boldly, daring him to make another move. She hoped he sensed a confidence and capability about her that she very much doubted within her own self.

Joseph did not seem dissuaded in the least. She doubted that he ever hesitated, even in the face of war. "Come on, Clara," he said, finally. "Let's go back to your father's house and sort through whatever wild ideas your pretty little head has about abolition and men's work on the war front. I've no doubt your father will have a thing or two to say on this matter—as well as the many lines you've crossed in your uncouth attachment to the slaves."

He started toward her, as though he might reach out and take her, but before he could, Rose grabbed Clara's lantern and threw it on the ground.

A perfect hit upon the rosebush, whose petals began to burn with the glory of secrets turned to ash.

Clara's mind raced to make sense of what was happening, for Rose was far quicker-moving than she. And she thought of Teddy's words on Edisto.

Fire is one of the most powerful weapons of war.

The fire licked at the notebook, destroying the names within. Joseph first stood in a stupor, then pulled his arms from his jacket and made haste attempting to suffocate the flame. But Joseph was too late. The notebook had been destroyed.

Clara's heart leapt with a mixture of terror and hope and relief. She now had no record of the other names in that notebook and would not be able to help them, *but* she had bought enough time to help Teddy and Ashley.

At least, so she hoped.

Maybe Oliver and Teddy could come up with a way to find out the other names. . . .

Soldiers now hurried closer. They could tarry here no longer.

The wind blew the embers, and the fire began to spread. As heat pierced the cold darkness, passersby began to yell. "Fire!" someone screamed. "Run!"

Clara grabbed hold of Rose. They would run to Harriet together, and she would not let go of Rose's hand for a moment. It would not be easy, but they would find a way out of here. They'd been relentless, and they'd be relentless still. She'd do well to remember it.

Radiant heat hurt Clara's face with its warmth, and she blinked through the smoke curling upwards. She hadn't expected the fire to spread so quickly, though perhaps she should've, given the strong winter winds tonight.

But something happened.

As she and Rose began to turn the corner, Joseph yelled out to them through the flames. "Go ahead and run!" he shouted. "I bought that woman's daughter, Clara—as a surprise for you, and tell you what—I'm going to keep her!"

Clara and Rose stilled, both stunned in horror at his words.

Though their backs were turned to him, Joseph yelled one final thing. And she need not look at him to know the steely determination in his wicked eyes. "Come after the slave girl—ever—and I'll kill her. You hear me? I'll kill her."

Rose's eyes met her own, flashing emotion like Clara had never seen before—panic and fury and passion all rolled into one.

She screamed. She screamed with a fierce desperation that Clara had never known before. And she looked as though she might run after Joseph and strangle him with her own two hands. But the fire was quickly encircling them. There was no time left to go after him—they had to run to Harriet.

Had to get to Teddy and Oliver and make some kind of plan before Joseph came after them too. It was only a matter of time before he tried to compromise their operation in helping those enslaved escape to freedom.

Surviving was the only way to preserve this woman's heritage for her daughter.

So Clara yanked Rose hard, away from the flames, and tugged her onward . . . faster than she'd ever run before. The harsh winds carried the blaze swiftly from one building to the next. Many people ran madly about, screaming as clouds of fire hovered.

The city was burning.

As Clara held on to Rose and wove through the street toward the carriage, she reached into her pocket for the little rose.

And then she prayed for rain.

TWENTY

New Orleans, Modern Day

Alice

After her unexpected breakfast with Sullivan this morning, Alice clipped stems for a petite arrangement of carnations and crimson-tipped roses, with a few sprays of purple wildflowers thrown in for good measure. She breathed in deeply, and the fragrance brought back the magic of the first Valentine's flowers she received from a crush back in high school.

It was one of many things she loved about flowers—their ability to pull you out of the present and into the past, then back into the present once more, better for having remembered something lovely.

The bouquet had turned out perfectly.

Now, hours later and cradled on a wrought-iron bench beneath a canopy of ancient oak trees, Alice looked out over the water in New Orleans City Park and enjoyed the last light of the day. She always came here when she needed a sense of calm.

Usually, she found it.

Not today. Not after that conversation with Sullivan and the possibility that her mother was playing at Preservation

Hall. She'd spent the better part of the afternoon staying busy at The Prickly Rose, helping customers and putting together subscription orders. She had managed to avoid the depth of emotion about the sudden possibility she might actually see her mother once more.

But now that she was here, breathing in air that smelled like new leaves and promise, pulling her cardigan a little closer to protect from the chill, she couldn't avoid it any longer.

Alice buried her face in her hands, closed her eyes, and began to sob, as the tears she'd held inside so long came rushing forth. The flood of emotion was so strong, nothing could hold it back.

She kept hearing Sullivan's words in her mind again and again.

"She told me she recognized you from a band that plays at Preservation Hall."

So hard to believe that after all these years, Alice and her mother still could be mistaken for one another . . . and yet, at the same time, it wasn't hard to believe at all. In some ways, it felt as though Alice had simply blinked and been transported through time.

Alice began to rock back and forth on the bench, her face still in her hands. She shook her head. She'd accepted that her mother might not have survived, and she had made peace with that reality. Okay, maybe not *peace*, exactly, but she'd come to terms with it. They'd searched for her after the storm, but even the Coast Guard had limited rescue ability in certain areas.

Alice shuddered.

They'd never stopped looking. And in her heart of hearts, she had always wondered if her mother was still out there, thus the furtive prayers just in case.

Alice had never forgotten the letter her mom left her.

She wiped the still-falling tears from her eyes. A robin fluttered its wings, swooping down from a solid oak limb to the leafy ground. Its flight was free, its belly the color of autumn.

She had let people believe that the storm had taken her mother because, even if she was alive, in a way, a storm had. It just wasn't Hurricane Katrina.

As a child, Alice would often dance and sing with her mother in the kitchen, making muffulettas and waiting for her father to come home. One day, he had—with a bouquet full of carnations. Pink for Alice. Red for her mom.

Those memories were some of her sweetest.

She hadn't thought of them in so long.

Alice wiped her nose on the arm of her sweater, trying to collect herself. She leaned back against the park bench and watched ducks waddle toward the pond. Several brave souls guided kayaks through the murky water, and children chased one another across the bridge just beyond.

The world kept moving just as it always had. The tide pulled forward; the tide pulled back. But Alice sat still, stuck somewhere in between.

A strong wave tugged the flow of her thoughts—the same doubt she'd been having over and over. If her mother was still alive, why had she never come home? But the question filled Alice with such unease, she pushed it quickly from her mind and closed her eyes.

Please let her be okay. Please let her be okay. Please let her be okay.

The sound of her cell phone ringing jarred Alice from her prayer. She checked the number but didn't recognize it. "Hello?"

"Alice?" The male voice was deep and warm. "It's Sullivan."

"Oh, hi, Sullivan." Her heart jumped at the sound of his

voice. After their breakfast this morning, he'd promised to call later to make plans.

"Hey, uh . . . Declan is staying with a buddy while he's here and there's this cat—I don't even know whose cat it is, honestly—but the thing escaped. I'm over here at the house to pick something up while he and Lucy get dinner, and I can't find the cat anywhere. If I don't get it back inside before Declan comes back, he's going to kill me. And then Lucy is going to tell my Grandma Beth, and I'm never going to live a happy life. You're the only one I knew to call. Can you help?"

Alice found herself smirking. "Sullivan, give me the address, and I'll leave now."

Sullivan

Of course the cat would escape while Declan and Lucy were out. This was what Sullivan got for offering to pick up the groomsmen's tuxedo rentals and return them to the store. Declan had insisted it was fine for Sullivan to run in and out of the house while his buddy was gone and he and Lucy were off at dinner. He mentioned the cat being there but *failed* to mention the cat was a ninja.

Stupid feline.

The air was thick with humidity, but the mist of the rain was cool against Sullivan's face as his shoes crunched the gravel below the deck. He breathed in the welcome chill of the rain, a respite from the record heat earlier this afternoon.

"Hey, Sinatra?" He pointed a flashlight under the deck. "Where are you?" The cat had burst through the open back door nearly an hour ago. Probably knew full well Sullivan would come after him.

The rain that followed Sullivan's SOS call to Alice had just been a bonus. He pulled the hood of his sweatshirt up over the top of his head as the storm began to pick up.

"Sinatra," he tried again, jingling one of the bell toys he'd found inside. "I'm serious . . . I've got cat food in the house." He didn't know anything about cats. . . . Could they be bribed with food?

Sullivan moved the flashlight to illuminate the large oak near the porch. He had visions of buying an extension ladder to get Sinatra down from a tall branch. But nothing. "Come on, cat. Enough is enough."

Lightning flashed across the Mississippi, as the thunder followed the water closer to shore. The weather was starting to get bad, and Sullivan's clothes were dripping rainwater now.

"Sinatra!" Sullivan called louder.

"Frank!" Alice's voice startled him, and Sullivan jumped. She wore exercise clothes, tennis shoes, and a humored grin. She was beautiful, even in the rain. Maybe especially in the rain.

"Thank goodness you're here."

"Frank *is* his first name, right? Does he have blue eyes or something?"

"Don't look at me—I didn't come up with it." Sullivan turned the flashlight to more trees in the backyard. "He ran out the door when I came in from the patio."

"So you're saying he's looking for strangers in the night."

Sullivan turned to her, stone-faced.

"Or is it possible he's got you . . . under his skin?" Alice's tight-lipped grin broke into a full round of laughter.

Sullivan couldn't help himself. Slowly, he began to laugh too.

"Where's Declan? He left you alone to cat sit?" Alice wiped the rain from her eyelashes. Her eyes were red . . . but why? Had she been crying? He hoped he hadn't upset her by explaining what happened with that woman at the wedding and bringing up her mother.

"He and Lucy are at dinner. I got the impression it was fancy, so I didn't want to interrupt them. His buddy who owns the house is gone too." Sullivan shook his head.

"Hand me the flashlight." Alice cleared her throat. "Maybe luck will be a lady tonight."

"I'm beginning to regret asking you over here."

Alice playfully swiped the flashlight from his hand. "Do you want my help or not?" Not waiting for an answer, she pointed the flashlight at the wooden porch extending from the back of the house. "Did you check up here?"

"Under it."

Alice seemed to have her own ideas of where to search. "Cats can sense changes in barometric pressure and like to hide when storms are coming. He's probably hunkered down somewhere close."

She took the steps up the porch and pointed the flashlight at the house.

Sullivan pocketed his hands in his wet jeans. The rain had soaked through his sweatshirt. "Don't you think I would've seen him if he were sitting on the porch?"

Alice was not deterred. "Cats can hide in some pretty small spaces." She crouched down by an oversized planter. About a foot of space separated the intricate metal lattice-work from the deck.

"Mhmm," she said. "Just as I suspected."

Curled up underneath the elevated planter was Sinatra, wiping his little cat whiskers with his paws and meowing as if his escape act were perfectly executed according to plan.

Alice patted the ground beside him. "Come here, sweet-heart."

Within a few moments, she'd coaxed the cat out, and Sullivan retrieved a dry towel from inside to wrap around him. But Sinatra hissed whenever Sullivan neared.

Alice laughed. "Guess I'll help you get him inside."

"That'd be great."

Once the two had gotten the rebellious feline dry-ish and settled in his cat bed, Alice made her way back through the patio door to leave, and Sullivan shut it behind them. He realized his mistake as soon as he heard the click.

Oh man . . .

"Everything okay?" Alice asked.

Humiliation heating his cheeks, Sullivan raked one hand through his wet hair and looked down. "I'm pretty sure I just locked myself out of the house."

"My, how funny . . ." Alice smiled. Then she murmured, "Valentine."

She proceeded to hum. But it wasn't until she winked at him that Sullivan recognized the rest of the song. And he didn't want to admit just how much he was enjoying all her renditions . . . maybe the best was yet to come.

TWENTY-ONE

Charleston, December 1861

Clara

The carriage clamored to a stop in front of Mary and Oliver's house, and the three of them—Clara, Rose, and Harriet—all emerged as though they'd aged ten years apiece on the journey. Teddy, Mary, and Oliver ran out of the house, the darkness of evening fast upon them all.

"Where have you been?" Oliver's tone was filled with worry. From the glow of the lantern Teddy carried, Clara could see relief in Mary's eyes.

"Oh, Teddy," Clara said. "It was awful." She shook her head. "It was awful . . ."

"What happened?" Teddy met Clara's gaze directly.

Where should she even begin?

Clara swallowed, looking over at Rose. Her heart tugged in her chest so painfully, she thought she might break in two—she could not imagine the pain Rose was experiencing.

"Why didn't you send word where you were?" Teddy asked, before she had a chance to answer his other question. "Do you know how concerned you had us? Did you know there is a fire spreading through Charleston?"

Clara's lips parted as she tried to find the words. She wiped her sooty hands against what had previously been one of her best dresses. "Earlier today, a series of events unfolded that led Rose and I to the realization Joseph is working in some kind of intelligence capacity and reporting to General Lee. I've made a horrible mistake, Teddy. . . ." Clara looked at him then closed her eyes, covering them with her hands. "I compromised everything. Or I could've, at least."

When she opened her eyes, she found him staring at her—not with judgment but with concern. "Clara, what do you mean?" He reached out, touching her elbow gently with his callused fingertips. She didn't remember his skin being so rough before the war, and she thought to herself what an image that was—how they, all of them, had developed rough spots to cover the delicate places beneath. War did, indeed, do maddening things.

She swallowed. "In my haste, I put the little note you wrote me inside my pocket. I *did* plan to destroy it, as protocol mandates, but I wanted to first treasure it—for a little while, at least." She shook her head. "But apparently the note fell out of my pocket, and Joseph found it, and then Rose caught him writing something in a notebook. When he left the room, she discovered he had written your name. *Your* name, Teddy. And plenty of other names were in there as well." Clara met his eyes, pleading with him to understand. "That's why we wanted to apprehend it. We wanted to bring the names to you, so you could offer protection. And to protect the work you and Oliver have done. We had to act as fast as we did."

Teddy chose his words carefully. But even in the gentle glow of the lantern, she could see the deep worry lines in his expression. "You mean to tell me . . ." He cleared his throat. "That you and Rose took on this mission without so much as a word sent to Oliver and I, requesting assistance?"

"A lot of good that would have done!" Clara retorted. "The man was after you. Had he seen you, he might have killed you instantly."

"Better me than you," Teddy said without hesitation.

"Hardly." Clara sighed, reaching up to softly touch Teddy's shoulders. "You must think beyond chivalry to your larger role in helping those who seek freedom. Your role in this cause at the war level. And besides"—she shook her head emphatically—"there simply was no time to send word. It all happened very quickly. Why, we were lucky to even arrange for Harriet with the carriage."

Teddy rubbed his eyes with his hands. "I distinctly remember you agreeing not to put yourself in danger."

"We both knew it was a mere platitude." Clara crossed her arms, looking up at him. "But you should know that Joseph came upon us, just as I was preparing to swipe the notebook. Rose thought quickly, destroying the evidence with the fire of the lantern, and Joseph was too dumbfounded to react in time to retrieve it." Clara released a deep sigh, her eyes stinging. "But as we ran to escape, he yelled out over the roar of the flames that he has Ashley in his possession . . . well, as much as one human being can possess another human being, that is." She gritted her teeth. "He apparently purchased her for me as a surprise after I inquired about Rose's relations. And he told us if we ever tried to come for her, he would kill her in retribution."

Teddy blinked. "We'd planned Ashley's escape for tomorrow."

Clara's stomach soured.

"Do you think he's bluffing?" Teddy asked.

Clara ran the tip of her tongue over her dry lips. "Unfortunately, Joseph never bluffs about anything." Of that much, she was sure.

By the moonlight and with the steady drip of her tears, Clara rooted the little rose she'd plucked downtown inside a small container using dirt from Mary's garden. She'd lost track of the time, of the world, but her nose and her throat still burned with the smell of the smoke, and her skin had begun to blister in the spots where the flames had lapped. Mary had lent her fresh garments, but the smell of the smoke was in Clara's hair, and she doubted she would ever get it out.

It was probably only a few hours until dawn, but a new day meant little to her when all it would bring was fresh despair and more loss.

She knew what it meant to be broken now.

Joseph would, no doubt, tell her parents of her involvement with the fire and Teddy and the Union cause. They would likely be on their way to find her any time now.

And she would do anything to go back to yesterday and use more care retrieving the notebook. Oh, there were so many ways she could have prevented it. To start with, if she had simply destroyed Teddy's note in the first place, as he asked her to do with all correspondence.

Why did Rose have to pay for Clara's foolish error? For the first time she could remember, Clara wished she had the opportunity to give her own future for someone else's—for she cared that much about what happened to Rose and Ashley.

A man stepped out of Mary's house, toward the garden where Clara knelt. She knew it was Teddy immediately because his presence soothed the singes in her heart.

"Can I sit with you a while?" he asked.

Clara nodded. "Have you and Oliver finished crafting a new plan?"

Teddy stepped forward, then sat on the ground beside her. He nodded. "We have." He hugged his arms around his knees. "I was watching the moon from the window of the parlor when I saw you out here, and I wanted to talk with you about it."

Clara pushed the soil around the little rose, praying it would sprout roots, then stood. "I'm so sorry, Teddy. I've endangered all of us." His somber eyes stared back at her, reflecting the moonlight's glow. "I never should have held on to that note. I never should've hesitated to follow protocol. At the time it seemed harmless enough. Joseph was so difficult to be around, so pompous, and I felt as though I couldn't go another day keeping up the charade, another day without you. And then your note . . . well, it reminded me the cause was bigger than my own comfort. The thought of your love waiting for me was what I needed to keep going."

Teddy's shoulders lifted with his slow and steady inhale. "Clara, the fault is not yours to bear. It's mine." Teddy shook his head. "I could have conveyed my sentiments to you in a myriad of other ways, or kept them to myself a short time longer. I never should have put you in this position to begin with. It was impulsive of me, unfair to you, and I apologize. I hope you can forgive me for what I've done."

Clara reached out and took hold of his arm. "'Tis nothing to forgive." She said the words slowly, hoping he would take time to absorb them into his heart. For she truly believed she was the one singularly in the wrong. "The note must have fallen out of my pocket. I don't know how else he would've gotten hold of it."

Teddy watched Clara with tenderness in his eyes. "Blaming yourself will do no good. You can't look forward with your head turned over your shoulder." He tugged a small stick through the dirt beside them, swirling it into patterns Clara tried to make sense of before she realized there was no meaning to be found.

Clara stared at the little rose she'd just planted. "Tell me of your plan. What do we do now?"

Teddy met her eyes and watched her for some time. "Clara, there's something I want to propose. Such circumstances are far from the romantic ideations I'd ruminated on, but I assure you my words hold no less sincerity than they would in another context." He brushed the singed hair from Clara's forehead and tucked several strands behind her ear, unflinching despite what she knew to be a harsh look and feel and smell. "I have already expressed my adoration for you, and perhaps it's fanciful thinking but I've gotten the impression you've interest in me as well. So it should come as no surprise, sweet Clara, to hear the words come from my mouth—I love you, and I can commit to saying I always will. My hope, my greatest desire, is that we may join our lives together through the joys, and the hardships, and the trials."

Clara's thoughts began to race once she understood his proposal. Beneath a bright moon, both of them seated firmly upon the earth's soil—planted, as it were, by all that had been upturned before them and hoping beyond all hope something beautiful might grow, despite everything. She watched him as he continued, and told herself to soak in every grace-filled word like water upon that soil. Her heart leapt with anticipation even as it fell in grief, so that she began to tumble. And she thought of the leaves she saw yesterday as she and Rose buried the silver underground.

Sometimes even somersaulting leaves can look like butterflies.

"Would you marry me, Clara?" Teddy asked. The moonlight reflected a sliver, a narrow half-moon along the rim of his eyes. "Oliver is ordained as a minister. We could have a small ceremony in an hour, then leave together with Rose—if that's what she would like."

Clara's heart and mind continued to tumble, and she blinked to slow them down. "Marry you . . . now?"

Teddy pressed a kiss to her forehead, and suddenly all

the frenzy around her began to still as she realized this was exactly what she wanted—to marry Teddy and spend the rest of her life with him. "We will have to move fast. Your father and Joseph will come for you by daylight. Save for the vastness of the fire's reach, I've no doubt they would have already come by now." He reached out to gently stroke his thumb along her jaw.

"But what of yours and Oliver's plan?" she asked.

"This *is* the plan. Should you find it agreeable, then you, Rose, and I will travel to my family in New York before Joseph has the chance to connect my work with Oliver's. Oliver and Mary will reach out to your family in your absence and keep a close eye upon Ashley as best they can. We will probably enlist Harriet's help since Joseph may now be suspicious of direct contact with your relatives. In time—once tensions have subsided—we'll try to make a plan to free her, even if that means by a purchasing price."

"Sounds like it could work . . . though knowing Joseph's wickedness, I doubt his willingness to go along with it."

"Perhaps." Teddy turned his head to the side. "But at least it's a start." He hesitated. "That said, I don't mean to coerce you if you're unsure about matrimony. Of course there are other routes . . ."

"No!" Clara caught even herself off guard with the authority in her tone, and he raised his eyebrows. "Teddy, do not misunderstand. I have wanted to marry you from the day we met. Being wed to you is the greatest thing I could imagine, especially among the grief of all that's been lost."

He gave her a steady half grin. "Okay, then. We have a plan."

"Yes." Clara smiled back at him. "We have a plan."

And at these words, the first bird of the morning made its holy call, awaiting the coming glory of the dawn.

TWENTY-TWO

New Orleans, Modern Day

Alice

Sullivan was embarrassed.

Before tonight, she wouldn't have thought it was possible.

Alice blinked a couple times so the raindrops collecting on her eyelids would clear from her vision. She nodded in the direction of the driveway in front of Declan's friend's house. "Look, why don't I drive you back to my place? We have a dryer, you know. You can wait out the rest of the storm, and then when Declan gets back from his date, he can get your keys from inside. I'm assuming your hotel key is in there too?"

"Guilty as charged." He held up both hands. "Are you sure about this? I don't want to put you out."

"Absolutely. It's not a far drive." She squeezed her dripping ponytail, which was beginning to feel heavy against her neck, and hit the unlock button on her car keys. "But I guess you know that."

Sullivan smiled. "Yes, I do." He continued. "I did a little more market research today, and if you'd like, when we get back to your house, I can show you some screenshots of comparable stores and some features I think you could implement for The Prickly Rose at minimal cost."

"That sounds great." Settled inside her car, Alice turned up the heater as Sullivan rubbed the water from his arms. She caught herself staring at him sitting there, in her passenger seat, all tall and trim and messy-haired, and she forced herself to shift the car into reverse.

She turned onto the main road.

Well, this was certainly an interesting turn of events.

"Hey, I really appreciate you coming tonight. Had I known you were way out at the park, I wouldn't have . . ."

Alice held up one hand. "Really, don't mention it. The distraction was welcome. I was way too lost in my thoughts."

"Still." Sullivan shook his head. "You're such a cat expert."

Alice swatted his arm. "You don't have to act so surprised."

"I'm not surprised. I'm just . . ."

She tilted her head, waiting for more as she watched the road.

Sullivan hesitated, considering his words. "I've never met anyone quite like you, Alice."

She didn't tell him she only knew the cat thing because Aunt Charlotte had rescued so many of them, or that she was actually allergic to cats herself. Instead, she smiled.

She flipped on her blinker and rounded her little corner of Magazine Street. Within a few minutes, they'd arrived. Turning off the ignition, she put her hand on the door handle and turned to look at Sullivan. "Exit on three. One . . . two . . ."

"Three!" he yelled, laughing.

Puddles splashed from their two-at-a-time footsteps as she and Sullivan hurried past bushes with a few stray, blooming azaleas. Out of breath and laughing, Alice reached for the front door of her home. But when she opened it, she discovered quite a surprise.

It appeared another visitor was already in the house.

The Great Dane wore a bone-shaped dog tag, several black splotches on his otherwise-white coat, and a slobbery grin as he greeted them at the door, wagging his nubby tail all the while.

"Aunt Charlotte," Alice murmured through gritted teeth. She loved animals—truly loved them—but sometimes Aunt Charlotte seemed to confuse their home with a full-fledged animal rescue organization.

The huge dog jumped up on Alice, his paws to her shoulders.

Yes, this was one of those "sometimes."

Sullivan shut the door the rest of the way behind them.

"Who do we have here?" He clapped his hands, and the dog came lumbering over. "This guy wasn't here earlier, was he?"

"Nope. He definitely was not." A note on the back of the door caught her eye. Alice stepped past Sullivan as the dog leaned against his hip, enjoying some scratching. She pulled the taped piece of paper from the door.

> *Alice,*
> *Found the dog outside. He's scared of the storm. His name is Mighty Mouse. I know we said we can't afford to bring in any more fosters right now, but this one really is temporary. I called the number on his collar—his owner is out of town and coming in the morning.*
> *Went out for cookie dough. See you soon.*
>
> *—Aunt Charlotte*

Temporary. Alice had heard that word before. Sounded a lot like the way they'd gotten Aunt Charlotte's permanent foster, Freckles. And the orphaned squirrel. And the three-legged lizard.

Alice balled up the note in her hand, then pushed it through the revolving lid of the trash can. "It would appear Mighty Mouse is staying the night."

Sullivan raised his eyebrows. "Mighty Mouse?"

"The dog, Sullivan—try to keep up."

He chuckled. A small puddle had formed beneath him from his dripping sweatshirt, and the dog stepped out of the way to avoid getting wet.

"You need dry clothes." She gestured at the hallway on their right. "Just through the first door, you'll find the guest bedroom slash office slash animal rehabilitation area, which seems to be what we're running here, and an adjoining bathroom. If you want to grab a shower, just leave your wet clothes in the bedroom, and I'll toss them in the dryer for you."

"Appreciate it." Sullivan rubbed his facial stubble, which she had to admit, was filling in nicely. The trimmed, dark beard suited him. When he turned, Alice watched him walk down the hall. She tilted her head to get one extra glimpse of him before he disappeared around the door.

Alice sighed. Why did he have to live in Charleston? She had nearly forgiven him for his Valentine's Day blunder, too, just in time for him to head back home next week.

She gave him a few moments to get settled, wiping up the puddle by the entryway, then opening the door to find his wet clothes draped over the large dog crate rather than balled up on the wooden floor as she expected.

It was a small gesture, but his thoughtfulness in keeping his dripping clothes from warping the hundred-year-old flooring did not go unnoticed. She grabbed his clothes, dropped them into the dyer, and headed back to her own bathroom on the other side of the loft, a little skip in her step despite herself. There she found Freckles huddled into a ball on her bed. She scratched her head. "I'm sorry, girl. Is there a pony in your living room?"

Freckles looked up at her, wide-eyed.

"You should appreciate that Aunt Charlotte does this, though," Alice tugged on her favorite pair of leggings and an oversized sweater. "After all, you were once a stray too, you know."

Freckles turned her head to the left, her little paws tucked under a pillow.

"Yes, I know you can't remember that time in your life. But trust me," she swiped a tinted lip balm over her lips and smacked them once. "You were even more pity-worthy than Mighty Mouse."

Alice patted the dog once more. "He'll be gone in the morning, and the house will be all yours again."

I hope.

She shut the door to give Freckles some privacy for her evening nap.

Since she'd beat Sullivan to the living room, she decided to have a little fun and synced her wireless speaker to a Frank Sinatra streaming station on her phone.

With a chuckle, she cozied onto the couch and propped her feet up on the repurposed coffee table as Old Blue Eyes crooned about a summer wind. But nothing could've prepared her for the sight of Sullivan.

He adjusted the hem of her vintage-wash Louis Armstrong tee against a pair of oversized joggers. Well, they were oversized on her, but fit him nicely.

"Suits me, don't you think?"

"I'm so sorry," Alice said, giggling. "That was all I had that would fit you."

Sullivan sank down beside her on the couch. "Hey, it's surprisingly comfortable."

Louis Armstrong's face on that T-shirt had never looked so good.

Sullivan shifted toward her. She tried to concentrate. He

smelled like coffee and rain, and her head was spinning more than she'd care to admit from how close he was sitting. "Hey, I know I said it earlier, but seriously. Thanks for coming to help."

Alice waved away the comment with her hand. "Really, don't mention it."

As the music changed to "Come Fly with Me," so did Sullivan's expression, from genuine appreciation to humor. He recognized the song.

"I thought you'd like a little mood music for the evening," she quipped.

Sullivan's jaw set, and he shook his head, but she saw the sparks of amusement in his eyes. Before he could say anything else, the lights flickered, and the music stopped. In the darkness, she could see the outline of him.

He stepped toward the windows at the front of the house. "As suspected."

Alice bit her bottom lip. "Power's out?"

"Down the whole block."

Storms made Alice nervous. She didn't like the dark. "I'll get a candle . . . and I think we've got some matches in the drawer by the sink."

"Good. I'm going to get something to drink, if you don't mind—" Sullivan opened the refrigerator door and left it open while choosing a beverage. Alice shut it quickly and grabbed his hand.

"You can't leave the fridge open like that when the power is out—there's only so much chill in there to go around." With a grin, she added, "Clearly, you've been living in buildings with fancy generators too long."

Slowly, Sullivan returned her grin.

It wasn't until a full moment later that Alice realized she'd never let go of his hand.

Their eyes locked. He watched her intently. And for a moment, Alice felt as if her heart were a puzzle piece sliding into its match. What must've been only a moment felt like so much more.

The air hung between them, heavy with the pulse of attraction. She swallowed hard, looking up at him, and felt her whole body settle at his touch. Slowly, he leaned forward, pushing through that heavy air with movements so slight, they were nearly imperceptible. Her eyes were beginning to adjust to the darkness, and she could make out the flicker in his eyes and his strong jaw.

In an instant, the kitchen lights flashed. The power flickered back on, and the moment was gone.

Only, for Alice, it wasn't gone.

Not at all.

Sullivan raised his chin, and Alice watched as his chest, so close, broadened with his inhale.

The dryer dinged.

Alice blinked. "Sounds like your clothes are ready."

Sullivan raked his hand through the damp, messy waves of his hair, and smiled slightly—the whiteness of his teeth a sharp contrast to the dark beard that framed them. "Great," he murmured.

She couldn't decide if the disappointment in his tone was merely wishful thinking on her part. Mighty Mouse chose that moment to come running toward them and nearly tackled Alice to the ground, as if seeing her for the first time.

Sullivan rubbed the dog's back as Alice pulled herself to standing. "Scared of the dark?"

The question was meant for the dog, but Alice, too, had grown weary of storms. She left the two of them and stepped into the laundry room just behind the kitchen. After removing Sullivan's warm jeans from the dryer, Alice breathed in deeply for the first time in so long.

And in that moment, she realized something huge.

Despite the darkness, and the grief, and the questions, and the fear—tonight she'd fallen from her perfect perch between comfort and denial. She'd looked into Sullivan's eyes. And tonight, she'd felt alive.

She returned the warm clothes to Sullivan just as Declan's call buzzed from his phone. He confessed to Declan what'd happened with the cat, then scooped up his clothes in one arm and headed down the hall to change.

Within a few minutes, they arrived back at Declan's rental house. Sullivan unlatched his seatbelt and shifted to face her. "So tomorrow . . . do you want to hit up some tourist sites before we go to Preservation Hall?"

Alice smiled at him. In her mind she smelled roses, though she didn't know why. "Only if you promise not to lose another cat."

TWENTY-THREE

New Orleans, Modern Day

Alice

The following day, Alice stood at the open doorway of her house, staring at Sullivan. He wore black slim-fit chinos, a white button-down under a cocoa sweater with just the tail of the hem peeking out, and a pea coat with his tortoiseshell glasses. To say she was a fan of the look would be an understatement.

The morning rain had given way to a sticky-yet-cooler afternoon, and the pulse of sunshine beat down on the small puddles outside her entryway.

"Hello," Sullivan said, hands casually tucked into the pockets of his coat.

"Hello."

Alice internally chided herself for her *An Affair to Remember* moment, then cleared her throat. She pulled at the hem of her sweater and stuck her hands into the pockets of her skinny jeans, rocking back on the heels of her Converse sneakers. "Let me just grab my coat, and we can head out."

Alice slid her purse over her head, lifting her freshly curled hair from her shoulder as she stepped under his arm and through the doorframe.

She was intoxicated by his nearness, and for a moment she wondered why she was torturing herself like this when he was only in town for a short while. But even Cinderella went to the ball for a few hours, and Alice couldn't fault her heart for dreaming of more.

Sullivan followed behind her on the steps down from her house and ducked under a large oak limb as he stepped down onto Magazine Street.

Alice turned to him. "Where do you want to go this afternoon?"

"You're the New Orleans resident. You tell me." His grin could've charmed the sun into shining, and Alice melted under its warmth.

She nodded, looking down at the sidewalk to avoid the unraveling effect his gaze had on her. "How about the French Quarter then, and all the tourist sites?"

"Sounds good to me."

"We obviously don't have time for everything, but maybe Jackson Square, Café du Monde for beignets, and hear some jazz on Royal Street?"

"You've got a date," he said, so naturally. But the words plunked like a marble in her heart, rolling round and round with echoes of meaning.

A date. With Sullivan.

She knew he didn't mean it like that—of course he didn't mean it like that—but still, she couldn't help the sudden leap of anticipation she felt.

"We'll walk up a few blocks and take the St. Charles streetcar." Alice turned and headed toward a smattering of cottage shops trimmed in gingerbread millwork.

"Spoken like a local." Sullivan winked.

Alice glanced up at him and smiled as they walked in stride.

They passed several antique stores and coffee shops in easy rhythm with each other. Alice inhaled the fragrance of espresso deeply, hoping to capture the scent before they got to the startling olfactory experience the French Quarter always offered. She didn't even want to think about the multiple variables contributing to that smell.

But beignets made it all worthwhile.

In no time, they'd reached the trolley stop and lucked out when the streetcar approached just as they did. Alice boarded and dug three dollars out of her purse, then told the driver to keep the change.

Sullivan followed close behind and chose a mahogany bench in the middle of the trolley. "I'm sorry I didn't think to carry cash."

"Consider it payback for my donut yesterday." She took the aisle spot so he could see out the window of the oldest continuously operating streetcar in the world.

Sullivan studied her a long second—his eyes alight with something—and Alice wondered what he was thinking.

The trolley bell rang, and they gently swayed back and forth as the car rolled down the street. Sullivan reached his arm over the back of the bench and turned so their knees touched. "Alice?" he asked.

"Mmm?"

He watched out the window of the trolley as they rolled closer to the French Quarter. "Thanks for letting me tag along."

"Absolutely." She hadn't expected him to say that. The truth was, she was grateful for his company.

Stray perennial Mardi Gras beads glimmered from the branches of oak trees out the window as the trolley rumbled past. By the time they reached their stop in the French Quarter, Alice rubbed the arms of her sweater, wishing she'd thought to bring a coat. She'd underestimated how the earlier rain had chilled the air.

She stepped down from the old-fashioned green streetcar. Sullivan wasn't far behind. He must've noticed her shiver because he shimmied his arms out of his pea coat and set it over Alice's shoulders.

She warmed instantly, for more reasons than one.

Alice reached up to clutch the edges of the coat at her neck, and her hands grazed Sullivan's. Attraction spread over her with fury. Could he feel it as well?

"Won't you be cold?"

"Are you kidding? I've got a sweater on." He rubbed her arms with his hands. "You need it more than me."

Maybe she would pretend to continue being cold . . .

A whitewashed storefront with colorful accessories caught her attention as they passed. Alice slowed and reached out to touch a gauzy scarf with whimsical poppies. She always found herself attracted to this color because it brought out the red in her hair.

"You like it?"

She looked up at him and smiled. "It's gorgeous." Alice flipped the price tag over with her thumb. "But a little over-priced for me."

Sullivan pulled the scarf from the display and balled it up in his hand. "In that case, hang on a minute, would you?"

Before she realized what he was doing, Sullivan returned with the scarf in one hand and a receipt in the other. "You were cold." He shoved the receipt into his pocket, then gently wrapped the scarf around her neck.

Slowly, Sullivan stepped behind Alice and lifted the back of her hair from underneath her new scarf. She was beginning to like him. She was *really* beginning to like him.

Maybe Aunt Charlotte had made the right decision opening the door on Valentine's Day after all.

Sullivan

Sullivan and Alice sat under the green-striped tent of Café du Monde and ordered three beignets, a French roast coffee, and a hot chocolate. Moments later, their server returned, balancing a plate full of beignets with heaps of powdered sugar and carrying a drink in each hand.

Sullivan thanked the woman and took a sip from his coffee. When he'd come a few days ago, he'd tried the chicory blend, but the French roast was every bit as rich, with a New Orleans flavor.

Alice blew on her hot chocolate, the steam visibly rising from her cup.

She wore a long cream-colored sweater with gold threads that skimmed over the curves of her body, tapered jeans, and a pair of Converse All Stars that suggested she was not one to fool around with walking miles in heels.

He loved everything about the way she looked. Which wasn't surprising, because he loved everything about Alice. She was like a red-haired Mary Poppins. She'd captivated him, and he didn't know what he was going to do without her when he went back home. Sullivan took another sip from his coffee. He wouldn't think about that right now. Right now, he would just enjoy the time he had with her.

Alice pulled several napkins from the dispenser and spread them across her lap neatly. Then she reached for a beignet.

"You know the trick about the sugar, right?"

Sullivan took another drink from his coffee. "There's a trick?"

"Yeah, so you don't get it all over you."

He looked down at his black pants and thought back to the last time he'd eaten beignets. Previous history would suggest he needed Alice's secret.

Alice adjusted his black pea coat on the back of her seat, a safe distance from the powdered sugar all over the plate, table, and ground below. "Don't breathe."

Sullivan laughed. "That sounds easy enough."

"I'm serious! Hold your breath while you take a bite. Otherwise . . . well, if you exhale, the sugar goes everywhere, and if you inhale . . . let's just say your nose will be burning for days. Don't ask me how I know that."

Sullivan set his coffee down and reached for his own beignet, eager to try her trick. He raised the pastry to his mouth as a sly grin slipped across Alice's lips.

"What is it?" he asked.

She shook her head. "Nothing. I was just thinking about the first time we had beignets together—the day we met."

"I must've left a lasting impression."

"I thought you were blowing off a Valentine's date and told my aunt not to let you inside."

Sullivan's laughter escaped him before he had a chance to think better of it. A cloud of powdered sugar floated up from his beignet in a moment of weightlessness before gravity did its work.

Alice's eyes went wide. She set her own beignet down and jumped up from her seat, trying to escape. But it was too late. The damage had already been done.

White sugar coated them both, as well as their table, and the already-sugary ground at their feet.

"Sullivan!" she hissed, but her laughter made her disapproval hard to believe.

"It's your own fault for being so funny." He licked the sugar from his lips.

Alice held up the napkins that had been in her lap. "Guess I don't have much need for these anymore." She brushed the sugar off her seat and sat back down.

"I really am sorry." He grinned. "Mostly."

Alice tested the temperature of her hot chocolate with a small sip. "You're impossible."

"Thank you." He reached for the container of powdered sugar at the center of the table and dusted the now-bare beignet with an ample layer. "Now let me try this again."

"I'll do my best to be less amusing."

Sullivan chuckled—softly, this time. He successfully ate the beignet without any further issues, and he and Alice decided to split the third one since neither of them could eat the whole thing.

She put the lid back on her hot chocolate and stood, attempting to brush the sugar from her clothes to no avail. At least she wasn't wearing black pants. He looked ridiculous. He'd be lucky if an army of ants didn't follow him around town for the rest of the day.

Alice removed her new scarf from her neck and shook it to get the sugar off, then wrapped it back in place with a pat.

Had he been too bold in buying her the scarf? It wasn't as if she was his girlfriend. But she'd loved the thing, and she was cold, and he thought it would look beautiful on her.

He'd been right about that part, at least.

It took all of Sullivan's willpower not to take Alice's hand as they strolled down the cracked sidewalks of Royal Street.

The smell of gumbo and fresh pralines wafted toward them as they passed tacky tourist shops and classy antique stores. He was surprised Alice hadn't wanted to go in more of the stores—but for the time being, she seemed content to simply window shop. He was relieved—antique shopping with his Grandma Beth had taught Sullivan there were only so many overpriced vases a man could look at before his feigned interest became decidedly less convincing.

But it was the jazz band playing under the wrought-iron

gables on the corner that ultimately caught Alice's attention. She was drawn to the upright bass, fiddle, and banjo as though she'd been magnetized.

And as the two of them stepped nearer to the crowd around the band in the middle of the street, Alice tilted her face up toward him with a smile. Her eyes alight with passion, she drew him even as the jazz drew her.

The crowd roared with applause when the band finished its song. A man Sullivan hadn't noticed before hopped from the bed of an old pickup truck that was parked behind the musicians. With a trumpet in hand, he began a jazz rendition of "Boogie Woogie Bugle Boy."

Alice reached for Sullivan's hand and turned to face him with a beaming grin. "Do you swing dance? I learned how at a wedding last year. Lucy's sister's wedding, actually."

He took her hand and spun her once. "Do I swing dance? What kind of a question is that?" He led her out into the crowd of dancers that was beginning to form.

The real answer would've been *no* if Grandma Beth hadn't forced him to watch all those episodes of *Dancing with the Stars* years ago. But Alice didn't need to know that.

Facing Alice with both her hands in his own, Sullivan waited for the next beat before stepping out. She followed him easily, so he stretched his arm around her head after the next rock step and pulled her to his side.

Alice laughed and took his lead as he rocked back to start the Charleston.

She puckered her lips slightly so her dimple showed and looked up at him with just the right amount of sass.

"Is that your dancing face?" He tried to play it cool, but the truth was, Alice did a number on him, and he wasn't sure he could keep up with her dancing skills so he tried to focus on which moves he should do next to keep from getting predictable.

"You haven't seen my dancing face until you've seen me Lindy Hop." On his next forward kick, she angled her own kick under his knee.

"Fancy moves, Miss Florist."

Alice flipped her long curls out of her face, laughing. "I try."

From under her breath, Alice sang along freely. Her voice was enchanting. The depth of it stunned him, and she had a brightness about her tone that he'd never heard from anyone before.

Sullivan drew in the sound, memorizing it and the feel of her in his arms.

She fit perfectly. And the truth was, she drew out a part of him he'd long put aside. The jazz-loving guy who dreamed of a committed relationship and didn't really mind that he still had powdered sugar all over his pants.

He'd really missed being that guy. He hadn't realized it until he met Alice. But she had this effect on him, even without knowing the man he used to be before the heartbreaks of life and relationships caused him to pull back from commitment.

"You sing beautifully."

She looked up at him. "Thank you."

The song neared its end, and Sullivan spun Alice close. He would dance with her as long as she'd let him. She smelled like lavender and honey, and for a minute he wondered if maybe she was interested, if maybe they could make a long-distance relationship work.

Sullivan stretched out his knee and pivoted Alice into a low dip from his arms. Her eyes fluttered closed as if she, too, were savoring the moment.

Then she opened her eyes with a look of enchantment and surprise, and the moment got the best of him. His fingers intertwined in her curls, Sullivan held the back of her head with his hands and started to close the space between them. The band started a new song—a slow song—but he didn't care. Her presence was a tunnel, and everything around them faded away.

He longed to kiss her but stopped himself.

Because today wasn't about him. Today was about finding her mother. Sullivan pulled her upright even though every fraction of him protested. But as he moved, Alice stiffened from his arms. Had she too sensed how close they'd been to sharing their first kiss?

Suddenly the moment—light as the afternoon's powdered sugar cloud—sunk with the weight of reality. Sullivan drew in a deep breath, trying to steady himself from the strong sway of the attraction he felt to her.

"We . . . um . . . we should probably make a plan." Sullivan pushed his hair back from his forehead as sweat trickled down his back, despite the chill in the air. "For tonight . . . and all."

Alice pulled her arms from out of his coat and handed it back. She might as well keep it, because he would never be able to wear the thing again without seeing her in his mind and remembering that almost-kiss. "Actually, I was thinking about it, and I'm going to go to Preservation Hall tonight by myself."

"Are you sure? I can go with you." Sullivan slid his hands into his pockets as the two of them slowly meandered away from the band.

She watched him a long moment. "Yeah . . . it's probably best I take this one on my own."

He watched her a while, really wanting to talk his way into coming along tonight . . . and really wanting a second chance at kissing her as well.

The magnetism of their almost-kiss had clearly taken them both by surprise. But maybe it was best nothing happened. She had so much going on, and he was headed back to Charleston in a week's time.

"I hope you find her, and the reunion is all you'd like it to be," he said, trying to respect her wishes in wanting to go to Preservation Hall alone.

"Thank you." She smiled sweetly up at him as if she, too, did not know what to say next.

"Maybe I'll see you tomorrow, then?" he asked.

"Sure. Maybe." She nodded as she adjusted the scarf around her neck. "See you, Sullivan."

"See you, Alice."

He walked, and he walked, and he walked—all the way back to his hotel because he couldn't stomach the thought of getting back on that streetcar. He didn't even think about an Uber until he made it back an hour later.

He already missed her.

He missed her so much, in fact, that he wondered how he could be happy in Charleston without her.

TWENTY-FOUR

Charleston, December 1861

Clara

Mary placed a lacy shawl over Clara's bare shoulders. The wedding dress had a scooped neckline and a layer of ruffles at the bust that mirrored the ruffles in the full skirt of the gown.

Mary had worn the dress with two petticoats when she married Oliver, but Clara could not fit into them both, so one would have to do. But she didn't mind. She was glad to be able to wear the dress at all—both to borrow it from her cousin and to have the occasion in the first place. The circumstances of the last twenty-four hours had blurred all sense of time and space, but there was one thing that had only grown clearer in Clara's mind, and that was her desire to marry Teddy and do right in the world.

When she and Teddy had returned inside from the garden, Mary sprung into action, offering Clara her own garments and even clipping a small bouquet of flowers for Clara to carry. She'd carefully placed the flowers into a silver tussie-mussie as Rose combed Clara's hair. Mary even made sure to clip a few extra flowers to pin in Clara's hair along her veil.

As she set to work readying the bride, Mary lamented. "My

sweet Clara, I'm so sorry I have no fruitcake to celebrate, and no favors to be hidden and baked inside. Although I suppose we have no guests to find them, either."

Clara raised a small heirloom mirror and looked at her reflection. "Cousin, don't be silly. You have been so gracious to both Teddy and I already. Besides, I never much cared for the tradition of baking little tokens into the cake, rings and buttons and pennies—for I've always worried I may miss one and choke upon it. Not to mention, the havoc such a messy search leaves on women's gloves."

"Want to hear something humorous?" Mary fastened a strand of pearls around Clara's neck. "Years ago, on the morning I met Oliver, we had both attended an early wedding and were enjoying the breakfast reception afterward when I *did* the very thing you mention—I missed a little token, took a bite, and nearly swallowed it."

Clara laughed, looking at her dear cousin through the mirror. "What type of token was it?"

"A ring." Mary sighed wistfully, seemingly lost in the memory. "Oliver kept it for months and used it when he proposed to me. Of course, he gave me a knot ring as well, but the sentiment of keeping the little token all that time . . . it was lovely."

Clara reached for her cousin's hand. "Then I fear, dear Mary, that even if we *did* have guests or tokens to offer, nothing would compare to your story, for it may be the most charming I've heard."

Mary met her gaze, her smile, soft. "Oliver is a kind man. As is Teddy. Actually, Teddy has made quite the favorable impression upon us while staying here." She and Rose began pinning flowers in Clara's hair. "I know you've had to make some difficult choices leaving behind your family, but Clara, I want you to know that I *am* your family too, and I will always be here for you. I am proud of you, so proud of you, and am honored to be part of this day as we celebrate your union to Teddy."

Clara's eyes stung with tears. Mary's words were a balm to her soul—a balm she didn't know how much she needed until the sentiments were spoken. "I love you, Mary."

"I love you too." Mary patted her hand. "Now let's get you downstairs to the garden, where your groom is waiting."

$\sim$

Teddy

Teddy never expected to be married under a garden trellis on a plantation outside of Charleston, South Carolina. He never expected there would be no guests, no pomp and circumstance, no honeymoon.

But he also never expected the birdsong or the way the breeze would lift the ends of his bride's beautiful hair. Never expected how the heart inside of him would lift with that very breeze and float off into the air.

And for the first time, he understood why his mother always invited all those women to call back at home. She wanted him to experience this type of love, a commitment and adoration which far exceeded what he'd known before . . . far exceeded fickle feelings and selfish endeavors, and, ironically perhaps, filled him with more giddy glee than he had ever expected himself capable.

Clara was absolutely beautiful, in every way.

She carried a small bouquet of flowers contained by a silver tussie-mussie, her hair swept into an intricate design, and her cheeks with a tint of red, her natural blush. She smiled at him as she stepped closer, and her smile unraveled him at once.

She came to stand beside him, and Oliver too, who held an old Bible and prompted the sacred vows. They were fortunate to have a minister in Mary's husband. Otherwise, this plan might have been tricky . . . for Teddy and Clara may need to flee at any moment, should her father appear at the door. And if they were not yet wed, propriety would be far harder to follow.

Teddy repeated Oliver's words at his prompting. "I, Theodore, take you, Clara, to be my wife . . ." She seemed to glow with radiance as she looked back at him, and for a moment he forgot what he was saying. Oliver got him back on track, and Teddy continued the vows. "I promise to be faithful to you until death part us."

He took Clara's gentle hand in his own as she repeated the promises, still holding the little bouquet of flowers in her other hand. And somehow, taking these vows before the Lord during such a hard time made it feel as though the commitment would be easier to uphold when healing arrived. When and if it ever did arrive.

Who was he kidding? Teddy could not even predict what the day's end would bring, let alone what was to come thereafter. But he did know one thing—he loved Clara with a love that was ever-growing and grounded in faithfulness. And together, they were committed to doing whatever it took to make a difference within their time in history, within their corner of the world.

He was just about to offer a kiss to his new bride when from the side of his vision, he noticed movement on the horizon. He stiffened, squinting to get a better view. Clara, Mary, and Oliver took note of his concern and all turned to look as well.

"Is that a carriage?" Mary asked.

For a stunned moment, they all stood in silence.

Not only was it a carriage, but it was coming toward them.

Teddy held tightly to Clara's hand, not daring hesitate any longer. "Run!" he yelled. Clara grabbed onto Rose too, hitched up her skirts and ran like the wind, never letting go of either of them.

⤳

Clara

By the time they finally arrived in New York, Clara had decided she would be perfectly content if she never rode in another carriage again. She tried to salvage what little elegance she had left after the long journey, but her gloves were filthy, her frock was torn, and her stomach was in knots from the long and bumpy ride.

Teddy was as stalwart as he'd ever been, finding little general stores for provisions along the way and making plans for how they might integrate into New York society. Though New York City was far from Confederate ground, the spirit of the movement, unfortunately, was not so far from many people's hearts. The international slave trade—an illegal endeavor—still thrived from the city, and as Teddy explained it, even in New York, discrimination abounded. Discrimination that often turned violent, despite the state being the first one to pass a law in favor of total abolition.

Clara wrung her hands, looking at Rose as the carriage came to a stop in front of Teddy's parents' home. When they were in South Carolina, getting Rose away from the plantation and into a state where slavery was illegal seemed like such a straightforward step. But now . . . well, now Clara was beginning to realize Rose might not be safe here either.

Rose might not be safe anywhere, at least not for a long while.

How long would this war last? And how long would the

fight last, even beyond the war? Would it *ever* end? What type of future would Rose be able to secure for herself, and for her own family, and for their own family after that?

What once seemed simple seemed simple no more.

Teddy opened the door of the carriage, reaching upward to help both Clara and Rose out. The three of them huddled together as they ascended the steps toward the house.

Teddy knocked three times. When the door opened, an older woman wearing an ornate frock and sparkling gemstone earrings gasped in surprise, immediately drawing Teddy into her arms.

"You've come home," she said, then she said it again.

Several moments passed before she released him, turning at once to both Rose and Clara. "Where are my manners?" She squeezed Teddy's shoulders for good measure. "You must forgive me . . . I'm just so happy to have my son home."

"I can understand why." Clara smiled.

Teddy clasped his hands together, then reached for Clara. "Mother, you'll remember I said before I left that I wanted to find an adventure."

"I most certainly remember that, yes."

He looped his arm around her waist. "Well, I've brought quite a surprise along with me. I'm happy to introduce you to Clara." He hesitated, his grin, broad. "My wife."

His mother's eyes widened. "Your . . . your . . . you mean to say you got . . ." She pointed at Clara, clearly dumbfounded by the news. Clara actually felt a little bad for the woman.

"Married." Teddy supplied the missing word. "Yes. And I'm sorry you weren't able to attend. I do hope you'll forgive me for that part. But urgency was a necessity, as I'll explain in a moment."

His mother swallowed visibly. "You don't mean to imply . . ."

Clara vehemently shook her gloved hands. "Oh no. Definitely no."

Her relief was palpable. "So you *do* love each other, then?"

Clara and Teddy met one another's gaze and shared a smile. Clara was lost in a moment—in the joy of his nearness—as the world faded around them.

"Very much yes," Teddy said.

Clara nodded, agreeing. She gently placed her hand on Rose's shoulder. "And this is Rose. She has bravely escaped with us."

Teddy's mother watched Rose, her mind obviously working to fit all the pieces together. "Welcome, then, Rose, to you as well. Should we all continue this conversation inside? I'm sure your father will be delighted to see you."

"Absolutely." Teddy motioned for the ladies to enter before him, then whispered into the hair above Clara's ear. "She likes you. I can tell. But of course, who wouldn't?"

Her heart warmed so deeply, she wondered if she wore the blush on her cheeks as well.

"I've been fretting over you, my dear boy, ever since news of the Charleston fire reached us. The papers reported it was quite a disaster." Teddy's mother spoke to her son.

"Yes," Teddy confirmed. "Watchmen lowered the red lantern from St. Michael's steeple as a warning the fire was spreading, but little could be done."

At the thought of St. Michael's, Clara could hear the church bells as though they were actually tolling. And she wondered about those bells—had they survived the fire? Would generations after hers stand near the church and pause, taking a breath from work and conversation to hear that beautiful, hope-filled sound?

Or had the bells cracked—to be heard no longer? The very future of their hope seemed to hang in the balance. What would come of her family back in Charleston? Of her home?

What would come of *her*? And Teddy, and Rose? And Ashley as well . . .

Clara blew out a deep breath. She needn't think long about what would happen if they were caught. They would certainly be tried, and possibly be killed. . . .

"The two of you must have been quite frightened to leave in such haste," Teddy's mother said to Rose and Clara.

But Clara was not sure whether she felt frightened or not. Aside from her joy over marrying Teddy, grief had clouded all other emotions, and she wondered whether she would ever again be able to feel something outside the spectrum of loss. Loss haunted her at every turn, it seemed . . . loss, and more loss. She was destabilized and spinning further, and holding Teddy's hand anchored her amidst the chaos. She could not fathom what Rose must be feeling, or how she was even getting by moment to moment.

"Scared? I don't know that I'm scared, exactly . . ." Clara's gaze scanned the ornate, marble-filled interior of their home, and she offered a sad smile. "But what I have learned is that I'm strong." What she really meant was that she was broken. Ironic, perhaps. But maybe that was all the more reason to remind herself that she *could* be strong. Strong beyond the grief, strong beyond the despair, strong beyond the heartache.

And maybe *strong* didn't mean what she once thought, at all.

"And you, Rose?" his mother asked when Rose did not speak up.

Rose said nothing for a long while, only looked down at the tiny coin purse she carried, the one that held the butterfly buttons inside. Finally, she sighed deeply. "I've been survivin' so long, I'm not sure I would recognize fear if I felt it. Fear is a privilege for those with hope on the horizon. And I've been watchin' the morning sun rise from behind a shade for far too long."

"Oliver's good at his job, Rose," Teddy tried to assure her.

"The very moment he has Ashley in his care, we will travel back to Charleston. You and Ashley can stay here with us in New York, or I can help connect you with other people who have escaped slavery down in South Carolina. Don't let the words of that pompous fool Joseph echo in your mind—it's exactly what he wants."

And yet, Clara knew Joseph's words were all Rose was thinking about, because she'd spent a good amount of time going over them herself—*I'll kill her*, he'd said.

They both knew he'd meant it.

TWENTY-FIVE

New Orleans, Modern Day

Alice

Alice knew what it meant to fear for a parent. She knew the loss of hope and the loss of dreams that so readily led to the loss of identity. She knew what it was to hurt so deeply you wondered if you would ever feel again, and the ripping away of all you ever knew yourself to be.

Somehow, despite all that, she was determined to find her mother. To find her way back to her dreams. She would let go of bitterness. And she would not waste another day of her life in the meantime.

Her passionate moment with Sullivan in the French Quarter had been jarring, to say the least. She was growing entirely too attached to him, when the relationship between them was clearly not going anywhere. He was afraid of commitment, and she was afraid of being abandoned all over again. They were far from a perfect match. It was kind of him to offer to come along tonight, and she knew he did mean to be supportive, but she just couldn't bear the thought of giving him another piece of her heart, only for him to turn back to Charleston and leave her behind.

So that evening, Alice waited alone in the line forming outside Preservation Hall. Across the street, neon red lights from a dilapidated storefront advertised tarot readings and voodoo. A man leading a ghost tour who himself looked to be an apparition stood out front.

But the sky. The sky just beyond Bourbon Street glowed with the setting of the sun, and clusters of white clouds filtered the rays over the French Quarter—light among the darkness, hope among the haze. And Alice's spirit lifted at the sight of it.

She handed the teenager behind the counter the exact cash amount for entry, then stepped onto the old wooden floors of Preservation Hall.

And she marveled.

Coming into this space was like walking directly into history, into a time when jazz first brought a city alive. And for Alice, it was also like coming home. A small swirl of dust floated up from the worn slats of the floor, aged with history and the legacy of song. Large portraits hung from the walls—artistic sketches of jazz greats. Small hand-painted signs on the walls asked patrons to refrain from using cell phones or taking photographs.

Alice stood at the back of the large crowd that had gathered around the musicians. The first fifteen or so people got dibs on seats, and the rest of the space was standing room only.

Near the band, a sign listed pricing for songs: five dollars for normal requests, ten dollars for special songs, and twenty dollars for "The Saints." Alice chuckled to herself. So, they were still charging twenty bucks to play the march. . . .

Ceiling fans spun from the exposed beams of the ceiling. Warm despite the walls needing a good scrubbing—warm, despite being worn—the space collected a unique kind of family. Old and young, diverse races and interests and walks of life—they were all moved by the rhythm.

Once the band had been introduced, a woman stood, moving from the maroon cushion of the wooden chair next to the saxophone player. She wore a Ramones shirt tied in a knot in the middle that accentuated her waistline, over the top of a pleated maxi skirt.

And Alice's heart sputtered at the sight.

She was thin—thinner than Alice remembered—and much older too.

And not just older in the way time tugs us forward, but older in the way of being closer to death than the last time you've seen someone. Her hair lacked its former luster, and the wrinkles of age had replaced the wrinkles of laughter around her eyes.

Alice grieved from the very depths of her heart.

Because all this time, her mother had been alive. And all this time, her mother had been alone. She hugged her arms to her chest and watched as her mother approached the microphone. The voice had never left her memory. The voice that had lulled her to sleep as a child.

But as Alice's mother sang, her voice had the opposite effect now . . . for it awakened Alice, shook her with memories that crumbled the walls between past and present.

And Alice wanted to weep in the middle of that large crowd and could scarcely hold herself back. For she had mourned her mother's voice—she had missed her mother's voice—but now . . .

Now her mother's voice had brought a rainbow of color back into her life.

As the band continued playing, Alice let go of all her burdens with every beat of the drum. Music had always been therapy to her, and this moment was no different.

For the first time in such a long time, Alice let herself fall fully in love with the song. She closed her eyes and swayed with her arms hugging her chest, and she forgot the world that surrounded her.

And as Alice rocked back and forth, she was a child again. Her broken voice and her broken heart were soothed by each note of her mother's song. Fully immersed in the music, her soul began to heal from the harmony.

Her eyes fluttered open as an old trumpet player laughed heartily. Holding his trumpet in the air, his grin was wide. Age and wisdom layered the tone of each note he played, and Alice was stunned by the precision of his skill.

Behind him, a young pianist ran his fingers over the keys with ease. And though he did not hold the experience of the trumpet player, his was a song of enthusiasm, and the hope that youth has to offer.

The sound deepened by each instrument, just as one generation builds off the last.

Her mother was the only woman in the band. The men all wore white button-down shirts with nice slacks, but they must have let her wear whatever she wanted, including her current skirt-and-vintage-T ensemble.

Alice lost herself in the set. When the band announced their last song, she blinked several times and suddenly realized darkness had fallen beyond the long ten-paned windows outside. She'd been so caught up in the music, she'd completely lost track of time.

The announcement pulled Alice out of her trance and stirred a whole new set of emotions. She was about to reunite with her mom . . . but could she find the courage to say something?

Alice twirled one of her long curls around her finger out of habit, then rubbed her clammy palms against the knees of her jeans.

As the band ended the song, the crowd erupted in applause. If their smiles were any indication, the musicians fed off the energy as they set their instruments down.

Alice pulled her phone out from her back pocket and checked the time.

Ten minutes until the band's next set, according to their posted schedule.

Could she approach her? Or should she watch them play all over again, hoping to feel a little stronger in an hour? Her gut clenched. She'd waited so long for this moment.

But Alice's decision was made for her when her mother's gaze scanned the crowd. Their eyes locked. And the moment set a fire inside Alice as someone dropped a sparking cigarette to the ground just beyond the darkened windowpane outside.

"Alice?"

Her mother ran to her with open arms.

They stood on the sidewalk outside Preservation Hall, the smell of smoke burning Alice's nostrils and the putrid stench of Bourbon Street turning her already-sick stomach.

How—*how*—had any of this happened? How had one night, one event, set the course for years upon years of mourning?

Her mother leaned against the ragged old building—this place where historical jazz was painstakingly honored but musicians flooded out each night into streets that were one day older and one day dirtier than the night before.

This place her mother had come, Lord only knew how many times, to escape into what was perhaps the only sense of beauty she had left in life. Into a space both figurative and literal, where the past was preserved and the melodies told its stories.

Maybe that's why her mother loved jazz so much.

Maybe that's why it was the only love she could fully accept.

And maybe—Alice swallowed past the lump in her throat at the thought—maybe that's why Alice loved jazz too.

"I found your letter after the storm," Alice murmured, her voice hoarse and barely audible over the bustle of Bourbon Street a short ways over. She looked down at the cracks in the sidewalk and the cigarette butts littering the pavement. She didn't dare look at her mom. "All this time, I thought you were gone."

Her mother took her time before responding.

Alice wanted to scream.

It was the opposite reaction she'd imagined she would feel in this moment—a moment she'd played in her mind hundreds of times.

But now—right now—she was angry.

Reality was setting in.

Her mother was alive! But also . . . her mother was alive.

How could she do such a thing? How could she abandon them? Reject Alice's love? She could forgive her mother for leaving, and even considering suicide. That, she understood, in her own way. She knew depression and she knew anxiety from the loss of her mother, and she could only imagine how much more challenging her mother's experience had been, given the loss of a child.

But to never come back? Alice wasn't sure she could forgive her for that.

"I needed you." Alice choked back tears.

It was a ridiculous thing to say. She should've asked *what happened?* Or *how?* Or even *why?* But she found herself adding, "I wanted you—in my life."

"I wanted you too. More than you'll ever know." Her mother's voice broke with a rasp.

"Then why would you stay gone?"

"Because I didn't have anything to offer." Alice's mother kicked her right foot from where it'd been perched against the wall and took one step closer. "Don't you understand? You think you needed me, but I wasn't the person you remember. I was broken. It was better for you if I stayed gone."

Alice's cheeks pulled into a grimace as she heaved with a sigh.

"Whoever said you needed something to offer, Mom?" Alice turned to face her mother and braved a glance into her bleak eyes. "You—just you—were always enough."

"I was a mess."

"You were my mother."

What part of this was she not understanding? That no matter what she'd done, no matter how she'd felt or how desperate she'd become—no matter how hopeless or broken or afraid—she was and would always be Alice's mom.

Nothing could change that. "You will always be my mother." Alice reached out and touched her shoulder. "No matter what."

Her mother looked like a child who was deeply afraid of the dark, and her eyes darted back and forth across the street corners. Then she stared off at nothing in particular. She tucked her hair behind her ears. "I don't know . . ."

Cymbals clashed from inside, and her mother turned, wiping tears that had begun to stream down her face. "Let me get back in, and I'll see if I can leave. I know we have a lot to talk about."

Alice shook her head. "That's okay. I'll stay and hear the rest of the set."

"Are you sure?"

"Absolutely." With the heaviness currently upon her soul, Alice could use a few hours of jazz right now.

Her mother held open the door for Alice to pass through. This time, Alice chose a spot near the front of the group to sit. The band welcomed the gathering crowd, and her mother waved in her direction. It was a small gesture, but a supremely normal one, and Alice didn't know what to make of how she felt.

Her mother stood before her. Singing. Alive.

So why did her heart still hurt so badly?

"This next song is one of my favorites." With a wide grin, the old trumpet player spoke into her mother's microphone. "We about to have church up in here, y'all."

The crowd laughed, electrified with the pulse of the music, and some of them even clapped.

"How many of you know the old spiritual 'Wade in the Water'?"

The question resulted in another roar from the room.

"When we play this one, I want you to think about what the Good Lord did to bring those Israelites out of slavery and into freedom. He did the same thing for my ancestors, and He does the same thing for us today. How many know what I'm talkin' about?"

"Quit your preachin', Simon!" the drummer yelled.

But the man just shook his head with a smile. He glanced back at the other band members. "Sounds to me like someone's feelin' convicted back there."

Without missing a beat, Simon turned to the crowd. "Harriet Tubman used this song on the Underground Railroad to let the slaves know they'd better jump in the water, away from the dogs. Now, what they singin' about? Why does the Lord trouble the waters? I'll tell you why—because it's *in* the waters, *in* the wading, that healing comes."

"Amen!" several people yelled out.

The man shook his head. The drummer wasn't kidding about this guy preaching. But Alice was mesmerized. She knew the song, but tried to remember the lyrics in her mind.

Only the refrain came back to her, nothing about any references to the Bible.

"When Moses led God's people out of slavery, God didn't take them around the Red Sea, did He? He took 'em *through* it. One step at a time." Simon looked back at the drummer once more. "Relax—I'm almost done."

His gaze trailed over the crowd, and he locked eyes with Alice. He spoke to all of them, and yet, somehow, he spoke directly to her. "Here in New Orleans, we know somethin' about troubled waters."

Alice swallowed hard. Her stomach turned as his words brought a flood of memories back, threatening to dismantle all the fragile ways she'd tied herself back together.

"As we play this song, I hope you know these aren't just the words of an old spiritual. We're singing for our city as well. We're singing for healing to come in the chaos."

Slowly, the drummer began, and the trumpet player joined in. But as her mother sang with Simon, the lyrics captivated Alice. Her very soul danced to the beat of the drum.

"You don't believe I've been redeemed," her mother sang, as Simon repeated, "Wade in the water."

"Just see the Holy Ghost looking for me." Her mother's tone was rich, deep, and beautifully wild. "God's gonna trouble the water."

Alice tapped along to the beat with the toes of her shoes, her spirit fully open to the words as the echo of the chorus began.

This is the answer to the prayers you thought fell on deaf ears. My pause a breath, never silence, as I waded into the waters with you.

Alice stilled.

The words were as clear in her heart as if they'd been spoken aloud. So many times, she'd begged for her healing from heartbreak. So many times, she'd asked God *why*. But as her mother's voice blended with Simon's, a new wisdom settled over Alice's soul, and she thought of Simon's words once more.

It's in the waters, in the wading, that healing comes.

Alice buried her face in her hands as the band brought the refrain to a crescendo. And the tears she'd held back for so long began to fall.

Tears for her mother. Tears for her own abandonment, and the broken pieces of her life and city. Tears of fear that she would never again find a place she belonged.

Tears for the weak moments, and tears for the strong.

Because—she realized—she'd asked for healing but had jumped out of the waters. She'd been begging God to show up for years, seeking restoration. But what if He'd been *in* the fire, and He'd been *in* the waters all along?

TWENTY-SIX

New York, 1861

Clara

The following afternoon, Clara, Rose, and her new mother-in-law were peering into the window display of Macy's dry-goods store, enjoying the brisk New York air as Teddy ran an errand across the street.

"Wouldn't it be something," Clara said, "if the city was filled with storefronts—and not just for the necessary sorts of things, but for frocks and fabrics? Someplace like the stores in London, where women could go and shop among themselves?"

"Unchaperoned?" Her mother-in-law spoke the words as though she couldn't picture it. "Just imagine all the trouble we might get in . . . all the dresses we might buy!"

Clara laughed, and Rose did as well. "I mean it, though," Clara said. "Surely the trend will come across the pond, as they say, eventually. Do you not think so?"

Teddy's mother sighed wistfully. "Sometimes I miss England."

Clara nodded. "Teddy has told me a little about it there, although I confess, I would love to hear more. I find British culture intriguing. From the tea to the countryside to the accents."

"Let me guess." Teddy's mother fussed with her gloves. "Did you acquire the interest from a certain Miss Jane Austen?"

Clara laughed. "How'd you know?"

"Because even *I*, who adores the city of London, want to run away to the countryside and to Pemberley anytime I read her fiction. The way she describes the estates, the dresses, the gardens is mesmerizing."

A woman on the arm of a distinguished gentleman passed them, nodding slightly at Teddy's mother and Clara before taking notice of Rose. She sneered.

"Do you have a problem?" Clara spoke the words boldly, before she considered the provocation could put them in danger. She was grieving with each hour—the loss of her old comforts and for Rose's sake, grieving Ashley—and right now, she happened to be processing her grief through anger. All the injustice of the world had lit her fury, and she was an inch away from letting this stranger know it.

The woman's derision was unabating. She rolled her eyes and put one hand to her hip. "Your rude manner speaks for itself *and* for the company you keep."

Rose was looking down, avoiding eye contact with the woman. Clara's heart hurt thinking about how many times Rose would have to do this. How many times she'd done this already. Well, it wasn't happening today.

Clara straightened her posture. "You are pretentious, heartless, and a fool if you think this free woman does not deserve her rightful place within society. What would President Lincoln say about displays like this one? He would call it shameful, that's what he would do. You ought to live in holy fear for believing yourself more valuable than other human beings—persons the Scriptures say are made in God's image."

Had the woman not held her gloved hand to her mouth, Clara was sure her jaw would have visibly dropped. She hoped her point would sink in through coming days.

"Or do you still believe in the illegal practice of slavery?" Clara added for good measure.

A smirk formed on Rose's lips at that.

"I believe in minding my own affairs," the woman retorted.

"Then mind them, and keep your condescension away," Clara said.

"That's enough now," the man said to his companion. "Let's continue on our way." Together, the two of them strolled down the block, not even once looking back.

Of course, socially speaking, such a display between women outside of a dry-goods store was both unacceptable and completely uncouth. Women did not linger at a window or within a store. They brought a list of items, handed it to a male clerk, waited patiently as he wrapped said items, and then hurried on their way.

But today felt like a good day for talking.

Clara looked back through the window one final time, catching the reflection of Teddy waving. The sound of horse hooves clomping announced the passing of another carriage, and Clara looked at all the dry goods, so neatly displayed.

Teddy stepped onto the sidewalk and waved the post in his hand. "I've word from Oliver here." She desperately hoped the letter her husband carried was from Charleston.

Clara did not miss the enthusiastic hope that flickered in Rose's eyes, her face alight with opportunity. Clara bit down on her bottom lip and fiddled with the buttons of her gloves. She so very much hoped the news from Charleston would be good news—but truthfully, she knew better than to expect it. Mary and Oliver were clever indeed, but Joseph? Joseph was wicked. So wicked, Clara feared his wickedness might defy all other resolve.

Teddy placed the letter in her hands. Clara read it aloud.

Teddy—

First of all, Mary and I send our warmest congratulations to you and Clara on your marriage. The three of you had to flee in such haste, I fear we did not adequately convey how happy we are for your matrimony. Despite the unique circumstances, we trust your marriage will be long lasting and a blessing to you both, as we have nothing but the highest level respect for you and your union.

As for the news on Ashley—I'm afraid it's both good and bad.

Clara hesitated, her breath catching as she noticed the tightening expression around Rose's eyes. She gathered her composure and continued reading, so as not to make this situation even harder for Rose than it already was.

The good is this: Harriet has made contact and learned Ashley is now a house slave and is no longer working the fields. By Harriet's observation, she appeared safe and as well as can be expected given the tragic circumstances. Ashley has also befriended a young woman in the house with whom Harriet has corresponded before, so we hope this connection will be a steady source of information for us.

As for the bad news, when Harriet made a comment to Joseph about his new house slave, he thanked her and said he plans to keep Ashley long-term—that she's a good worker and also that he's got a bet to win.

Clearly, we must devise a plan. But the truth is, Teddy, I'm not sure how we could even get a message to Ashley, let alone attempt an escape. A failed attempt would compromise her safety even further—Joseph is clearly a determined man.

In the meantime, Mary and I will arrange for Harriet to check up on Ashley as frequently as possible. Mary is trying to devise some reason Harriet would be needed at Joseph's estate, and you know my wife—she is bound to come up with something convincing.

Let me know your thoughts. And please give Rose our apologies for the limitations on our ability to help at this time. We don't want to endanger her daughter, but we will also never give up on her.

Sincerely,
Oliver

Slowly, Clara folded the letter and slid it back inside the envelope. Her gaze trailed toward Rose, hoping she might summon something wise or encouraging to offer the woman, though truthfully, she could think of nothing. But Rose's gaze was somewhere else . . . lost in another world.

Rose

It'd be hard puttin' into words how I felt as Clara read that letter. How would any mama feel, to hear her heart is alive and beating but can't be put inside her chest no more? To feel every bruise and every burden as a cut that won't stop bleeding, or else to wall oneself off to the world?

The truth is that all this time, I withstood unthinkable things in the name of holdin' on to the hope of a reunion with my daughter. I shoved humiliation and fear and anger and rage all deep down inside of me, so it wouldn't show on my face and so I *could* keep going. Didn't want nobody to raise an eye at me, didn't want nobody noticing that the one thing I always wanted more than anything was Ashley.

I really believed I would get to her someday.

Maybe I had to believe it—maybe the hope of the impossible was my only way to cope with reality. Really, my only way to keep living.

Weren't for Ashley, I would've been reckless a long time before now. I would've tried to escape without a plan, and they probably would've caught me and either killed me or sold me—and I certainly wouldn't have my "freedom" . . . whatever that word even means.

Because living in the shadows with your head down for fear somebody may recognize you . . . that doesn't feel free.

Everybody actin' like I'm still a slave, or as Clara does, like they owe me favors to make up for what's happened to me . . . that doesn't feel free.

No way to get my own baby because some man's convinced he owns her . . . that doesn't feel free.

Charleston feels so far from here, but it also feels like a blink.

And all I know is somehow, some way, I have got to see my girl.

So I'll wait for the war to be over if I've got to, because I'm sure the Yanks will win eventually and the law will say Ashley has to be released. I will stop at nothing to see her because if I ever stop trying, I can't imagine I'd be able to breathe.

My mind keeps spinnin' with the same old plans I've had for months now, none of which have amounted to anything. Well, I guess that's not true entirely—the work I did with Clara helped Oliver and Teddy heaps, and they in turn helped a good many folks escape into freedom, away from slavery.

Me and Clara and Teddy and Teddy's mother are back at their house now, and my eye catches the rosebush Clara brought with her from Charleston. Good thing she'd already stowed the flower away in the carriage before her weddin', or she never would've had time to grab that thing as we all fled from the plantation.

And looking at that rosebush, the circle I been going 'round and 'round in my mind breaks suddenly, and a new thought comes to me. Maybe I have more to offer than I think.

I may not be able to travel to Charleston and get my baby, but that don't mean I can't send a message to her.

"Clara," I say real quick, as the idea begins to take root.

She turns and looks at me, her eyes wide like she's caught off guard by me speaking up so suddenly and she's worried.

"The post . . . does Teddy plan to return a letter back to Oliver?"

"I'm not sure." She turns her chin slightly, clearly trying to make sense of what I'm saying. "I assume so. Why do you ask?"

"It's just, I have an idea." I take a deep breath, swallowing hard after. "My old dress . . . the one I was sold in . . ."

At the word *sold* Clara flinches slightly, and I know she feels uncomfortable at the thought of it, but this is my reality.

"What about it?" Clara asks.

"That's what I have to offer." Chills run down my arms as I try to catch the right words. "I'm going to cut up the fabric and stitch a rose on it—make it an applique or even a brooch or something. Do you think Harriet would wear it for me? Could she wear it around Ashley—even *give* it to Ashley?"

Clara reaches out and takes hold of both my forearms, gentle but real enthusiastic too. "Rose, you are brilliant. This is perfect." She nods her head. "Yes, Harriet would absolutely do that, and I'm sure she can find a way to get it to Ashley."

Unprovoked, Joseph's threat in the fire thunders within me. I hear him often, in my sleep and in my memory. Sometimes I wonder if I even hear him in my future. *"Come after the slave girl—ever—and I'll kill her. You hear me? I'll kill her."*

See the thing is, I've met men like Joseph before, and I

know he means the words. Much as I want my baby, I want her safe even more.

My heart begins to race, and I wonder if maybe—*maybe*—this will be my way to get back to her.

Maybe this is our hope.

TWENTY-SEVEN

New Orleans, Modern Day

Alice

When Alice returned home that night, she discovered Aunt Charlotte had fallen asleep on the couch—probably waiting up for Alice. And she knew she should probably wake her aunt, tell her all about what happened . . . but she wanted some time alone first, to sort through her emotions.

Because she should be happy.

She should be singularly, unequivocally, unbelievably happy.

She was not.

Guilty was more like it.

Guilty because of her anger, her persistent feeling of loss.

Guilty for not finding her mom until now.

Guilty for feeling guilty.

She thought of their conversation outside Preservation Hall and started to pray—

Please let her be okay. . . .

Then she stopped herself. Because God *had* helped her mother. Her mother was still alive.

So why, instead of relief, instead of gratitude, did Alice have a sense she was spiraling out of control? She felt a strong impulse to repeat the prayer, though she already knew the answer, and the compulsion overwhelmed her with discomfort when she didn't give in.

Next came a wave of something even stronger—an overwhelming sense of despair. The hopelessness that what was once right would be right no longer. And the powerlessness to make anything better.

Alice took off her shoes and hung her purse on the rack by the door.

She thought back to the night of the storm, the night her mother had left, realizing she had no control then, as a child, just as she had no control now. Her mother could vanish from her life all over again within a moment. What was to keep her mom from breaking her heart—ironically, the very thing her mother sought to avoid? And what was to keep Alice from crumbling under the pain?

Alice twirled her fiery red hair into a bun and tugged her yellow cardigan a little closer. She could feel a depressive episode coming on . . . as if she stood teetering on top of a well, dangerously close to falling inside. Her depression always seemed to worsen in the dead of night—in that quiet place before morning when monsters crawl out of hiding.

She'd been to counseling years ago, and the counselor had given her some advice for moving forward in these moments—calming her thoughts and grounding herself in the present reality by using breathing exercises and actively noticing her physical environment.

But now, she was tired. So tired. And not the kind of tired sleep could fix. Even in her dreams, she always saw her mother . . . felt the shattering of broken plans. And she woke up each morning more tired than the last. She couldn't imagine tonight's dreams would be any better.

She was tired in body, tired in spirit, and tired of letting everyone down.

She felt tired down to her bones—worthless, a letdown. Without hope of ever being that happy, talented version of herself again.

Alice grabbed her fuzzy robe, wrapped it around herself, and ambled into the kitchen. She kept replaying the conversation with her mother in her mind, trying to put each piece in its perfect spot as though arranging stems in a bouquet—trying them this way and that until the order formed some type of meaning, some type of cohesion.

Only, memories didn't work like that.

And no amount of replaying them could change what felt like a tainted part of the conversation—something that needed to be edited, corrected, for peace to come. She knew anxiety brought these strong compulsions to her mind but wished she could stop them from coming in the first place.

Sometimes she felt as though she was a prisoner to them. Giving in to the intrusive thoughts only made them more powerful, but fighting them was exhausting. Oh, the counselor would say she should let the waves pass rather than getting caught in the current—but she wondered if the counselor had ever been through a hurricane.

Alice mindlessly scrolled on her phone, looking for a diversion. But her newsfeed was anything but helpful. Photo after photo of friends with their hands on their hips, as if their arms weren't skinny enough to be photographed otherwise. Photo after photo of Pinterest-worthy homes. Swoon-worthy crushes.

All of the photos, so happy. So perfect. So filtered.

But her life was so . . . not.

Alice swallowed hard and shook her head. This was not helping at all. She felt empty and alone.

She had thought finding her mother would bring relief

and closure, but instead, it'd opened up a whole new kind of pain. Because now, in place of fearing for her mother's safety, she grieved her mother's absence—she grieved her mother's choice to stay gone. No matter that she claimed she was doing it to protect Alice from heartache.

Cataloguing all the details of the conversation with her mom, Alice began to critique herself. If this were the big reunion moment, had she enjoyed it enough? Been present enough? Said the right things and felt the right things and noticed all the nuances? She was sure she had missed some of the nuances.

She wanted that conversation to be perfect, but she couldn't make the memory just right, no matter how many times she went over it in her mind. In fact, every rehearsal of their dialogue only made her feel worse—only reminded her how hurt she'd been and how powerless she felt to change history.

She knew she was probably putting too much pressure on herself to be hyper-present, but she felt an inexplicably strong need to hoard all the details, packing them away like her overly full sweater drawer just in case she might need to recall them later. What if she tried to remember the color of the night sky, or the timbre in her mother's voice, or the type of shoes she was wearing, or how she felt precisely when she saw her, and she couldn't? How helpless would she feel, in her inability to capture that moment?

It was almost as though she expected herself to halt time and preserve it, and she knew that was not possible. But still she pushed against the bending of memory with every ounce of resistance she could muster.

Simply put, she hated change.

She hated to lose the past and the people in it as well. And while other people may be excited about their new chapters—relationships and interests and careers—she had always been the type to mourn chapters gone. Probably because she knew all too well the *grief* of chapters gone.

She had never been able to move forward knowing she didn't have her mother.

Alice took a deep breath and set her phone down on the counter.

Maybe a cup of tea would help.

Barefoot, she stepped into the kitchen and opened the pantry door. Aunt Charlotte had restocked their tea supply because the boxes were overflowing. Loose-leaf black tea in bags, and decaf . . . ginger, peach, green, and Sleepytime tea boxes lined the pantry shelves.

Alice pulled the canister with loose-leaf tea down, opened it, and looked into the mountain of tea leaves. She usually preferred to steep this instead of using a bag because it tasted so much better that way, but with all the anxiety she'd been having of late, maybe she'd be better off with decaf. . . .

Alice replaced the lid and put the canister back on the shelf. She reached for the decaf box, then stopped.

She could do peach. . . . it was blended with white tea and didn't have much caffeine. But did she really want a fruity flavor right now?

Alice blinked.

Indecision paralyzed her.

For a reason she could not explain, the choice between the teas seemed impossibly hard. Rationally, she knew it was ridiculous. But the stakes felt so high . . . as though a wrong decision might mean a missed opportunity with the power to forever shift her life.

Even the wrong cup of tea.

Everything—every little thing—came at a crescendo.

Indecision overwhelmed her, and she felt the subsequent panic. She stood in front of the open pantry door, frozen for a full four minutes in indecision, emotionless until she finally began to cry. And then the emotion welled.

Alice wiped the tears from her eyes with the back of her

hand and shut the pantry. Maybe tea wasn't such a good idea right now.

It was dawn—hours later—when Aunt Charlotte woke up and found her still in her robe and wearing llama pajamas, staring down at her computer.

"How long have you been looking at the Sephora website?" Aunt Charlotte quirked an eyebrow and crossed her arms as she studied Alice's laptop.

"Not that long."

Most of my morning was actually spent shopping for leggings.

Aunt Charlotte sat down beside Alice. She had dark circles under her eyes. Even Freckles wasn't awake yet.

"Did I wake you?" Alice asked.

"Don't worry about that. What's going on with you?" Her aunt hugged a pillow to her chest.

"She's all right. I saw her last night."

Aunt Charlotte breathed in deeply, as though for the first time in years. "So it's true. . . . she's okay." Tears began streaming down from her eyes, and she tucked her knees up under her. "How did she look?" She leaned toward Alice, as though desperate for more information.

"Decent, I guess. Older. But then again, she *is* older, and we are too." Alice traced the loose threads of her pajama shirt with her fingers. "I'm having a hard time with it all."

Aunt Charlotte simply pulled Alice to her chest and hugged her. Her nearness was a comfort—she didn't dismiss the reality of Alice's struggle nor did she try to offer advice. She simply sat there, a welcome presence who understood.

Maybe it was the early morning hour. Maybe it was the comfort of her aunt. But for whatever reason Alice couldn't explain, the floodgates opened, and she found the courage—and the words—to say her struggle out loud.

She was cold, so very cold, and she imagined it was the intense emotion mixed with anxiety causing the feeling.

"A lot of well-meaning people have said thoughtless things about my mother in the name of God over the years, and it's damaged my vision of Him, if I'm being honest. Things like 'there's a reason for everything.' Or 'God wouldn't give you more than you can handle.' Even reminders of the good: 'You're so blessed to have your aunt like a second mother.'" Alice shook her head. "And many more have suggested that if I just did a better job trusting Him, or if I just more faithfully pressed into my prayer life, I would unlock all the secrets of heaven and God would heal me, and heal my mother, and fix everything for my own comfort."

"I've heard a version or two of those sentiments myself." Aunt Charlotte reached out a trembling hand to squeeze Alice's own.

"What I don't understand"—Alice shook her head, surprising even herself by her sudden transparency—"is what I've done wrong. Why my prayers didn't work like they were supposed to. I believe in God, sure. But sometimes I still worry. Do I believe in Him *enough*—for heaven, for forgiveness, for peace, and restoration? And if God really knows me like the Bible says, then why do I sometimes feel like I don't know Him well in return? If God has truly redeemed me, why on some days do I still feel broken? And if Jesus has given me His mind and peace, why do I still have doubt about hard things?" Alice realized tears were streaming down her face, and she wiped them away. "I feel the weight, sometimes . . . a lot of times . . . of sustaining my faith by my own effort, even though I know that isn't what the Bible says we should do.

"And if I'm really being honest . . ." She lowered her voice to a whisper. "Sometimes I worry if I don't pray well or in a certain way, I'll accidentally miss the voice of God leading me, and that, in turn, will close a door He would've otherwise opened."

"I understand that feeling. I understand it well, actually."

Aunt Charlotte met her gaze and held it gently. "I think people mean well—I do," she said. "But sometimes they say things that are really shortsighted, and do more harm than good. And these things have hurt me too. If you really stop and think about it, even Jesus prayed a prayer in Gethsemane that wasn't answered the way He wanted it to be. Did He not believe enough in the Father? Did He not pray long enough, or hard enough, or with enough faith? Of course not! The mere thought is ridiculous. And so I wonder if maybe we need to shift our focus away from rosy platitudes that are, quite honestly, easier to say than the alternative—the hard work of keeping our hearts open in the pain. Recognizing that God is with us, whether or not He calms the waves."

Aunt Charlotte patted Alice's hand once more. "And that's not to say fear is what God wants for us, because I don't believe that's true. But it *is* to say you aren't alone in it, Alice. Not hardly. God has never left you, and I haven't either."

"You're right . . ." Alice's voice trailed off as she cozied deeper into the sofa. "I've never thought about it like that before, but even Jesus prayed there'd be some other way than the suffering He endured, and He was the Son of God. And even Lazarus died eventually. Death always comes before resurrection. All this time, I've been so focused on praying my mom back to health that I've missed out on the big picture. It's not about whether I pray fervently enough to unlock some blessing through the right combination of words. It's about God walking with us in our brokenness—a brokenness the Bible warns that in this world, we will all endure. Maybe instead of trying to sidestep the pain, I need to feel it instead, and ask God to help me find a way through."

Another wave of anxiety came, but this time, Alice recognized it for what it was—trauma triggered by seeing her mother yesterday. The intrusive thoughts continued to pass through her mind, but she remembered the thoughts didn't have to make a home there.

Because the thing was, God never promised no more tears this side of heaven. He did not promise that in the here-and-now, He'd fix the world or end the wars or cure our circumstances. He promised to be with us.

And sometimes His with-us felt like an overwhelming sense of His presence, or a breakthrough, or rainbows coming through clouds and long-prayed-for miracles.

But sometimes, it did not.

Sometimes with-us fell silent, amid the roar of an oh-so-broken world.

And we'd err to believe that in either scenario, He is no longer Emmanuel.

And instead of wondering why she wasn't doing enough for Him to take the pain away, Alice, like Job, began to see Him differently. To realize the miraculous is not the only testimony worth sharing.

That Emmanuel, God-with-us, has *kept* us, and from day to day and century to century has *remained* with us through everything.

Through fire, through flood—through hope and despair. Never leaving, never forsaking, even when we doubt very much He is there.

TWENTY-EIGHT

Charleston, January 1862

Ashley

I been a house slave two months now, but even still my fingers shake when I reach for things 'cause I'm so afraid to make a mistake. I don't want to go back to those fields, not ever. Really I just want my mama back, but I know now that will never happen.

See, I've grown up a whole lot in this last year. I'm ten years old now, and I understand how the world works. People like me, when they lose their families, they don't see each other no more.

What breaks my heart the most is that sometimes, it's hard to remember the sound of her voice. And then if I'm real quiet and pay attention, I hear her singin' again, and it breaks my heart all over, only this time for different reasons, and I'm not sure which one's worse.

So today I'm near the front door tidying when a man and woman arrive to have tea with Mister Joseph and his mother. I've seen the man and woman before, and the lady smiled at me which I thought was real curious. I think her name is Harriet.

They both slide their arms out of jackets, and as I prepare to take the coats, that's when I see what the woman is wearing, and honest to goodness it hits me so hard I can't speak because I'm in such a stupor.

Then the lady catches my gaze and holds it there a real long time, though white people ain't supposed to do this, and it's like she's trying to tell me something, and then she nods her head once—very, very slowly like she's sayin' *yes, it's your mama's.*

On this woman's dress is a brooch made out of fabric. And that wouldn't be sayin' much noteworthy, except for the fabric it is. 'Cause that brooch is made out of my mama's old dress, and I would recognize it anywhere.

The brooch is shaped as a small heart, and on it, a tiny embroidered rose.

Rose.

The connection to my mama's name is obvious, like a signature of her love.

A love that floods my heart with warmth and color, bright as the promise of the rainbow, and just as sure. With its wave, emotion washes over my body, and I think I may be faint because I know—I *know*—I just got a message from her.

When Mister Joseph and his mother enter the room, the woman does something real unexpected. She takes her fingers so gentle-like and removes the pin from her collar before anyone but me can take notice. She covers it with her hand, and in one stealth move slides it under my own as she offers me her jacket.

The fabric brings back a familiarity, a sense of comfort, that I thought was lost forever. The security of knowing no matter what happened, my mother was always—*always*—going to seek me out and find a way for reconciliation.

No matter the fires, no matter the floods.

I would never be far from her.

It wasn't until later that night when I got settled on the cot in my room that I dared take a closer look at the brooch and realized it had a pocket.

Inside that pocket were two butterfly buttons, so beautiful they looked as though they may catch flight and carry me away from here. At least they would do so in my imagination, and in my memory.

See, these buttons, they represent somethin' real important to me. A love that's never failing. Beauty that just keeps on. And a hope for the future.

My mother's buttons.

My mother's heart, in me.

Somehow, she found me, here at Mister Joseph's house. And I don't know if she is coming for me or if she *can* ever come for me, but in this moment, my heart swells to know I am loved and seen.

Maybe I can get a message back to her, if that lady ever comes back for tea . . . 'cause I have a feeling I'm only at the beginning of this story.

New York City, March 1862

Clara

When Teddy came around the corner into the library, Clara was sitting beside a window, reading from her new book *Uncle Tom's Cabin*. She immediately noticed the envelope in his hands, set her book down, and stood.

"Is that a letter?" she asked him.

He pressed a kiss to her temple, sending a shimmy of sensations down the back of her neck. "It is," he said, a glimmer in his eyes.

Clara tilted her head. "Why do you seem so eager?"

He opened her palm and set the letter inside. "You'll soon see."

Anxious anticipation rose in Clara, and she consciously stilled herself as she opened the envelope and took a peek inside. Immediately, she knew she needed to find Rose.

As it turned out, Rose was outside in the little garden when Clara went looking for her. Rose turned from the plant she was pruning as Clara hurried toward her.

"What's got you in such a hurry?" she asked.

Clara practically skipped forward, holding out the envelope. "Rose, you have to see this. We just received a letter from Charleston. Or should I say, *you* just received a letter from Charleston."

Rose frowned quizzically, wiping the soil from her hands against her dress before reaching for the correspondence. "What do you mean?" But she held the envelope and reached inside before Clara could respond. Soon, her fingers found the fabric, and she pulled it the rest of the way from the envelope.

Rose covered her mouth with her other hand, and her shoulders began to tremble, a clear indication Clara's suspicion had been right.

"This is from Ashley," she whispered, holding the tiny embroidered sampler as though it were Britannia metal or the rarest of gems. "What a fine job she did on it too." Rose handed the envelope back to Clara and traced the embroidery with her thumb.

On the tiny sampler was a carefully stitched heart beside a small rose—a clear message of love for her mother—as well as an orange flame and a little bird perched on the rosebush. A swallow, perhaps?

"I hope I'm not being presumptuous," Clara said. "But what does it mean?"

Rose breathed in the gentlest of breaths, her shoulders lifting as though a weight had been lifted from them and the corners of her lips lifting softly too. "Hope," she said, simply.

"Hope?" Clara repeated.

Rose nodded, pointing to the iconography. "The little flame represents the fire several months ago, most likely she's sayin' she came through it okay. And the bird?" Rose met Clara's eyes, her own filled with budding tears and wistful memory. "It's a swallow. Swallows are meant to represent safe homecoming." The tears in the corners of Rose's eyes fell, running down her cheeks and chin. In fact, they seemed to keep falling, as though the whole of them that'd been bottled up had suddenly come unstuck. "Clara, do you understand? This means . . ." Rose's voice trailed off, and she shook her head. "Well, it means Ashley *did* get the buttons, and she's come up with a way to contact me through Harriet. May not be what I'd hoped for in a reunion . . . but it's so much more than I'd feared. Having a way to contact her, even in this manner, changes everything."

Rose's words set a new hope within Clara, and she wondered if over time, Harriet may be able to pass or even teach Ashley a code similar to the one Rose and Clara had used. Maybe with something like that, they could pass even more complex messages—and maybe Ashley could even learn to read and write.

Maybe the war would eventually end, and abolition would eventually come. Maybe Ashley would be free by the law, and maybe Joseph's need for control would finally subside.

Maybe someday, Rose could return to Charleston. And Clara and Teddy could as well.

Maybe the future would look different from the past in all its wrongdoing, and similar to the past in all its virtue. Maybe a generation would come—generations, even—that would see value in Clara's hidden silver and in Rose and Ashley's precious buttons. The value in their stories.

And maybe—*maybe*—it could start right now.

Not when the war was over or when Ashley was free or when Clara and Teddy ceased being on the run from Joseph and her own family. But right now, in the midst of the hardship.

She remembered a verse from Isaiah. *"When thou passest through the waters, I will be with thee; and through the rivers, they shall not overflow thee: when thou walkest through the fire, thou shalt not be burned; neither shall the flame kindle upon thee."*

Clara had never appreciated the Scripture's application until now, nor had she understood its further articulation—*"Fear not,"* the passage said. *"For I am with thee."*

In waters, in rivers, in flames.

And what did that mean, exactly? Perhaps empowering the feet of the faithful to keep going toward reconciliation, both divine and earthly.

Alighting with the hope of the reunion.

Emerging from the chrysalis of hardship, having been given the wings of faith.

From age to age, always passing through.

"Do you think we might be able to send more messages to Ashley?" Rose's hopeful note brought Clara's attention back to their conversation.

"Yes, Rose," Clara said, putting a gloved hand at the structured waistline of her dress. "I think we might send *many*."

And Rose cradled the embroidery to her chest, a correspondence from a once-lost daughter who was so deeply treasured.

TWENTY-NINE

New Orleans, Modern Day

Alice

Alice adjusted the cross-body satchel at her hip and looked up at the ironwork of the second story of her mother's apartment building. Alice was familiar with the area because of its proximity to the French Quarter, but this marked her first time on this particular corner, at this particular apartment.

She buzzed the front security panel for access, and from upstairs, her mother put her through.

Alice decided to climb the stairs rather than take the elevator—a choice she regretted by the time she made it all the way to the top, slightly out of breath as she stood at her mother's door.

A wave of panic washed over her. What was she doing? Was this really the right decision? But she shook her head. She would not allow herself to overthink this. Instead, she lifted her fist and knocked three times on the front door.

When her mother opened it, with a bright smile and holding a cup of coffee, Alice had to admit—she was a little taken aback by how good her mother looked. "Hi, Mom," she said, her heart swelling with gratitude that last night's meeting had not been a mirage and that her mother had not disappeared thereafter.

"Hi, sweetheart," she said, gesturing past the doorway. "Please, come in."

Alice did just that, and discovered another mug of coffee had been set out on the corner of the small kitchen bar. Before she could ask, her mother confirmed she'd poured it for her. Needing no further prompting, Alice took a sip.

It was then she smelled the Elizabeth Arden perfume. Everything familiar and good about her childhood and her mother's comfort washed over her in one fell swoop.

She took another sip of the coffee, looking around the apartment.

It was the size of a mouse house but decorated with cute colors. She spied a full bath the usual size of a half bath and imagined it must be original to the historic building. One central room had just enough space for a couch, two chairs, and a circular kitchen table, and just behind that was a modest kitchen.

The space was decorated in a very bohemian style, which was right up Alice's alley. She loved the two fiddle-leaf fig trees her mother was growing near the window, and the large art pieces on display too.

It was all very tidy, though a little disorganized, and it reminded Alice of her mother's personality—at least as Alice had once known her.

Her mother turned toward the kitchen bar and grabbed a box of pastries. "I have some cinnamon rolls here—do you want one with your coffee?"

Alice took a seat in one of the kitchen chairs, being careful that her coffee didn't drip. "That'd be great. Thank you."

Her mother warmed the cinnamon rolls for a few seconds before bringing them to the table. The fragrance was heavenly.

She held her fork midair, ready to take a bite. "Hey . . . I recognize you're probably looking for answers, and that I've caused you so much pain." She set her fork down, pulling her long hair from her shoulders and twisting it into a bun at the nape of her neck. "I'm so sorry, Alice. You'll never know how sorry I am. I hope you can believe that."

Alice hesitated, trying to find the right words. "I do . . . of course I do."

Her mother reached for her coffee mug with both hands. "Good." She took a deep breath, as though finding her resolve. "Then I guess we should start at the beginning." Her gaze trailed somewhere past Alice entirely. "How much do you already know?"

"Just that Juliet stopped you from jumping off a bridge." Alice pushed the cinnamon roll back and forth on her plate, taking tiny bits of frosting onto her fork, as the sweet nibbles were all she could stomach after saying those words.

Her mother ran one hand over her eyes. "Not my proudest moment, but yes." She met Alice's gaze. "You have to understand the backstory. . . . I had just lost your brother several months into my pregnancy, and I found out your father was cheating on me. I had clinical depression as a result of the miscarriage, but postpartum depression isn't something people talk about when there's no living baby, and so for a long time I suffered in silence. The infidelity was the final straw. I just felt so worthless, so helpless, without hope that things would ever get any better." She shook her head. "Depression is like that, if you've never experienced it—it plays cruel games with your mind, and getting healthy is overwhelming when you feel so weak."

Alice bit down on her bottom lip. "What happened after you saw Juliet?" What she really wanted to ask was *Why did you never come back for me?* But there would be a good time for that question, and this was not it.

Her mother took a bite of her cinnamon roll. She hesitated a long moment. "To be completely honest, Alice, I went through some things I still don't like talking about." With that, she took another drink of her coffee. "I ended up in St. Bernard Parish at a friend's house, but when I got there, I realized she had evacuated. So I was all alone with her cat . . . and actually, that cat saved me. I don't know what came upon me, but when I heard that loud boom and the levees broke, and the waters started rising so quickly, all I could think was that I had to get that cat out of there. I had to get it to safety."

Alice shook her head. "You come by it honestly, I guess—if you only knew how many animals Aunt Charlotte saved after the storm."

Her mother smiled.

"Go on," Alice urged.

Slowly, her mother nodded. "First we climbed up onto the refrigerator, but I quickly realized that wouldn't be tall enough, and so I grabbed the biggest kitchen knife I could find and cut a hole through the ceiling, then the roof. Debris was flying everywhere . . . houses too. Some of them seemed to simply disappear." Her expression turned absent. "Not many people survived in the Parish."

A cold sweat ran down Alice's back at the thought of her mother waiting for help on a rooftop, just like those people in the photos she'd seen on the news. "How long were you up there?"

"About a day. Then a volunteer firefighter came by in a boat—but some people had to wait far longer. I got out of there before the oil spilled and the water was toxic. Not long after my rescue, all the crews had to wear hazmat suits. It was really bad there, Alice." When she met her gaze, Alice knew *really bad* meant *worse than you can imagine*—and a tremble came over Alice as she considered what kind of horrible trauma her mother had gone through during that storm.

"I did try to come home at one point, about a week later. I was so worried about you." Her mother took another sip of her coffee, and Alice did too, thankful it gave her something to do with her shaking hands.

"What happened?" Alice asked. But she knew.

"You were already gone by then. A neighbor told me you'd come through the storm just fine and that your Aunt Charlotte had you." She swallowed visibly. "This is the part that's hard to understand, but Alice, when I heard you were with my sister, I knew I needed so much help and I really and truly believed you were better off with her, which is why I disappeared."

Finally, they were getting into the heart of what Alice had wondered for so long. But the answers didn't sit well with her, souring the coffee in her stomach. "Even if you thought Aunt Charlotte was more stable or capable or whatever, why would you *ever* think you could just vanish from my life as though you were never there?"

Her mother let the bun out of her hair and loose waves cascaded beautifully down. "If I had showed back up, you would've come to live with me, and you would've suffered for it."

"What?" Alice shook her head. "How could you believe you had so little value to me?" She decided to say what she was thinking. "I'm sorry, I don't mean to be harsh. I know what you went through was very real trauma and it couldn't have been easy. It's just that . . . I needed you."

Her mother didn't hesitate. "I needed you too."

Alice closed her eyes. The words, though painful, were also a balm to a wound that had been open for years. They would get through this now, one way or another—they would grieve the years they missed while maybe finally having hope for a different future.

"Was there a turning point for you?" Alice asked her.

"Yes. That friend I was trying to meet in the Parish the night of Katrina? Years later, I told her I felt God had left me and I was invisible. She looked into my eyes and said—*'What if the problem isn't that you aren't valuable to God, but that you assumed going through hardship meant He'd abandoned you?'* When she said that, something clicked. Now, don't misunderstand—it wasn't an instant fix or anything. I still struggled for a long while after that, and to some extent, I struggle still . . . but that realization shifted something in me. It was the moment I realized the circumstances of my life, both good and bad, are not an indication of the presence or absence of God."

These words struck a chord in Alice like no other.

She simply blinked in response to them.

Because this was exactly, in her own way, what she had believed about God and her mother. And this was exactly the truth she needed to hear.

"Mom," Alice said, reaching out to take her mother's hand across the table. "I love you." Tears began to stream down her face, and tears streamed down her mother's too.

"Oh Alice," her mother said, a wobbly smile on her lips. "If only you knew how I love you. How I've always loved you. How I always will."

Three hours after their heart-to-heart, a hummingbird flitted to the rosebush and jasmine Alice's mother was growing on the little patio outside, and Alice thought of Juliet. She remembered she had meant to ask about the needlepoints while here, so she pulled up the photos of them on her phone.

"You wouldn't happen to recognize these from the attic of the old house, would you?"

Alice's mother leaned closer, getting a better look. "Actually, I do. I was always interested in those samplers and even took some of them with me. A couple weeks after the storm, I got brave one day and returned to the house . . . but of course you were already staying with your aunt, and your father was out on the oil rig. The weeks after Hurricane Katrina were so chaotic, it was hard to know where people had gone." She shook her head. "Anyway, I went up to the attic and grabbed the needlepoints, as well as a few other sentimental items I'd been storing up there. But my mind was still in a thousand different places, and I left behind the heirlooms that you recently found. I always meant to come back for them. . . ."

She stood up straighter, turning toward the bookcase. "Do you want the ledger?"

Alice's heart began to race. "The *ledger*?"

"Yeah . . ." Her mother pulled an old leather notebook from a bookshelf and brushed off a layer of dust from it. "This was stored along with those needlepoints when I first found them. I always thought it seemed like a codebook, but I couldn't make heads or tales of the meanings."

Alice nearly leapt out of her chair to get her hands on that notebook. "Would you mind if I take a look?"

"Be my guest." Her mother smiled, holding out the ledger.

And when Alice carefully opened the antique pages, she knew she'd found just what she was looking for.

Later that afternoon, Alice parked her bicycle outside The Prickly Rose and tightened the lock cable, slipping the key into the pocket of her cherry-patterned skirt. The jasmine vine blooming from a pot outside the flower shop mingled with the fragrance of the clipped flowers indoors as she pulled the door open and stepped through.

The bell chimed at her arrival, and she smiled at Aunt

Charlotte, who was behind the counter, putting an arrangement together.

"How did that go?" Aunt Charlotte asked, clipping a pink strawflower. They were able to get so many strawflowers last week, they'd kept some for arrangements and had dried others to use in wreaths. Strawflowers held their color despite being dried, and the wreaths always turned out beautiful. Time consuming, yes, but beautiful. Great for the transition from winter to spring. Alice once saw an Etsy listing that called similar wreaths everlasting strawflowers, and she liked the phrasing so much she'd thought of them that way ever since.

"Remarkably well. She wants to have you over sometime in the next few days if you're up for it."

Aunt Charlotte raised her eyebrows. "That . . . that would be wonderful." Taking Alice's hands in her own, she got choked up with emotion. "Actually, Alice. That would be a gift."

Alice nodded, squeezing her aunt's hands in return. "Have I ever told you how much I appreciate all that you've done for me?"

Her aunt pulled her into a tight hug. "I'd like to have you believe that, but the truth is, I'm the one who owes you big time. I don't know where I'd be without you." She looked around the store. "I don't know where the flower shop would be without you, either."

Alice grinned. "So you want to hear something amazing? Do you remember those needlepoints I told you about? The ones I found in the attic of the old house—that Juliet encouraged me to study?"

"Of course." Aunt Charlotte paused in the middle of her work, her eyes wide. "Did you find something?"

"Yes!" Alice tried to keep from jumping up and down inside the store. "Turns out, my mother had a ledger for the arbitrary symbols like names and locations, and I was able to put that together with what I already knew about the floriology."

"And . . . ?"

Alice stepped closer to the counter where Aunt Charlotte was working. "I confirmed that Sullivan's ancestor was a spy, just like Juliet suspected, and that their families knew each other way back when. I also uncovered a ton of interesting war-related messages that show Clara was working for the Union while living in a Confederate household and engaged to a Confederate soldier. But most fascinating of all . . . I learned that Millie and Juliet's ancestors *did* communicate with each other, even though they were sold to different places. The circumstances were heartbreaking, but in a way, they still found each other." Alice set to work organizing individual stems into their respective containers, creating a mosaic of fragrant color. "I'm going to stop by Juliet's house later today and let her know. She and Millie are going to be amazed."

Aunt Charlotte set down her clippers. "I'm so glad you pursued this."

"Me too," Alice said. "And this is just the beginning. I want to learn more about them, now that I know where they lived and that Clara was involved in espionage." She snapped her fingers, remembering one more thing. "I can't believe I almost forgot this part! As it turns out, the rosebush at Juliet's house—the one she said holds secrets? Well, it's a cultivar that goes all the way back to the Civil War when Clara pulled it out of the ground, just before the Great Fire of 1861 destroyed much of Charleston. So not only did it survive through Hurricane Katrina, but it also survived through that fire. The very last rose there—yet it continues to thrive and bloom."

"What a beautiful image. Sounds like a story waiting to be written," Aunt Charlotte said. "Maybe you could write it with a certain tall and handsome business consultant."

Alice rolled her eyes and smirked. "You just never give up, do you?"

"I'm sorry." Aunt Charlotte laughed, holding up both hands. "I couldn't resist."

But truthfully, Alice delighted in the talk about Sullivan. She had missed him the last couple days and wanted to give him a full update but didn't know what would be appropriate, given the awkward way they'd parted ways.

He was never far from her mind, and thoughts of him made her heart all aflutter, no matter how hard she'd tried to push them away. Getting over him was going to be easier said than done once he went back to Charleston, and she was dreading it.

Both Alice and Aunt Charlotte had gone back to their work when the bell above the door chimed, and Declan came in, wearing khakis, a Polo, and loafers, like he was on his way to a job interview.

Alice turned her head. "Hi, Declan! Can't say I expected to see you here. Would you like to get Lucy a bouquet?" He was always making sweeping romantic gestures, and she wouldn't be at all surprised if he planned to get Lucy a just-because arrangement. Alice loved hearing all Lucy's updates about their relationship as the two of them had gotten more serious. Lucy had the patience of a saint, putting up with all of Declan's passionate and stubborn ideas, but she was rewarded for it by him treating her like royalty.

"Actually . . ." Declan stepped closer, taking in the canisters of different types of flowers that were bundled together like a fragrant, beautiful perimeter all around the room. "I was wondering if it's possible to order five hundred roses before we leave for Charleston."

Alice had learned to expect the unexpected with Declan, but *that* . . . well, that was unexpected. "I'm sorry. Did you say five *hundred* roses?"

Declan slid his hands into his pockets and grinned widely. "I did. . . ."

Alice's eyes widened with realization, and chills ran down her arms as she ran from where she was standing to throw her arms around Declan in celebration. "Yes, I can absolutely get them for you. There are several flower markets up the way that we source special orders from, and roses are common enough that we shouldn't have any trouble getting that many. Oh my goodness, Declan. You're going to propose!"

He nodded, still grinning. "Tomorrow, if you can get the flowers by then. I don't know how I'm going to keep it a secret."

"Me neither!" But Alice did know she couldn't wait to see what tomorrow would hold for her best friend Lucy. And maybe for her too . . . because she still hadn't talked with Sullivan.

THIRTY

New Orleans, Modern Day

Alice

It took some doing—driving to multiple flower markets and filling up the delivery van top to bottom—but Alice did manage to find five hundred roses for Declan's proposal, and she even managed to do it with twelve hours to spare.

Sullivan had volunteered to help her get all the flowers set up in the shop, just *before* closing time, and any minute now, Declan and Lucy would be here.

The plan was for Declan to text Sullivan when they'd found a parking spot so that Sullivan and Alice could make themselves scarce for the big romantic reveal. Then they'd pop out of hiding to get some pictures while the moments were still memorable.

Alice stepped into the "room" where they kept bouquets that were complete and ready for delivery. It was no larger than a closet, really—and was stocked top to bottom with an array of flowers that'd been prepared for weddings, special orders, and subscription services. The fragrance of all those beautiful sentiments bound up in one little corner was so strong yet airy, Alice's heart did a little skip of joy every time she came in here. It very well might be her favorite place in the world.

On her way in, she grabbed a praline from a basket Aunt Charlotte had set out and broke off a small piece, savoring the sugar-glazed pecan on her tongue as she scanned the rows of complete bouquets. Yes, everything looked to be in its place and ready for tomorrow. She should be okay to lock up and leave the store right after the engagement for the party after.

She took another bite of her praline, turning to exit the room when somebody hurried inside and shut the door.

"Sullivan?"

"Sorry, I panicked. They're on their way."

The little room was barely big enough for one person to be comfortable, let alone two. Not that she was complaining. The fragrance of the flowers mingled with the smell of his shampoo and a hint of coffee she guessed came from the cup he was carrying around earlier.

She took another bite of her praline.

"Do we have time to go outside and take cover?" she asked.

"I don't think so . . . not without walking through the middle of the store," he whispered, his face inches from her own. "Declan wasn't specific about how long their walk here would be."

A wave of jitters flooded Alice at the thought of her dear friend getting engaged any minute. She was living vicariously through Lucy, and she was loving it.

"Well, I guess there are worse places to be stuck."

He caught her gaze, and she couldn't put it into words, exactly, but something shifted in that moment between them. He swallowed visibly. "Definitely," he murmured.

Suddenly nervous, Alice started chattering. "Is this exciting or what? It's so romantic, don't you think? All those flowers—it's like roses as far as the eye can see." *Roses as far as the eye can see—really?* She chided herself for saying something so silly.

Sullivan shrugged. "I guess so. If you're into that kind of thing." He bit down on his bottom lip, never looking away from her gaze. Now her heart did a twirl for another reason entirely. "Not really my style, though."

"Oh really?" Wide-eyed, Alice looked back at him, blinking. "What *would* your style be, then, Sullivan?"

He tucked one wild auburn curl behind her ear, and her pulse began to pick up pace. She wondered if she was imagining this whole thing, or if it was really happening.

She leaned against the closed door of the little bouquet room.

He took a half step closer to her. "I lead with a few less theatrics."

"Hmm," she nodded, smiling up at him. "Just like your late arrival on Valentine's Day."

His eyes twinkled in humor. "You still let me in, didn't you?" He put one hand on the door, his grin widening.

"You do realize we are having this conversation in a closet full of flowers, which is pretty much as dramatic as it gets, don't you?"

He raised his eyebrows, his gaze lowering to her lips. "Are you quite done giving me a hard time?"

"I don't think I'm ever going to be done—"

The bell above the entryway chimed, signaling Declan and Lucy were here. But as Sullivan moved closer toward Alice, she could process nothing else besides the thrill of anticipation she felt about his kiss. His lips found her own, and she was breathless, caught up in the magic of the moment and his nearness. When he ended the kiss, she grabbed his shirt and pulled him back for another.

Though their lips only touched a moment, everything

around them was a blur—a spinning bunch of flowers full of fragrance and hope and promises to come.

It was Lucy's shout of glee from the other room that brought her back to reality.

Alice caught her breath, grinning and looking up at him. She patted his shirt casually. "We better get back out there."

"Mhmm." He looped his arm around her waist and kissed her once more on the tip of her nose.

She reached for the door handle, turning to look up at him over her shoulder. "For the record, Sullivan, I'm a fan of your style."

His grin was dangerous, and she didn't know how she was going to go take engagement photos for Lucy when all she could think about was when he would kiss her again.

"Did I mention I'm moving to New Orleans?" He murmured. "I was offered a marketing job here."

He had her full attention. But who was she kidding? He always had. "I hope you're not following a girl. You know, they say never to do that."

"I don't know—she's pretty reliable." He brushed a kiss to the top of her head. "And in the words of Frank Sinatra, I have a feeling the best is yet to come."

$\backsim$

Charleston, Modern Day
Six Months Later

Alice

Alice and Sullivan found themselves in the bridal party for yet another wedding, as Declan and Lucy prepared to take vows to one another in the garden of Lucy's historic home on Longitude Lane in Charleston.

Life had changed in many ways since her kiss with Sullivan inside the flower shop. Her mom had begun coming to Sunday dinners with Alice and her aunt, and was seeking treatment for her chronic depression. Alice and Sullivan had been happily dating for months. And Alice had begun volunteering by doing music classes. She was even considering pursuing qualifications for leading music therapy.

Lucy and Declan had planned a small but intimate ceremony, with a white runner and folding chairs set up along the middle of the garden which Lucy had explained once belonged to her ancestor, Eliza. The carriage house and brick wall beyond them added an extra appeal of historical romance, as did the fairy lights they'd draped along the bricks.

But at heart, the most beautiful thing were the flowers—flowers in every shade and shape, from roses to jasmine, the roots growing deep. Alice took a deep breath of the fragrance—for every garden had its own unique blend of florals, and this one was no exception.

The ceremony was set for late afternoon, when the birds would be singing from the trees. It was the most magical time of day in the garden, Lucy said.

Alice took a seat beside Juliet's mother, Millie, who was a dear friend to both the bride and groom through their connections to Peter and Harper, as well as through the extended families.

Alice watched a butterfly float through the air just behind Millie. It flew on whimsy's wings toward the roses, and its wings of orange and yellow glowed in the scattering of sunlight through the trees.

The butterfly perched, and Alice stood in awe of the mighty roses where it landed—Clara's roses. The rosebush that spanned one and a half centuries, and the spread of blooms that boasted their age.

Alice marveled at the flowers. Huge, fragrant, God-praising blooms. That rose, transplanted and broken, giving beauty to this ground. The dirt and the seed, the flood and the flame, all writing a story of where we belong.

Where roses grow, but more than that. Where roses bloom, and where life—full and glorious at its crescendo—finds its meaning over and over again.

Maybe the important thing was the same root bound them through any circumstance and any ground. And after a few months, or maybe a few years, the rose would bloom again.

The rose always bloomed again.

Because somewhere, deep within that plant, was life—abundantly.

Alice looked out beyond the roses, to that hazy space on the horizon between the heavens and the earth where the two became one.

"How are you today, Millie?" She smiled, setting her hand on Millie's knee. The woman wore a beautiful gown of crimson fabric that was vintage in style and matched the red cloche on her head.

"I'm well, thank you." Millie's smile was warm. She shifted in her seat to face Alice. "I've been meaning to thank you for all you did to help Juliet uncover the story behind those needlepoints. I've wondered about Rose my entire life. . . ." Millie shook her head. "I've only known her as my Grandma Ashley's mama, and truth be told, she seemed more legend than real to me." Millie breathed deeply. "But not anymore. Now I know her story. And I see how threads from it have woven through my own life, and—I hope—also through my daughters'."

"You're very welcome, Millie." Alice patted Millie's knee. "I really enjoyed learning more about their history. Thank you for the privilege of knowing it."

"Did Juliet tell you they're going to put a historical marker in front of this house? Since that's where Rose and Clara ferried the messages to the Union army?"

"No way!" Alice adjusted her pearl necklace. "What a great way to honor them."

"I thought so too," Millie said.

"On that topic, there's actually something I want to show you." Alice pulled the ledger her mother had given her from her purse, turning to the page she had marked. She handed it to Millie so the woman could read the diary-style entry for the first time.

"What's this?" Millie took the ledger from Alice and held it gently.

"You'll see." Alice smiled.

Millie began to read Clara's entry aloud.

This morning, we returned to the house on Longitude Lane, which I now own. We brought the rosebush with us, and Rose and I planted it close to where we buried the silver. A quiet hush settled over us in that holy moment as we thought of the fire. I know we were both grieving for all that happened. That rosebush, poetically speaking, was sort of like our hope for the future. It'd been ripped up and transplanted, shaken and moved around. And yet, as Rose said, it bloomed. And will continue blooming still.

From the broken ground, somehow those delicate, vibrant petals came anew, offering a fragrance that might catch on the breeze and carry down the street to where the bluebirds flew.

And that rosebush carries with it a heritage, too—from the ground where the last rose blooms.

"Well, isn't that something." Tears glistened from the corners of Millie's eyes. She offered the ledger back to Alice, but Alice shook her head.

"Why don't you keep it?"

Millie hesitated. "Are you sure?"

"Absolutely." Alice grinned. "After all, their story is yours."

"Thank you, sweetheart." Millie tapped her red-painted

fingernails against the ledger. "You know, it's funny how through it all—the failures that tear at us from the seams, and the gardens of our lives, and the fires and the floods and the people who long for one another . . . through it all, the theme was always reconciliation. And maybe even as we long for these reconciliations, there's a deeper redemption to be had there."

Alice sat back in her chair, mesmerized by Millie's words as the sentiments took root. "You have a lot of wisdom, Millie. I'd love to hear more about your story someday."

Millie grinned back at her, adjusting her cloche. "Good— because I intend on living a lot more of it."

Alice chuckled at her words, always inspired by her tenacity, and watched as the approaching twilight colored the horizon. A hazy, fiery sunset fell upon the fountain waters, and the steady dripping reflected the clouds. All the flowers, all the pieces, all the fragments, blended into the bigger picture, and the picture became something of beauty.

But what if it was beautiful all along?

A NOTE ON HISTORICAL ACCURACY

The rose in this story was inspired by a cultivar that survived during Hurricane Katrina, despite being submerged under saltwater for two weeks. That rose became a symbol of hope to many, as its cuttings were sold through the Peggy Martin Rose Fund with proceeds given to help rehabilitation and beautification efforts post-Katrina. Cultivars of that rosebush are now growing all over the Gulf Coast, as a message of hope and survival.

Edisto Island was evacuated near the beginning of the Civil War because General Lee thought the island too difficult to try to defend. Many formerly enslaved people went free as a result, on this island once renowned for its sea island cotton. While in the story, the fires burning on Edisto occur in May of 1861, in real life this happened several months later. I adjusted the dates a bit to make the development of Teddy and Clara's relationship less hurried, but it is true that cotton planters set fire to their own homes on the island before they evacuated. As the war continued, the Union did their share of crop-burning as well. By November, most of the planters were gone, and refugee camps were created by and for those who had escaped from slavery.

In December of 1861, as the Civil War was escalating, a mysterious fire destroyed a large portion of Charleston, South Carolina, and may have ultimately helped the Union win the Civil War. St. Andrews Hall, where Clara and her family attend the ball early in the story, was among the many buildings that were destroyed. All that remains of St. Andrews Hall is the fence around the property.

To date, no one knows what started the fire.

A NOTE TO READERS

Dear reader,

It's a bit surreal to think this is the final novel for our HEIRLOOM SECRETS friends. These characters have been with me so long, in different ways. I want to thank all of you who have read and supported this series—it's truly been a privilege to share these stories with you, and an absolute dream come true.

A special thank you to each and every one of you who has reached out to tell me what these stories have meant to you.

I want to make a very important note that if you find yourself identifying with Alice or her mother's mental health struggles, you are not alone. Please reach out to your doctor about counseling and/or medication. Help is readily available.

Where the Last Rose Blooms was actually written before I drafted *The Dress Shop on King Street*. Wouldn't you know that the edits of this story would come years later, at the end of the year 2020? I was in a season where the ground seemed unsteady beneath my feet, and I wondered at times what I had to offer readers from the brokenhearted place I was in after a very difficult loss in my life. But through it all, I sensed a deeper message anchoring this story and me, too—that God is with us, no matter what we walk through. We may at times feel disoriented by life, and that's okay. We don't have to "fix" our circumstances or our feelings to rest in His faithfulness—and sometimes, admitting doubt and fear and struggle can be the loudest witness to His grace.

But make no mistake—God is with us. He is with us in whatever we walk through, walking through it too and loving us just the same.

I hope to connect with you through social media and through my newsletter, which you can sign up for at www .ashleyclarkbooks.com. May the Lord bless you, strengthen you, and remind you that whatever you face, He loves you and is there beside you.

—Ashley Clark

If you or someone you know is struggling with mental illness, help is just a call or text away.

Text "HELLO" to 741741 for the Crisis Text Line, or call 1-800-273-TALK (8255) for the National Suicide Prevention Lifeline to speak with someone who can help you.

BOOK CLUB QUESTIONS

1. Which setting did you prefer, New Orleans or Charleston? Have you ever been to either of these places?

2. Rose and Ashley's story was difficult to write because I knew their fictional journey represented many people's actual lives during that time in history. What do you think happens to Rose and Ashley after the end of the novel?

3. Why is Alice so annoyed by Sullivan showing up late to the flower shop? Why is reliability so important to her? Can you relate to either her or Sullivan?

4. The book juxtaposes the natural disasters of fire and flood throughout the storylines. What do you think these things represent, and how do they relate to the verse (Psalm 66:12) at the beginning of the book?

5. Millie from *The Dress Shop on King Street* makes several appearances in this story. If you read *The Dress Shop on King Street*, how would you say Rose and Ashley's story relates to her own?

6. You may remember Eliza's character from *Paint and Nectar*. Were you surprised to find she is Clara's granddaughter? What characteristics do you think she shares with Clara?

7. Did you find yourself empathetic toward Alice's mother? In what ways? Does she share any characteristics with Rose?

8. Did any moments in the story surprise you? Which ones and why?

9. Aunt Charlotte is a fun character who's always there when Alice needs her. How do you think Alice's story—both on and off the page—would have been different without her aunt?

10. The title of this book, *Where the Last Rose Blooms*, refers to the rose Clara plucks from the scene of the fire. After having finished the story, what do you think the title means?

ACKNOWLEDGMENTS

This series represents so many prayers and dreams and hopes come true. To everyone who has been a part of that journey, thank you. I have been abundantly blessed by you, and am abundantly grateful God has allowed me the opportunity to steward these stories.

What a gift it has been to come alongside Bethany House in getting these stories to readers. Everything Bethany House does, from cover design to editing, they do with excellence. It's been such a privilege to be part of their publishing family.

Thank you to Raela Schoenherr—you take my whimsical rambling and make it coherent. You believed in me and my stories before I ever had any readers. You bring experience, wisdom, and creativity to everything you do. These stories never would have become what they are without you. Time has only brought me more respect for you, and I'm so thankful you're my editor.

Elizabeth Frazier—I am so grateful for you and your skillset . . . from the family tree you created to your eye for detail, you keep my stories straight. Both I and readers would be lost without you!

Amy Lokkesmoe, Noelle Chew, Brooke Vikla, Serena

Hanson, Rachael Wing, and all the others in marketing and publicity—thank you so much for your hard work getting my books out into the world. You are incredible.

Karen Solem—you encouraged me to hold fast to my dreams and believed in my stories every step of the way. Thank you for everything you do. I am so glad to have you in my corner.

Angie Dicken—do you remember our first writing conference? I will never forget it. Thank you for keeping in step with me through all the breakthroughs and all the failures and all the in-between moments along the way. I am so grateful for you.

Betsy St. Amant Haddox—you are a gem. Our fun chats and your hilarious memes during the ups and downs of crafting this novel have meant so much to me. Thank you for "getting" me.

My parents, Steve and Laurie Young—you encouraged my love of stories from a young age and still support it in meaningful ways. I couldn't have dreamed up better parents than you, and I am so thankful for the laughter and love our family shares.

My husband, Matthew—you have stood beside me every step of my writing career, from making dinner to encouraging me to sit down and edit to sharing Charleston adventures. Thank you for always believing this would happen someday.

My son, Nate—I am so proud of the person you are. You are one of the funniest, kindest, most enthusiastic people I know, and I am so glad to be your mama. You brighten my days and challenge me to see the world differently.

Thanks be to Jesus, for the gift of these stories.

And thank you, sweet readers, for coming alongside me. I hope these books have ministered to you and encouraged you in your own dreams.

Enjoy an excerpt from another book
in the HEIRLOOM SECRETS series

The Dress Shop on King Street

ASHLEY CLARK

PROLOGUE

Charleston, South Carolina, 1860
The candlelight sent a shadow of Rose up against the wooden wall. From the shadow, Rose looked taller. Stronger. Funny thing about shadows. They made even the smallest things into monsters or fairies or whatever folks wanted.

Even a caterpillar could have the wings of a butterfly.

Her daughter, Ashley, used to be scared of shadows when the girl woke to Rose fixin' their dresses by candlelight. Rose tried to teach her to find the familiar shapes of happy things—flowers or ribbons or the sea. But Ashley had never seen the sea. And sometimes she still woke up Rose when bad dreams made her kick her feet.

Rose pressed her own coarse hair back from her sweating forehead using her palm. She wrung her hands and paced the dirt floor of the little room where she and Ashley slept.

Sold. She could hardly think the word, much less speak it aloud.

Her daughter. *Her* daughter.

Only nine years old.

With all of life ahead of her, and none of it hers to live.

Rose swallowed back the bile in her throat. Her hands

fisted, and she squeezed so tightly her fingernails soon brought drops of blood to her palms. That wicked, wicked man. Even from the grave, he ruined her.

First, ten years ago—when Rose herself was a child. And now, with his wife . . . who'd finally connected the dots about the girl.

The slave girl whose father was a white man.

That's all she was to them. A slave.

But to Rose, Ashley was a daughter. Her daughter.

Careful not to wake the little girl, Rose took a small blade from the table. For the briefest moment, she considered using it for another purpose, but shook her head. If God thought her life worth living without her daughter, who was she to question His timing?

Rose held the dull knife to the tip of her own braid, then cut slowly through the hair. She would put the lock of hair, a token of memory, with the rest of her daughter's things.

Her hands began to tremble as she looked over at Ashley, the braid still in her hand. In that moment, Rose's daughter was a baby all over again. Those sweet, round eyes and the hushed rise and fall of her breath.

And Rose would do anything to keep her like this forever, because her baby girl knew nothing of tomorrow's horror.

Rose reached for the empty feed sack and set the braid of hair inside. She folded Ashley's best dress with care, then put it inside too, along with three handfuls of pecans.

The candle flickered, and the shadows grew along the wall, and Rose knew this still wasn't enough.

She looked around the room at their meager belongings, then down at her own dress. Of course. The butterfly buttons Ashley had always admired.

The one thing Rose owned of beauty.

Rose snapped the two buttons from the cuffs of her worn cotton dress and dropped them into the bag. She closed the sack tight and set it down on the table beside her sleeping daughter.

She crawled into bed and slipped her arm around Ashley as she'd done every night of the child's life.

"The sack ain't much, child," she whispered. "But it be filled with my love always."

Rose held her daughter until the morning sun rose—an eternity between the night and dawn, and yet an eternity that passed in a moment. She memorized the size of the little girl's hands and the way she pulled the blankets to her chin.

And as Ashley stirred, Rose smiled—not for any joy, but these might be their final moments, and she wanted her daughter to remember them warmly.

She smiled because she'd no tears left to cry.

"Mornin', baby." Rose brushed her daughter's hair from her eyes. "Momma's got somethin' to tell you 'bout."

ONE

Downtown Charleston, 1946
Millicent Middleton.

That's the name Mama told her to give if anyone asked. Half of it was honest, at least.

Millie supposed her mama was being overcautious like all folks do when they've got an aching spot in heart or body, but she didn't mind playing along. She, too, still grieved for her daddy from what she remembered of him and sometimes wondered . . . if only they'd been more careful, well maybe he wouldn't have died.

Millie straightened the red cloche pinned to her bob-cut curls and peered into the window of the dress shop on King Street. The grey-blue of her dress complemented the deep olive of her skin, and her skirt swooshed a bit as she stood on her tiptoes to get a better look inside.

Ever since she first saw her mama's buttons, Millie had been fascinated by dresses and the stories of the women who wore them.

Mama collected buttons—said each had a hole to match—but there were two butterfly buttons in particular that she kept a close eye on and never saw fit to use.

Senseless, really. Buttons with that kind of beauty just lyin' around. Maybe they were waiting for just the right garment.

Inside the shop, a blond woman reached for a peach silk number on display. What Millie would give to go inside the store and let her own fingers graze the fabric of that gown.

Layers of peach silk draped down the back of the dress, then fell into a line of buttons along the fitted waistline and hips. The whole gown was like a summer dream.

Millie sighed.

Maybe someday.

Just as she was swooning, a young man tripped down the sidewalk and bumped into her arm. He righted her elbow immediately, and the two locked eyes.

He was handsome—Millie immediately noticed it—and he looked like just the sort who might've returned from war with Germany.

His blue eyes glimmered, his blond hair shone, and his pinstriped vest accentuated broad shoulders.

Millie smiled at him.

He returned her grin.

Her heart fluttered with all the possibilities of having been noticed.

"Looking for a wedding dress?" he asked, a glimmer in his eye. "My father owns the place, you know."

"Yes . . . I mean . . . oh no." Millie waved her hand, trying to clarify her meaning. "I'm looking, but no intent to buy." She held up her left hand for his inspection. "What I mean to say is I was daydreaming about the dresses. The fabrics. Sewing gowns like these."

He laughed at the response and seemed flattered to have flustered her. Then he took her hand in his own as if inspecting it more closely. "Now, you tell me—why does a woman as beautiful as yourself have such a lonesome ring finger?"

He was probably all talk, and Millie knew it, but she

didn't care. She'd never experienced such blatant flattery from a boy before, and she was going to enjoy it while she could.

Millie pulled her hand from his, not wanting to draw attention to herself and this stranger, despite how she'd secretly enjoyed his touch.

She rubbed the sleeve of her dress where it scratched her wrist, and for a moment she wondered . . . didn't he know? Could he not tell what was different about her?

But it wasn't the sort of thing someone said. Not aloud, anyway.

And what did it really matter? It wasn't as if she planned to marry him.

"I'm Harry." The boy rocked back on the heels of his loafers. "Harry Calhoun. And you?"

"Millicent Middleton."

Harry nodded once. "Pleasure to make your acquaintance, Millie." He glanced down the street and gestured his head toward the soda fountain on the corner. "Don't suppose you'd want to get an ice cream, or maybe a Coca-Cola with me? My treat."

Millie gulped back the panic that began rising in her throat.

Speaking with this boy was one thing, but brazenly walking into the pharmacy with him? For all eyes to see? That was another.

She straightened the cloche on her head, though it didn't need straightening. "I appreciate the invitation, but I . . ."

Harry ducked down several inches to catch her gaze once more. "Aw, c'mon. It's just some ice cream."

She did love ice cream. And she hadn't tasted any in ages. Folks on the radio were always talking about the economic depression and the war and the country's recovery; but for Millie's family, growin' up in the decades prior hadn't exactly been rolled in luxury.

Actually, she couldn't remember the last time she'd had a sundae. Maybe a year? Her last birthday?

She could almost taste the chocolate fudge sauce dripping over the vanilla ice cream.

Millie sighed. She was set to meet Mama at five o'clock on the dot. So long as Mama and Harry didn't meet, maybe . . .

"Sure." The word left her lips before she had a chance to reconsider.

"Excellent." Harry sounded as if he'd never expected any other answer from her. His smile caught gleams of sunlight.

He started down the sidewalk and glanced over his shoulder, clearly expecting her to follow. "Have you ever been to this soda fountain?"

It was safe to say she hadn't.

Millie hesitated. "I don't think so."

"They make a great sundae. I always get coconut shavings on mine."

An automobile puffed a cloud of exhaust as it rumbled down the cobblestones of King Street. Harry waited for it, then checked both ways before crossing. Millie stayed close by his side, the skirt of her dress bouncing with each step.

Moments later, they'd reached the pharmacy. Harry held open the door for her, and Millie stepped through.

She'd never been on the other side of the glass before. A jukebox played a cheery tune from the corner, and patrons sat atop stools around the bar. It was everything she'd always envisioned, except alive. Real. And it smelled absolutely delicious.

Millie smiled.

This was going to be a good afternoon. For a few moments, she could live a different kind of reality.

"Welcome, kids. Have a seat." The man behind the counter scooped heaps of ice cream into fancy glass bowls and poured flavored syrups over them.

Harry chose a seat near the center of the bar, and Millie gladly slid onto the stool beside him.

Hand-painted signs for soda, chocolate milk, and ice cream hung on the wall behind the bar, and the checkered black-and-white tile floor brought an air of whimsy.

Millie swiveled right and left on her stool.

"What can I get you?" The man at the counter pulled a pen from behind his ear and a pad of paper from his apron.

"I'll have a sundae with chocolate fudge on top." Millie tried not to sound as enthusiastic as she felt—for she knew she was Cinderella in this dream, and she didn't want it ending a second sooner than it must. The last thing she needed was Harry thinking she didn't belong in a place like this.

Even though she didn't.

"You got it." The man tapped his fingers against the bar. "And you?"

Harry ordered the same, plus coconut shavings. As the man readied their orders, Harry turned to Millie with that dangerous grin again.

"So, if you aren't planning a wedding of your own, do tell me, Millie Middleton, what were you doing peering into a bridal shop? Spying on somebody?"

Millie laughed. "Don't be ridiculous."

"Then what?" Harry asked again. The man set both sundaes on the counter, and Harry plunged his spoon into the ice cream.

"You'll think it's silly." Millie felt her cheeks warming and wondered how much color might show. Not that she was embarrassed of it in the least, but she also wouldn't give Harry the satisfaction.

"Maybe," he said with a raise of his eyebrows. "But you never know until you say it out loud."

Millie took her first bite of ice cream. The vanilla melted

sweetly on her tongue. Her dream was just as sweet—but also as much of a luxury.

"I want to own my own dress shop someday." Millie found boldness as she said the words aloud. "I want to be a seamstress."

Harry crossed his arms. "I don't see what's so silly about that."

No . . . you wouldn't, would you?

"Is it because you're a woman?" he asked.

Millie looked down at her sundae.

"Because no doubt, with a name like Middleton and a smile like yours, you'll marry well. I'm sure you'll find a man who will make it happen for you."

"What if I told you I want to make it happen for myself?" Her racing pulse defied the sass of her words.

Harry chuckled, then locked eyes with her. "Oh, you were serious."

"I was, and I am."

"Then I would say I admire your ambition." He hesitated a long moment. "But I would remind you that such idealism is precisely why we can't have women prancing around, running businesses. The idea may be alluring, but it will never happen in American society."

Millie clenched her teeth but managed a tight-lipped smile. Should've known better than to test him. She was normally not so foolish. Long ago, her mama explained why certain dreams and certain people were just not worth her time.

Millie took another bite of her ice cream, then mixed the chocolate fudge into the melting vanilla with her spoon. Blending the two together like a milkshake was her favorite part of a sundae—the hot and the cool, the rich and the sweet. Opposites blended deliciously.

"Tell me more about yourself. What brings you here this afternoon?"

Harry swept his blond hair back with his hand. "I'm studying at the College of Charleston so I can take on the family business someday. But with the pleasant weather today, I skipped class and took a walk down King Street. Perhaps it was fate that led to us meeting." He took a bite of his ice cream. "Do you live nearby?" he asked.

"Radcliffeborough."

"Really?" Harry sat up straighter.

"You sound surprised." Millie swallowed another bite of her sundae, determined not to let one drop go to waste. She ran her thumb beneath her lower lip to remove any traces of chocolate.

"I am, to be honest." Harry pivoted his stool to face her more directly. "I guess I just assumed you lived on Middleton Plantation or South of Broad. I'm surprised to hear you live uptown."

Oh, Millie. Why did you have to go and rattle that off?

"Despite that"—Harry inched ever so slightly closer—"I'd really like to see you again. Can I take you to dinner sometime?"

Millie frowned. "Did you just say *despite that*?"

"Did you not hear me say I'd like to take you to dinner?"

Millie simply stared at him. The clock had struck midnight, and it was time for Cinderella to leave.

"Thank you for the sundae, Harry." Millie stood from the stool and brushed the hem of her dress back into place.

"I . . . I don't understand." Harry dropped coins on the counter for the sundaes. In an instant, he was standing beside her, grabbing her arm, and turning her to face him. "I thought things were going well. Was I wrong?"

Heels planted firmly against the checkered tile, Millie raised her chin. "If you don't like persons from uptown, and you don't believe a woman can run a business, then I can tell you truthfully, Harry, you are not going to like me. Because you don't know the half of it if you find those things off-putting."

The ceiling fan above them pushed the air into a swirl.

"What does that mean, Millie?" Harry shook his head. "Are you trying to keep me guessing?"

Millie reached toward the door, but Harry wouldn't let go. "Please, just tell me."

Millie's gaze scanned the pharmacy—the girls wearing beautiful dresses and the boys trying to impress them and the artwork that just moments ago, she'd studied so intently.

She'd never come here again. So what was the point of keeping it a secret, anyway?

She lowered her voice so as not to cause a scene. At least now, she might let go of the breath she'd been holding.

"Middleton was my great-grandmother's name. She was born a slave and had no other surname."

Harry blinked. Millie watched as realization slowly changed his expression from pleasantry to disgust.

He let go of his hold on her arm then, wiping his hand on the leg of his trousers. "Get away from me, you filthy girl," he hissed.

No one was watching them. No one was listening. Millie had made sure of it.

So no one saw when he pushed her on his way out the door, or when she righted her balance with her foot to keep from falling down onto the tile.

No one saw the tear on her sleeve from Harry's grip, the turmoil in her heart, or the resolve on her face as she left the pharmacy a wiser woman than when she'd come.

But most of all, no one knew Millie was a Black girl pretending to be white.

Ashley Clark writes romantic women's fiction set in the South and is the acclaimed author of *The Dress Shop on King Street* and *Paint and Nectar*. With a master's degree in creative writing, Ashley teaches literature and writing courses at the University of West Florida. Ashley has been an active member of American Christian Fiction Writers for over a decade. She lives with her husband, son, and a rescued cocker spaniel off Florida's Gulf Coast. When she's not writing, she's dreaming of Charleston and drinking all the English breakfast tea she can get her hands on. Be sure to visit her website at www.ashleyclarkbooks.com.

Sign Up for Ashley's Newsletter

Keep up to date with Ashley's news on book releases and events by signing up for her email list at ashleyclarkbooks.com.

More from Ashley Clark

In 1946, Millie Middleton left home to keep her heritage hidden, carrying the dream of owning a dress store. Decades later, when Harper Dupree's future in fashion falls apart, she visits her mentor, Millie. As the revelation of a family secret leads them to Charleston and a rare opportunity, can they overcome doubts and failures for a chance at their dreams?

The Dress Shop on King Street
Heirloom Secrets

You May Also Like . . .

In 1929, a spark forms between Eliza, a talented watercolorist, and William, a young man whose family has a longstanding feud with hers over a missing treasure. Decades later, after inheriting Eliza's house and all its secrets from a mysterious patron, Lucy is determined to preserve the property, not only for history's sake but also for her own.

Paint and Nectar by Ashley Clark
HEIRLOOM SECRETS
ashleyclarkbooks.com

Mireilles finds her world rocked when the Great War comes crashing into the idyllic home she has always known, taking much from her. When Platoon Sergeant Matthew Petticrew discovers her in the Forest of Argonne, three things are clear: she is alone in the world, she cannot stay, and he and his two companions might be the only ones who can get her to safety.

Yours Is the Night by Amanda Dykes
amandadykes.com

Cassie George has stayed away from her small hometown ever since her unplanned pregnancy. But when she hears that her aunt suffered a stroke and has been hiding a Parkinson's diagnosis, she must return. Greeted by a mysterious package, Cassie will discover that who she thought she was, and who she wants to become, are all about to change.

Shaped by the Waves by Christina Suzann Nelson
christinasuzannnelson.com

◆ BETHANYHOUSE

More from Bethany House

After moving cross-country with her son and accepting a filmmaker's mentorship, Val Locklier is caught between her insecurities and new possibilities. Miles McKenzie returns home to find a new tenant is living upstairs and he's been banished to a ministry on life support. As sparks fly, they discover that authentic love and sacrifice must go hand in hand.

All That It Takes by Nicole Deese
nicoledeese.com

After promising a town he'd find them water and then failing, Sullivan Harris is on the run; but he grows uneasy when one success makes folks ask him to find other things—like missing items or sons. When men are killed digging the Hawk's Nest Tunnel, Sully is compelled to help, and it becomes the catalyst for finding what even he has forgotten—hope.

The Finder of Forgotten Things by Sarah Loudin Thomas
sarahloudinthomas.com

Wren Blythe enjoys life in the Northwoods, but when a girl goes missing, her search leads to a shocking discovery shrouded in the lore of the murderess Eva Coons. Decades earlier, the real Eva struggles with the mystery of her past—and that all of its clues point to murder. Both will find that, to save the innocent, they must face an insidious evil.

The Souls of Lost Lake by Jaime Jo Wright
jaimewrightbooks.com

◆ BETHANYHOUSE